SPOILED BRAT

GEORGE ONSTOT

FOR EVERYONE
EVERYWHERE:

MAY YOU GET WHAT YOU WANT,
AND STILL WANT IT ONCE YOU GET
IT

Chapter 1
Frances

Francesca Roff admired herself in a huge mirror as she got ready for her "date" with the adolescent son of an Arab oil sheikh. A date that would pay her fifty thousand dollars. She'd already gotten the money, in fact, and locked it in her safe.

Francesca checked out her big blonde smile, thinking, *How come I got so fine?* Well, she knew how she had gotten so fine: A rhinoplasty, breast enhancement and minor touch-ups as required, and they *were* required. But it had all paid off, and to top it all off, she had grown to a statuesque five-nine. Her mother hugged, kissed and beamed at her, believing that a woman who lacked beauty had no chance for a decent life.

Francesca didn't mind being swarthy even though she was from California, a place that worshipped blue-eyed blondes. What blonde beach bimbo could compete with Francesca's thick black hair, almond-shaped brown hair and lovely caramel-colored body?

Yes, she thought, staring at her perfect, heart-shaped bottom as she gazed from the mirror in front of her to the one behind, I am worth every dollar that every man pays to make love to me.

Of course, she did not usually do these things herself, but Adel Nasrallah, the boy's father, said, "I want Francesca to be Karim's first. He will begin his sex life with the best." After demurring a time or two, she had finally relented—as long as her fee was acceptable.

Fifty thousand dollars, she thought with a chuckle. And how long would this encounter take? Fifteen, twenty minutes? The boy would probably be impotent, or ejaculate immediately, and she would hold him in her arms as he kissed her breasts for an hour. Then they would part company and agree to say, when asked, that theirs had been a lovemaking session to be remembered forever.

She certainly could have referred to her sheikh and his boy to one of her dozens of spectacularly pretty twenty-thousand-per-hour girls, but sometimes it was fun to do a job herself—especially when the men who wanted her included movie stars, royalty, sports heroes and billionaire CEOs.

Yes, Francesca Roff—born Frances Rofstein; she used her mother's professional name, Roff—ran the most exclusive and prestigious "escort service" in Manhattan. She had moved there from Los Angeles, her city of birth, where she had grown up in all the luxury and excess her two rich parents could provide.

Each day Francesca felt grateful to have escaped those two tyrants—Mother, the most insufferable of nitpickers and Father, the hip, stylish producer of obscenely popular, trashy TV series. Everyone who didn't know those two envied Francesca for being their daughter.

Frances, restless, had dropped out of Bard College and drifted into New York, and her parents, three thousand miles away, had cared not at all. Both the Rofsteins were freaked out about getting old and neither wanted to acknowledge having an adult daughter, so they sent her a monthly check and told her to do her thing.

She did just that—and her thing at that time was checking out the Manhattan nightclub scene. For a while she'd found it gratifying, dancing her ass off and guzzling beer paid for by the guy she'd just danced with. Then one night someone introduced her to De Vito Silvera, a hugely popular disc jockey who worked at private parties and whichever nightclub he deemed worthy of his services. Frances took one look at him and said to herself, 'He's Mr. Right. Or at least Mr. Right Now."

Originally from "here and there," De Vito reminded Frances of Tony Manero, John Travolta's character in *Saturday Night Fever*—tall and lithe, with short dark hair and incandescent blue eyes.

De Vito's big problem was a cash shortage due to his addiction to crack cocaine. Frances wanted him because he was handsome and as virile as a porn star, qualities that she prized at that time in her life. She knew little of his background and couldn't have cared less. She wanted him, period.

After a few weeks of hanging out together, he moved into her SoHo loft without her objections. Alas, he hit her up for crack money nearly every day. "How do you expect me to keep this up?" she asked, and he said, "Call your daddy and lay a guilt trip on him. He'll come through with the bucks."

Saul Rofstein, who'd started out with zero and busted his ass to get most of what he had, said nix when Frances telephone him for a handout. "I made my own money. You make yours. Your mother and I have already spoiled you rotten. You want money? Go get a job."

"Fuck you, too, Daddy dearest," Frances muttered after hanging up. *You make retarded TV shows for a living! You call that* work? *Your problem is that you just don't give a shit about your only child.*

She and De Vito soon came up with a get-rich-quick plan. They had been lying in bed one Sunday morning, watching TV. One of her greatest joys in life was staying up late and sleeping till she felt damned good and ready to get out of bed.

The news story on CNN was about a married politician who had been caught having sex with high-priced prostitutes.

"His problem was that he paid them with personal checks," De Vito said. "That's the dumbest thing you can do."

Frances nodded. "With those girls, you pay cash."

"We know that because we know so many of those girls."

She giggled. "Most of our friends are prostitutes or beautiful girls who would sell sex if the price was right."

"We know the right people," he said. "We know the people who want to buy sex and the people who want to sell sex. You think we're onto something here?"

She smiled. "Yeah. Let's get started."

At first, they tried it on a very small scale, both smirking at each other, but soon they had a very serious and successful call-girl business.

Delighted by her success, Frances became two

people, sort of: She remained Frances Rofstein, a girl struggling to begin a career as a fashion designer. As Francesca Roff (she loved how foreign and exotic her alias sounded), she was an enigmatic lady who could make a telephone call or two and make each client's fantasy a reality.

If he could afford it.

And not every man had that kind of money.

Frances' girls were *not* whores. They were chic, sexy, articulate career women who wanted (and sometimes needed) extra income. All of her girls were models, singers, actresses or dancers, some of them already fairly prominent and all of them classy, intelligent and discreet.

She said, "You need to wear masks on your dates. The men will like the mysterious touch, and you'll like how it protects your identity."

Finding the right girls was remarkably easy. De Vito, an accomplished stud before he met Frances, knew all of the most desirable young women and gave them his best sales pitch, which was quite good indeed.

"See, here's the gig. You go to bed with him and make a shitload of cash. It's all cash, no receipts, no record of the transaction, so as far as the tax man is concerned, the transaction didn't happen. You're a beautiful woman, so you get laid a lot for free. So what's the big deal about getting laid *and* getting paid?"

De Vito spoke to all the rich men he knew who would fork out big money for the pleasure of screwing a beautiful woman, and Frances took the names of numbers of women who wanted in on the action. De Vito and Frances got 60 percent of the revenue, so soon they were flush with cash. And naturally it was *always* cash.

After a year or so, the two laughed at how well their plan had worked, mainly because at the outset they had thought, 'If it seems too good to be true, it probably is.' But they acknowledged that they now required assistance.

De Vito procrastinated on recruiting help but eventually hired Barbara Tonucci, his bookkeeper out in Brooklyn. He simply said, 'Wanna work for me? Wanna answer the phones and book the appointments?' and knew her answer would be yes, because she had always been deeply in like with him. So she quit her job and went to work for Cousin De Vito.

Barbara was a huge woman with a twenty-year-old son named Chick. She considered De Vito the handsomest man alive and working for him was a dream come true, even if she didn't like his stuck-up girlfriend and she knew they were running a brothel.

Frances trusted Barbara but thought Chick was a lazy son of a bitch who felt the world owed him a living. She thought he was in danger of turning out to be another De Vito, minus the good looks and charisma. They decided to put Chick to work, too, if only to go for beer-and-sandwich runs and drive them places.

"Don't sweat it," De Vito said to Frances. "They're my family. They would never fuck us over."

"Money is money, people are people. Don't put anything past anyone."

"Franny! Barbara is in love with me! We're paying her big money to keep her yap shut. Like I said, she's my biggest fan. She would never act against my best interests."

"Famous last words."

After making sure that she looked her most irresistible, Francesca headed into the elevator and pushed the lobby button. Her main hangout was a Park Avenue suite in which she and De Vito spent most of their time, but she still had her SoHo loft, which was where she entertained her parents whenever they flew out to visit, which was seldom. They called every few weeks and asked few questions about their daughter's lifestyle. Frances had a handful of old friends but was largely indifferent to them. She had a new life now, full of people who didn't know she was Saul Rofstein's daughter and had grown up in Los Angeles. She liked it just fine that way.

De Vito had driven out to Atlantic City to hang out with a couple of pals, Nelson Skalbania and his business partner, Artie Jay Mitchell. Frances knew Nelson and Artie Jay from when the bunch of them had attended Beverly High. Yeah, man, good times. Nelson and Artie Jay were a year older than Frances but she remembered prom night, when the three of them had gotten baked on weed and she'd made out with both guys.

Ugh. The things you do when you're high as a kite. None of them had ever spoken of that evening, and were content to shut up about it for the next 150 years.

Then, one evening in Manhattan, she'd walked into a nightclub and there they were, Nelson and Artie Jay At first she thought of pretending she didn't see them, but presently they got to talking and laughing about old times. Then Artie Jay introduced her to De Vito.

She'd nothing to De Vito about being felt up and French-kissed in high school by his two pals, because that was none of his business. Also, De Vito had a motherfucker of a temper, and one never knew what would set him off. Probably *that* high-school makeout session would; De Vito considered Frances the most beautiful of women and disliked it when other men ogled her too much; if he knew that his pals had gotten too friendly with her back in high school, he might punch them out all those years later. You just never knew.

Gambling was De Vito's new thing, so Frances thought it O.K. that he had diddled off to Atlantic City for the weekend. He could be a handful to live with even on his best days, so she welcomed an evening by herself.

The man at the desk nodded that her car was outside. She nodded back and handed him twenty-dollar bill. He smiled and pocketed the cash; it was scarcely the best tip he'd ever gotten nor certainly the worst. She didn't mind greasing him; she could afford to do such things.

She felt quite exhilarated about the prospect of deflowering the sheikh's son. His father required a different girl every other night and was one of her most reliable clients, as were the Oscar-winning actor and the rock-music legend who loved to have girls sit on his face.

"Good afternoon, Miz Roff," said the doorman. She was certainly a stunner, and he tried hard not to stare at her braless breasts. And she was *so* mysterious! Nobody in the building could figure out just what, if anything, she or her handsome boyfriend did for a living. All anyone knew was that they were both young and rich and had many good-looking friends.

Frances walked over and slid into the back seat of the new Rolls Royce they had bought. She felt pleased that her date with the Arab boy was an afternoon activity, because she wanted to go to Saks afterwards and buy the Louis Vuitton purse she'd seen online. Also, because De Vito kept forgetting that a girl enjoyed receiving gifts from her man, she thought she might just go into her favorite jewelry stores and see if they had anything new she couldn't live without.

She closed her eyes and smiled. *Yes, that sounds like a plan. After I get the Arab boy to shoot his load, I'll go buy myself a few nice things. What's the point of having money if you can't spoil yourself?*

"Hey baby what's goin' on?" asked Chick, shooting her a big I-know-what-you're-about wink.

"Just drive the car," she told him.

"Boy, someone's on the rag."

She rolled her eyes. *Someone's got to fire this chump,* she thought. *The sooner the better.*

Chapter 2
Kayce

Pleased to meet you. My name is Kayce White. I am twenty-five years old, an attorney whose job will be to defend Saul Rofstein, a legendary TV producer, if the police arrest him.

The victim is Gina Roff, a beautiful actor who would never have condescended to appear in her husband's TV shows. Shot in the face. Beautiful no more. Closed casket.

It is early December, and the smog is as thick as ever as I drive up to the Rofsteins' house, a property I have known and visited for years, starting when I was a skinny whelp of a child who wanted to be best friends with the most popular kid I knew, Frances Rofstein.

"Why do you have cotton everywhere?" I asked her upon my first visit to her mansion.

"It's supposed to be snow," she said. "We don't get snow here in Beverly Hills, so this will have to do."

I had just moved there from the Midwest. I knew plenty about snow. "You haven't missed anything. Real snow is a drag."

"I've gone skiing in Switzerland," she told me. "I

know about real snow."

I nodded. My dad was a lawyer who'd worked for William Kunstler. My mom was a women's activist and poet. I wondered what they would have thought of Frances' fake snow and her TV mogul dad.

We went inside and watched TV. That was when we were kids, and now we are adults. Still, I will never forget Frances' wrinkled nose and impatience with my inability to understand why her family would want fake snow in their driveway. I haven't seen her in many years and seldom think about her. We went our separate ways right after high school, mainly because we had nothing more to say to each other. A friend of a friend told me that Frances had left Los Angeles to attend Bard College, and after getting bored and dropping out she'd moseyed on down to Manhattan and was trying to break into the fashion business. When I first heard that, I thought, 'Her old man is Saul Rofstein. Can't he just make a phone call and get her hired at the House of Versace or someplace? Isn't that how rich people in this country do things?'

I wondered where Frances had ended up and if we could see each other again. Our friendship had been brief. She was good-looking and hip and fashionably ignorant, while I had been homely, abnormally intelligent and indifferent to the dross of the world. Her thing was to go up and down Rodeo Drive and score that perfect pair of boots or belt. Boots, belts and jeans all looked alike to me. Even if I had liked Melrose Avenue accessories, I couldn't have afforded to go shopping with her. I felt better about myself when Frances shunned me and started doing her thing with the other rich girls whose daddies

17

worked in entertainment law or show business.

The termination of my friendship with Frances struck me as beyond trivial. My mother dismissed her as another snob who'd been blessed—or cursed—with good looks and affluent parents. My mom felt better when I hooked up with Hayley Coleman, a brainiac whose father was a plastic surgeon and whose mother ran a local children's charity. As soon as she graduated from high school, Hayley, instead of taking the summer off, found an internship in Washington, D.C., and is now the personal assistant of Senator Strom Greggins. We are still tight even though we live a few thousand miles apart. We email each other every other day even though we're both busy as all hell. She has promised to do her best to fly out here for the holidays, even though her schedule keeps her going like a madwoman all day and half the night.

She's the best friend I've ever had, and I'm really eager to hook up with her as soon as possible. We've recently called it quits with our boyfriends. She dumped Mark because, as she put it, "he was just too generous with his cock."

My guy, Pete, a family doctor, broke up with me because he said I always put my job before our relationship, and even when I was with him, I wasn't really *there*.

"Your problem," he'd told me, "is that you just don't love me enough. And that sort of makes it *my* problem, too."

I had to admit that he was right.

We had been together for a few years, so our breakup disoriented me but did not break my heart. I miss having a man in my life who liked many of the things that turned me on: Sharing items on our his-and-her iPads, taking long walks, watching *Californication* and *Orange Is the New Black* and devouring meat-and-seafood pizzas

It took me fifteen minutes to forget about our sex life. When we started getting it on, I had been relatively inexperienced and therefore getting naked and messing around was still hot, sticky, raunchy and terribly exciting. But after six months, well, he knew my best moves and I knew his, and our passion disappeared like bathroom steam dissipating after the shutoff of hot water.

Where did our love—or lust—go? I suppose it ended because it wasn't meant to last. Although hardly a seasoned lover, I had a couple of torrid flings in college, the first with a married professor and the other with a jock who ended up in the NFL. Both men made me scream in the sack, so I had some inkling of just how great sex could be. Being the Other Woman with that married man freaked me out, though. Too many lies to keep track of, too much sneaking around.

I often think our dog, Kurt Cobain, misses Mark more than I do. We found him wandering around on the beach, underfed and overstressed, and since he insisted on walking with us, we took him home and fattened him up. I named him Kurt Cobain because when we first met, we could hear *Smells Like Teen Spirit* blaring from someone's boombox. Plus, our new pet *did* smell like teen spirit.

When Mark said he was leaving me, I said, "I'm keeping Kurt. You'll never see him again." What I wanted to say was, *How dare you dump me, you son of a bitch! Don't you know that I'm much better than you deserve?*

He got up in my face a little about Kurt Cobain—"What gives *you* sole custody of him? We found him at the same time!"—but left without the pooch. Well, I hope Mark *wanted* his freedom, because that's exactly what he got. There was none of that 'I hope we can still be friends' nonsense; I had no intention of seeing him ever again.

My mother was displeased. She liked Mark, thought him a good catch, and my brothers always enjoyed having him around.

Well, I thought, that's a damn shame. Maybe Mom or my brothers should start dating him. All I knew was, Mark was a fine man and we had something great once but it didn't last, so now I needed to find something fresh with someone new. And I wanted my next man to be someone with whom I could spend the rest of my life.

So, Kayce, I have asked myself on myriad occasions, *who might that man be?* Beats the shit out of me. Not sure I'm going to find him in Los Angeles, either. I'm a lawyer, so most of the men I meet are clients, and the overwhelming majority are married, gay or both. The drug lawyers who drive the fanciest cars? They want the barely legal blondes with naturally jutting young breasts and aspirations to Hollywood stardom.

Not that I have anything to apologize for in the looks department. Fuck no. If I lived outside of southern California I suppose people would consider me the prettiest of women. I have long, wavy brown hair, light blue eyes (and the biggest, blondest smile around!). I'm just a hair under five-eight and wear a size eight dress (O.K., I have big bones).

All right, I'm not a blonde California beach

cutie—but those beach cuties, most of them, aren't natural blondes. I don't want to buy fake lips, breasts cheekbones or a chin. Why would any woman do that to herself? Yuck!

I have to admit that if Mark hadn't left me, I would have left him, because as a couple we were getting stale and I was feeling the urge to shake him loose and see who else was out there. I would need time to find that special man, and I'm not sure how I would free up that time because I am *such* a fiendish worker.

Our split happened a few months back, and an acquaintance told me that Mark has already found a new squeeze.—some emaciated blonde esthetician he met in a bar. I'm happy for him, I think. Actually, I don't think I give a shit.

Right now I'm feeling that there is no hurry to find a special new man. Maybe I should think like a Buddhist—"When you are ready for that special new man, he will appear at just the right moment."

"You're two minutes late," said my boss, Bryan "Frosty" Forst. We've nicknamed him Frosty because of his cool, aloof demeanor. A dedicated weightlifter, he is tall and muscular, with a full head of curly gray hair. He owns a piece of agricultural land and plows his own field. At work he wears garish Brioni suits and lizard-skin shoes. Folks think he's quite an eccentric.

Forst, Horne and Nurenberg is the name of the firm. I started clerking for them as a law student; after I graduated and passed the bar exam, they took me on as an associate. Within a few years, they promoted me to senior associate, mainly because I could, and would, outwork everyone else.

Also, I am so damned good at my job that Frosty loves me, at least to the extent that he loves anyone. I am sort of the daughter he wishes he'd had. He can rely on me to whatever needs doing, and I will always do it right the first time. "Kayce's on it," he'll say, "so we have nothing to worry about."

Bryan Forst is the best lawyer I have ever met, so I pay little attention to his clothes and shoes and concentrate on his legal brilliance. He's an astute teacher and I'm the most eager of students, so it's a win-win situation. I expect another big promotion soon.

Mark was right: My career is my top priority, and right now that's a very good thing.

I glanced at my watch—a Rolex, given to me by Frosty. Labels and brand names are not a big deal to me, but Frosty assured me that this particular watch was far, far better than any other timepiece I had ever owned.

"I'm a couple of minutes late," I told him. "Nothing to get excited about."

"Time is money."

"How original."

He shook his head. "Always full of backtalk."

"You say that like it's a bad thing."

"Let's go this way. We have much to do."

In L.A. legal circles, I am considered a rising star because lately I have defended, with remarkable success, two prominent men. The first one, a public-radio personality, had gotten into sex games with interns and female producers who later accused him of raping them. The American news media had great fun crucifying that radio host, arresting, trying and hanging him by the balls. My team and I, upon being retained by the radio host, investigated the matter, concluded that as a legal matter it was just the women's claims against his, and we went to court. No sweat. No jury, just a judge. What a joke; the judge naturally acquitted my client, and the press lauded me as some kind of young female Clarence Darrow.

Everyone at the firm seemed quite pleased with the way I'd handled the whole matter, and presently I received another case, this one concerning a comedian who had been caught in a public restroom jerking off to photographs of naked children. I had a jury this time, and I made those folks smile about all the funny routines he had performed. He was no pedophile, I assured them—although in reality I felt quite certain that he *was*—and this case was just a big misunderstanding. This funny, talented man had a wife and children he adored and legions of devoted fans who'd laughed till their sides ached. This wonderful man, I assured that jury, would never *do* anything like that.

They set him free.

Now I had a murder case: Saul Rofstein had allegedly murdered his wife. He hadn't been arrested yet, but he had already called Bryan Forst about it, so it didn't look good.

"Tell me what I need to know," I said to Frosty as we entered the Rofsteins' huge, opulent mansion.

He stopped, frowned and leaned over a bit to whisper in my ear. "Saul Rofstein," he said, "is a very powerful TV producer." Which was about as helpful as saying, "Barack Obama is the president of the United States."

Frosty frowned some more. "I mean, he was a powerful producer. I think he's been semiretired for a while. All those sappy TV dramas everyone loved? He's made enough money from them to live a dozen lifetimes. Plus, he knows everyone worth knowing, so he would be the best friend or worst enemy you've ever had."

I wondered if it was the right time to tell him that I had already forgotten more about Saul Rofstein than he had ever learned, because I had been their daughter's confidante and frequent houseguest during high school. Then I decided to shut up about it—the Rofsteins probably wouldn't remember me anyway.

Frosty ran it down for me. The Rofsteins had gone to a big fundraiser that evening at one of the bigger Beverly Hills hotels. They had gotten home around midnight. Gina Roff had gone upstairs to bed right away, while her husband stayed downstairs to watch TV and sip bourbon. After about half an hour, he had gone outside to say goodnight to his two Rottweilers, large, muscular dogs that had been trained to attack strangers but be nice to their owner.

Just before two o'clock, he'd decided to retire and gone upstairs to his own bedroom—he and his missus kept separate bedrooms, a fairly common practice among rich Hollywood couples. He had sat up in bed and watched TV till falling asleep. At six, he got up and walked over to the private gymnasium at the back of his house; only when their Colombian housekeeper, Rosario, came screaming into the gym did Saul learn that his wife had been slain.

I nodded. "Gotcha. Have the police found a murder weapon?"

"Negative."

"Any signs of forced entry?"

"Negative."

"Were the Rofsteins having any domestic difficulties?"

"How the hell would I know? I'm sure we'll find out soon enough."

The mansion swarmed with cops and detectives and whatnot.

Rosario sat inside the house. I could hear her sobbing. Gina Roff still lay in bed, dead for hours. The police photographer would arrive soon.

I approached one of the detectives, a big black guy who looked like Laurence Fishburne, the actor who played Morpheus in the *Matrix* movies. A handsome man; I had an easy time assuming that he had moved here from another state because everyone told him he was so good-looking that he should go to Hollywood and break into movies or TV. Instead, he ended up on the police force. L.A. showbiz attracts vast numbers of people from everywhere; always has, always will. His partner was a pretty Chinese woman, Detective Wong. Maybe she had come out here to become the next Joan Chen and wound up in law enforcement. Happens to the best of 'em.

I wanted to ask if either of them had bothered to call Frances and give her the dreadful news.

All of a sudden I felt nauseous. What does it look like, and sound like, when somebody makes that call?

"Good afternoon, Miz Rofstein. This is the Beverly Hills Police Department, and we're calling to tell you that your mother is dead. She has been shot in the head, probably by your father. While I have your undivided attention, I would like to wish you a merry Christmas!"

"There a problem?" Frosty asked me. He demanded my undivided attention at all times, and just then he knew he didn't have it.

"Has the P.D. notified their daughter of this death in the family?"

Frosty frowned again. "How do you know they have a daughter?"

"Saul Rofstein is a rich, powerful, famous man. Everyone knows he has a daughter."

"So far as I know, nobody knows jackshit about this except you, me and the cops. But just wait till *Inside Edition* and *Entertainment Tonight* latch onto this thing. Damn, are they gonna run with the ball!"

"Think the cops are gonna bust Rofstein for this?"

"It's your job and mine to make sure that doesn't happen. There is no evidence indicating that he did it. None at all."

"But maybe he did it anyway," I wanted to say. But some things were better left unsaid.

Chapter 3
Hayley

"You," said Hayley Coleman, "are a lying son of a bitch. You told me you were going to leave your wife." She wiped tears from her big eyes as she glowered at her boss, the man she had adored and worshipped for the longest time. "But you're still together, so in my book that makes you a lying son of a bitch."

Senator Strom Greggins looked past the pretty girl who had tears streaming down her cheeks. He was a tall, sturdy man in his early fifties with thick gray hair and a politician's phony smile.

"Sweetheart—"

"Yes?" She arched an eyebrow.

"You need to listen to me."

"Oh, I have been listening to you since the moment we met. In fact all I ever do is listen to you. You said, 'We'll be together by Christmas. I promise you that. I swear it'll just be us this Christmas.'"

"Yes, but—"

"You lied! I'm sure your wife still doesn't know about us!" The tears kept running down her face as if they would never stop.

Strom Greggins looked away. The biggest pain

in his ass was a woman in tears. His wife wasn't the world's biggest crybaby, but she certainly had her moments. This new chick was starting to demand more and more from him. He didn't need this crap from her. He had just met a British or Irish TV news correspondent whose bones he wished to jump. The limey girl was young and blonde and sweet, and much prettier than Hayley, although Hayley did have one gorgeous pair of boobies, he had to admit. Hayley's whole body was delicious, which was one of the reasons he'd promised her whatever she wished to hear.

I'm going to divorce my wife and take up with you. Dream on, little girl.

In Washington, D.C., men had wives. They also had girlfriends. Their wives and girlfriends needed to be kept separate. Everyone who was a man, a wife or a girlfriend had to understand how these things worked.

"Don't cry," he said in a gentle voice.

"Don't lie," she retorted.

"Things will be different after the holidays."

"Not good enough. You promised what you promised."

"Lighten up, Hayley."

"If you don't tell her about us, *I* will."

He sighed. If only her boyfriend was still on the scene…but he had gotten tired of her whining and gone back home. So what did Kayce do? She clung to her boss and insisted that he say those things about leaving his wife for her, and now she was making threats. She was threatening *him*, Senator Strom Greggins, one of the most respected men around.

This little girl's conduct was objectionable and

he was damned if he'd put up with it.

"Do not carry on like this in my office."

"Don't be embarrassed. Very soon everyone will know the truth about us."

"Nobody will know."

"Wanna bet?"

Who the hell did this little shit think she was? The way she spoke to him! Didn't she know her place? Jesus!

"How will people learn about us?" he asked her, his voice cool and even.

"I'll tell. Your wife first and then everyone else who cares to know."

He shook his head. "You will not say anything to anyone. Don't even consider it an option."

"Can you stop me? I really don't think so."

He swallowed hard. "Why are you doing this to me right now?"

Jayce choked back tears and took a deep breath. She hadn't wanted this conversation to go this way, but it was what it was. She closed her eyes and said, "I'm pregnant."

His face went white and his mouth dropped open. "You're kidding."

"No jokes here." She liked how seriously he was taking her now.

"Impossible," he said. His lips curled this way and that, lie a stroke victim struggling to form words. "Contraception…"

"Doesn't always work."

He rolled his eyes. "Oh, *fuck*."

"Now it's you and me and baby makes three. Therefore, we have to go public about our situation."

He paced up and down, running his hand

through his hair. She had seen him do that a hundred times when he ended up in a vexing predicament. But she guessed he could never have imagined being put in such a spot by *her*. He had always assumed that *she* was on *his* side. He spun around and darted his eyes at her. "How do you know it's *mine*?"

She smiled, expecting him to say such a thing. That was his way—to pretend that trouble didn't exist or that it was someone else's problem. First rule of politics and life: Find someone else to blame.

The problem, the real problem, was that she loved him. Absolutely, positively loved him.

Now she had his child—*their* child—growing inside her body, and that made her feel, more than ever, that they should be together.

"It's yours, Strom. It's ours. Trust me on this."

"It could be Mark's," he muttered, disgusted with himself for being played like a fool and acting like one, too.

She shook her head and said, in a quiet voice, "Yours."

"How do you know? How do you really know?"

"I know in the same way that your wife knows your children are hers and yours." Then, "You're the only man I've been with in the past few months. It's yours."

"Unbelievable," he muttered. That was his thing—muttering about matters that were just too obscene to be spoken of in a normal tone of voice. "Why are you doing this to me?"

"Excuse me?" she retorted with a hot, red face. "Who did what to whom? It seems to me that you came to my apartment to shove your cock into me all those times."

30

"Don't talk like that," he said, sneering. "It makes you seem so trashy."

This was the conversation she'd planned to have with him. She wanted him to say, "That's terrific! You're having my baby! I'm going to divorce my wife and marry you!"

Dream on, girlfriend.

She was disappointed, but not surprised, by his reaction to this news. By saying, 'Leave your wife, marry me and we'll raise our child together,' wasn't she expecting a bit much from him?

At times like this she wished she had a go-to girl to confide in. But Strom had said to her, *No one must know about us*. She hadn't even mentioned her thing with him to Kayce White, her best friend from L.A. So far as Kayce knew, Hayley and her guy Mark had had a good thing going till it just sort of fell apart.

Good ol' Mark. Poor guy had no clue that his girl was getting it on with the senator she worked for. Mark had his apartment and she had hers, and their sleepovers happened at his pad, so her private goings-on were just that. Also, Mark would never have suspected that Senator Strom Greggins would cheat on his missus.

Now Hayley wanted, more than anything else, to tell the world about her relationship with the world, starting with Missus Greggins. Strom had told Hayley many times that Joni, his wife, was a cold, heartless woman who refused to pleasure her man. Hayley right away felt O.K. about being sexually intimate with a married man. Strom needed Hayley; Hayley needed Strom. They grew closer after every lovemaking session.

He walked around his office and ended up at

the window. He stared out the ugliness of Washington, D.C. and said nothing, which she took as her cue to speak.

"Strom..." She hoped he would be ethical, moral and scrupulous towards. But she couldn't be certain of that, since he was a career politician. "I think we both know what needs to happen next. You tell your wife or I will. She needs to know about us and this pregnancy."

He turned around and faced her. Killers' eyes did not grow colder. "Is that how you see this matter?"

She nodded. "Yes. That's how it is."

"Is that so?"

"I meant every word of what I just said."

He looked around the room, pursing his lips. She felt relieved that he wasn't yelling and screaming and throwing punches into the air, as she'd seen him do when he was supremely pissed.

After several minutes when neither of them said anything, he told her, "This was the wrong place for this conversation. We should have met in private."

"Yes." She felt pleased that he seemed prepared to deal with this matter in a logical and practical manner.

"You'll need to give me a couple of weeks to work this out. It's a big deal."

"I understand."

"This is a very difficult matter."

"But you can work it out, and then we can be together. We will have the baby and live happily ever after."

His eyes narrowed. "Have you told anyone about this?"

"Nobody."

"Are you sure?"

"I have told *nobody*."

"People talk. They have big mouths."

"Not me. I don't talk."

He wandered around the office some more. She stood there watching him, wishing her heart would stop pounding so hard.

"How far along are you?"

"Three months."

"Have you seen a doctor?"

"I'll see my gynie next week." She smiled, pleased at hearing him sound like an expectant father.

"No. I don't trust your 'gynie.' I'm going to make an appointment for you with my doctor. Our baby deserves no less than the very best medical care available."

She wiped away a tear and smile. *Our baby.* How wonderful. *Her* Strom. She thought back to the day when his family was away and he'd made love to her in his own bed. They had held each other afterwards and she thought she would never know such bliss again.

Hayley rushed up to him and jumped into his arms. "I'm terribly sorry for all this. I just want to be happy with you, Strom. That's all I want."

"So you've said."

"It'll be so much better after we're married and there'll be no more sneaking around."

"But until that day comes, you must let me handle things the way I think is best," he said.

"Yes, boss."

"Don't tell anyone about us. Not a word."

"As you wish, boss."

He felt his manhood stiffen, as it always done when he felt her arms around his neck and her kiss on his lips. He felt angry, betrayed and bullied, but that little bitch could always give him a king-sized boner.

He placed his hands over her breasts and began teasing her nipples erect.

"Better go lock the door," he whispered into her ear. She grinned and as she turned away, he swatted her ass.

Chapter 4
Nelson

Nelson Skalbania was someone whom women stared at whenever he entered a room. He was handsome and tall, with black hair and smoldering dark eyes. He had a way of standing and carrying himself that was quite his own; everyone agreed that he had superb personal style. His appeal wasn't just about his looks, though at twenty-five he was certainly *GQ* material; nor was it limited to his being the heir to an outrageous fortune, which he was. No, he just seemed to possess a combination of Prince William's regal bearing, Russell Williams' muscular athleticism, and Johnny Depp's bad-boy naughtiness.

His father, the late billionaire Theodakis Skalbania, had made his money in shipping, food storage and, later on, cruise lines. His motto, "Everything not absolutely necessary needs to be delegated, automated or eliminated," made him quite a maverick in industry. He bought struggling companies, cut away the fat and slimmed them down into lean, competitive enterprises. Nelson had no desire to emulate his father—the old man's businesses seemed much too boring—any more than he wished to do as his mother had done. Lovey Skalbania, a ravishing beauty, had built casinos on the Las Vegas strip and owned Sappho Pictures, a Hollywood movie studio, for a decade. Nelson looked around at the people in his life and realized they were all movers-and-shakers, go-getters and winners. His stepfather, Sid Stein, had made them scream with laughter in comedy clubs for years before becoming an Oscar-winning producer and director.

So, thought Nelson, how am I supposed to big things and dazzle the universe in my own right?

He didn't have to ponder these matters for long. He had a headful of ideas, and without consulting anyone, he'd dropped out of school, and with Artie Jay, his best friend—a black boy whose father was an orthopedic surgeon—the two approached some family friends and said, "We're going to invest in some things; want to invest in *us*?" Such people felt eager to help the two young men get started, and soon Nelson and Artie Jay opened *Attitude*, a private nightclub that within months became *the* late-night hangout in Manhattan.

Nelson had inherited his father's business acumen and forceful personality, as well as Lovey's charisma and tenacity. He knew he had gotten his folks' best qualities and not their impatience and volatility. He'd really lucked out.

Everyone, it seemed, yearned to be Nelson's friend or lover or both, but his mother had cautioned him, "Because of who you are, and what you have and how you look, people will want to be near you or with you. So you need to start being very selective about the people you let into your life. Wealth often attracts difficult, evil people. Look at poor Margot and all the riff raff she's hooked up with over the years."

Margot Skalbania, Nelson's aunt, was the daughter of Allegra, Nelson's late half-sister and the granddaughter of Theodakis Skalbania.

Nelson often wondered why so many members of the Skalbania family had died while young or middle-aged. He preferred to think of himself as the exception.

He liked Margot a great, great deal, but she seemed to have ridiculously poor taste in men and consequently had been exploited emotionally and economically many times.

Due to Margot's dysfunctional relationships and the anguish they had caused her, Nelson was very careful about which women he dated.

He had far more than his share of girlfriends, none of whom he loved, all of whom were spectacularly beautiful. Debutantes, fledgling models and actresses. He asked them out, they asked him. they hung out, dated, danced, had fun. They said goodbye; he met someone else. What was the harm in that?

Only one girl meant anything to him. Charisma, she called herself, and she'd obsessed him for over a year and a half. She'd dumped him and had a one-nighter with his pal, De Vito Silvera. Then she'd fucked off with her Eastern European husband and nobody had any idea where she was.

Then came Ria, a singer who the critics said had the finest voice since Barbra Streisand or Joan Baez. Ria, well into her thirties, had a sassy attitude and a sizable entourage she brought with her into *Attitude*. Invariably she came in holding hands with one pretty boy or another, and she'd drive Nelson bonkers by flirting with Nelson and batting her big dark eyes in his face, or she would simply pretend he wasn't there.

Nelson had such difficulty coping with her conflicting messages that he was amazed nobody sensed his schoolboy infatuation. He was especially astounded that he hadn't shared his feelings with Artie Jay or De Vito. De Vito—*particularly* him—who played the club's music and was the boyfriend of Frances Rofstein.

Nelson often asked himself, *Why am I friends with De Vito? We're so different it's unbelievable.*

De Vito lived for smoking crack and drinking tequila shooters.

Nelson didn't.

De Vito loved fucking around on Frances.

Nelson had turned away a hundred cuties when he was in relationships because he didn't want to cheat on his girlfriends.

De Vito believed in staying up till dawn, spending endless hours in bed and never doing anything that sounded boring or difficult.

Nelson packed as much busywork as possible into each day. He and Artie Jay wanted to open *Attitude* nightclubs in other cities.

Despite their lack of things in common, Nelson considered De Vito a genuine friend from way back who, most of the time, was a good listener and a first-rate disc jockey in an industry that had a hundred mediocre ones. Also, they both had carnal knowledge of Charisma, the beautiful model who was so snobbish and selective about men. They felt deeply flattered that she'd boned them both before taking off.

In private, Nelson had burst into tears many times

over the loss of Charisma.

He chose to keep his yap shut about Ria. He feared that Artie Jay and De Vito, if they knew of his hard-on for Ria, would mock him without mercy.

Still, he believed that he would feel better about things if he spoke to *someone* about his feelings for this woman. He wasn't that fond of spilling his guts to people about anything, but there were times when it could be helpful to sit down and rap with someone who knew about life and people and who wouldn't judge him.

Did Ria want him? Or was she just having fun jerking him around and making him feel like an asshole? He honestly didn't know.

What he *did* know was that the women who most captivated him were those who cast him aside as if he were a bloodied Tampax. Lovey's best friend, Luna—who'd treated him like a child. Charisma—who'd treated him like an overly affectionate pet. Ria was the latest; what did they see in each other?

A shrink could spend hours on that with him.

To forget about these women he loved and how they treated him like dog shit, he decided to accept De Vito and Artie Jay's invitation to spend the weekend in Atlantic City.

Perhaps Ria would notice he wasn't there and she'd miss him. But she would probably keep forgetting he even existed.

The drive to Atlantic City was a quick one. De Vito wanted to drive them there in his Ferrari, but Artie Jay reminded him that there simply was not room for three in that car. So they had piled into De Vito's black Mercedes instead. De Vito could easily drive any kind of car he wanted, but his thing was to avoid attracting attention, so he preferred a more conservative vehicle. Not long before, on his twenty-fifth birthday, he had inherited most of his father's wealth, so he knew he was filthy rich—he didn't need to advertise it to the world.

He and De Vito never talked about money. They made a point of never bringing it up. Very early on in their friendship De Vito asked for a loan, and Nelson said no. De Vito was a crackhead and Nelson was *damned* if he'd lend an addict money to buy rocks. During one of their mother-son talks, Lovey advised him never to lend money to friends. "You'll lose their friendship and they'll end up resenting you," she'd said. "So either *give* them the money without expecting repayment or turn them down altogether." He had followed her advice completely.

De Vito, the best disc jockey Nelson had ever met, said he had developed a side business with Frances.

Nelson and Artie Jay knew right away what De Vito's new thing was—when chicks were involved, no secret was safe for long. But they decided to wait till De Vito himself told them about it. They knew that he and Frances were doing great business with their new venture, because De Vito, who always bitched about having very little walking-around money, had just bought a new Ferrari.

Before driving out to Atlantic City, Nelson called Lovey in Vegas. If she wasn't in Sin City, she could be found in L.A. or wherever her husband was shooting his latest eagerly anticipated movie.

Lovey was running the Oasis, her newest creation,

an upscale hotel/apartment complex. The place was always full and the waiting list for apartments was two dozen names long.

Nelson smiled as his mother bragged about her latest success. No surprise there; Lovey always made things work, period. As her son, he knew that everyone was watching to see how competent *he* would be, compared to his parents. So he'd done the only logical thing—fucked off to New York and lived *his* life *his* way.

He had been smart enough to get involved in something he knew about and really liked—nightclubs. He and Artie Jay had a highly successful one in Manhattan and wanted to open a half-dozen others. He had a terrific apartment on the West Side, more friends than he could count, a very busy social life. He also had a mother, stepfather and many other relatives he genuinely loved. He had an ideal situation, mainly because he was in New York and his people were in California.

His inheritance was vast, but he decided to pretend it didn't exist—he would just let it sit there untouched until he was older and wiser about investments. For the moment, at age twenty-six, he lived comfortably on the revenue from his nightclub. Every time he thought about the success he'd had with *Attitude*, he wanted to reach over and give himself a big pat on the back. His inheritance—that huge sum of money he had done nothing to earn and in many ways felt he did not deserve—could just remain in his mind as a comforting thought: He had big bucks stashed away if he needed them. Nelson liked himself that much more whenever he thought, *You're a self-made man, dude.*

"Nelly!" Lovey said in a delighted voice. "What's my boy up to?"

"Off to Atlantic City to be very naughty."

"You sound like your grandfather."

"I'm going with De Vito and Artie Jay. I'm turning off my phone."

"Don't do that. You know I hate it when I can't reach you."

"Just for the weekend, Ma."

"O.K., then I promise not to worry."

"Good."

"I don't worry much about you, Nelly. I know you really have your shit together. The one I worry about is Margot. You spoken to her lately?"

"The other day. She seemed happy enough."

"She's family. I think she's very unhappy. I think you should keep an eye on her."

"We don't have much in common."

"You're family. That's plenty to have in common. You know what her problem is? She can't resist lowlifes. She needs someone to give her guidance and I'm not there."

"O.K. I'll call her when I get back from Atlantic City."

"You do that. Also, give my best to Artie Jay When are you two flying out here to spend the weekend with me? You know how much I like him."

"Yeah, we'll have to do that soon." Nelson, smiled, thinking about how tight he and Artie Jay had been and for how long. High school, college, then *Attitude*. They'd had many good times together, enjoyed countless long talks about women, careers, life. Since they had grown up with more money than they could spend in a dozen lifetimes, neither had anything to gain by knowing the other. They were friends because they liked one another, period.

"How's the Oasis?" Nelson asked, wanting to terminate this call and get his ass over to Atlantic City.

"It's the place to stay in Las Vegas. We're booked up till Armageddon. Even Guido loves it. I've given him his own special suite. Everyone here loves him. He's such a slut."

Grandfather Guido Sanducci, a contemporary of Meyer Lansky and Bugsy Siegel, had helped build Las Vegas into the world-class vacation destination. He had built major hotels, stood up to the most intimidating competitors and built an empire. He had also screwed many hundreds of women and, now in his nineties, enjoyed life as much as ever with his new wife, a woman young enough to be his granddaughter.

"Tell Guido I said hello," Nelson told his mother. He was quite in awe of his grandfather. He considered Guido a man to admire.

"You can tell him yourself. He's flying out your way soon."

"For real? I better start calling around for strippers and hookers."

"Joy won't like the sound of that." Joy was Guido's current wife.

They laughed, and Lovey said, "Sassy is eager to see you."

"How is the little thing?"

"Not so little any longer."

Nelson chuckled. "They grow up fast, huh?"

"They certainly do. And she is probably making out with her latest stud right now."

"Oh? How many studs does she have?"

"I've lost count."

"That many, huh? Well, I'll give her a call soon."

"Please do. I have a feeling she's ready to run off with some creep again and there's nothing I can do about it. She's saying, 'Fuck college,' if you'll pardon my French. She's nixing everything we suggest."

"She's a wild child, Ma, just like you."

"I had to fight to survive and it wasn't much fun."

"So you've said—many times. I'll call her and see what's up. You need to stay busy and keep out of trouble."

"You got it wrong; *I'm* supposed to say that to *you*."

"Yeah, Ma. We'll both take that advice."

Nelson grinned. His mother was a hoot. Still absolutely gorgeous and eager to take on the world. God's mercy on whoever tried to stop her from getting what she wanted.

Sassy, his half-sister just coming of age, was her mother's daughter. A fearless, brash beauty, she never was the kind to do as she was told and refused to let Lovey and Sid Stein protect her, even though she had been kidnapped a couple of years earlier. The sheltered life, Sassy might have said, was not worth living.

Nelson knew what that girl wanted: to fly to Manhattan and move in with him; she'd said as much a hundred times. But he didn't want a roommate, and sure as hell didn't want to become his half-sister's keeper.

She'd flown in the year before, all dolled up and ready to party down like a college coed on spring break. What a nightmare! All those guys at *Attitude* ogling her ass and titties, even De Vito. Nelson got her cute precocious booty back on the next flight home. And now she wanted to *move in with him?* Fuck that noise.

Still, Sassy was very special to him in many ways, and he enjoyed hanging out with her when she minded her manners…

Chapter 5
Frances

On her way to deflower the Arab boy, Frances took a deep breath. Her silk dress felt wonderful, and she wore no brassiere or underpants. Easy money, shy kid, no sweat. She shook her head and grinned.

Before knocking on the door, she'd put on her mask. Instantly she felt like Francesca Roff, ravishing woman of mystery. No longer was she Frances Rofstein, daughter of two rich, powerful people who would *shit* if they'd known what their little girl was up to.

She heard a click at the door and saw it flung open. Standing before her was a twentysomething fat guy wearing a fancy track suit, many gold chains and rings and wraparound sunglasses.

Bodyguard, she thought. *I made it clear—just me and the kid, nobody else.*

"I'm here for Karim Nasrallah," she said.

The man smiled. "Pleased to meet you."

"*You're* Karim?" she asked. "You're not fifteen."

He laughed hard and grabbed her wrist, pulling her inside. "Yeah, baby, fifteen an' way too ready for some hot lovin'." He shoved the door closed with his leather-shod foot. "We goin' do some *L.A. pumpin' away.* Hope yo' li'l blonde pussy be ready for mah big black cock."

De Vito Silvera knew how much his girlfriend Frances hated cell phones, and that was kind of too bad when you worked in their business. De Vito considered it crucial for a beautiful young woman to have a cell phone so that she wasn't totally helpless.

"What if shit happens?" he had asked her.

"Then I'll deal with it when I get home," she had replied.

What if you don't have that option? he'd been tempted to ask.

So after De Vito had checked into the hotel and seen the news report on the murder of Gina Roff, he regretted having no way of contacting Frances. She was in some thousand-dollar suite, holding a sobbing Arab boy in her arms after he'd just ejaculated between her thighs. Meanwhile, the poor girl's mother had been fatally shot in Los Angeles.

He tried to remember where her date was staying. The two of them had laughed so long and hard about her upcoming session with a fifteen-year-old Arab boy that he couldn't recall much else about it. He knew that the father had forked over fifty large so that the kid could shoot a load into Frances' vagina. De Vito, who had shot hundreds of loads into Frances' vagina, wasn't at all sure that she—or any other woman—was worth that kind of money.

"Ask Karim if he has a sister," De Vito had joked. "Tell him I'll bust her cherry for fifty large."

"Like hell you will!" As far as she was concerned, it was all right for her to sexually service as many big spenders as possible…but for *De Vito* to sell himself to another woman? She would consider it the ultimate betrayal.

De Vito secretly laughed at, but accepted, Frances' hypocritical attitude. After all, she was the best thing that had ever happened to him.

"Fuck," he muttered, thinking, *What am I supposed to do? Her mother was just discovered murdered, and I have no way of reaching her. If I could contact her, what would she say? Probably she would tell me to get my ass out to Los Angeles.*

He was in Atlantic City for fun and nothing else, and would probably resent Frances for telling him to drive back to New York for moral support. It wasn't like she'd had much use for her parents, anyway.

He concluded that since Gina's death as all over the news and probably the Internet, too, he didn't necessarily have to be the one to tell Frances. She would find out when she found out, and when she called him to talk about it, he could pretend that he hadn't heard.

Yeah, that sounded like a plan. He would enjoy himself over the weekend and, when he got home, deal with whatever shit came along.

De Vito, he told himself, *you're a fuckin' genius.*

He resolved not to think about this bad stuff as he rejoined Artie Jay and Nelson.

"Where were you?" asked Artie Jay. "Have a seat. Order a drink. Enjoy life."

With his crewcut, whiter-than-white teeth and big brown eyes, Artie Jay was a man whom women found most appealing. At first they wanted to take him home and mother him, but once they got his clothes off they got other ideas. Artie Jay could pleasure a woman in many ways.

"I was dropping a deuce," De Vito said.

"Little more information than I needed," Artie

Jay said. "Nelson's been winning since he sat down, and I've been losing. Damn."

De Vito nodded. He sat down and bought chips from the dealer. Nelson got his attention and drew a finger across his upper lip—*Wipe the cocaine off your nose.*

De Vito did as instructed. It made him mad that Nelson didn't toot up, too. De Vito was a heavy cocaine user who felt energized and focused only when high. Once he came down, he found himself in the grip of a hellish depression.

He'd started getting friendly with Nelson and Artie Jay after being hired as their disc jockey a year earlier. Artie Jay had gotten De Vito to play the music at several private parties, and soon enough Nelson and Artie Jay discovered that they were dicking the same gal: Charisma. She'd thought she was pitting them against each other, but once Nelson and De Vito found out they were banging the same chick, they felt they had something meaningful in common despite coming from vastly different backgrounds.

Nelson's family had huge money, while De Vito, a native Chicagoan, started out in life with less than zero. De Vito's mother was terrified of her husband, and while trying one evening to prevent his father from beating his mother insensate, De Vito got the worst of it and required hospitalization. Several weeks later, upon being discharged, he'd gone home for two minutes, kissed his mother goodbye and, with fifty bucks in his pocket, skedaddled to New York City. The only times he'd ever thought about Chi-town were those many instances when he savored fantasies about going back and blowing his father's brains all over Wabash Avenue. De Vito might have impressed most people as cool, calm and collected, but just below the surface boiled a murderous rage.

"Can't win for losin'," he said, throwing down his cards in disgust.

Artie Jay nodded—he was losing, too—but Nelson continued winning one hand after another.

Nelson tossed the dealer a one-hundred-dollar chip and said, "Nice to meet you." To his friends, he said, "Look, if this isn't fun for you, let's go somewhere else."

"Let's split," said De Vito, getting up and feeling only a little bit guilty that on the worst day of Frances' life he wasn't there by her side.

What the fuck? He wasn't about to walk away from a fun day with two pals, and they might even pick up a few girls because what Frances didn't know wouldn't hurt her.

Frances didn't know what the hell to think. This big black dude in the rapper getup with his tats and 'tude certainly wasn't a painfully shy fifteen-year-old Arab virgin she'd been hired to boink. Why had she been told that he *was* such a person?

She resented the way he'd picked her up like a rag doll and practically thrown her onto the sofa.

"You are *not* Karim," she said, taking a deep breath, looking this way and that for the nearest exit No sex with this big black bruiser. *Not gonna happen, dude.*

"You callin' me a *liar?*" He scowled at her, his stance confrontational, legs spread, arms folded. "My old man paid you *top dolla*, and he warn't payin' you to ax me dumb-ass questions. Now git yo' body naked and let's do dat wild thang."

She shook her head. "I can't. There's been a huge mistake…"

"Ain't no *mistake* goin' on, girlfrien'. You got yo' money. You here, I here, an' we bof' know *why*."

He was right about one thing—she *had* gotten all of her money, every dolla of it in cash that the IRS didn't need to know about, all of it locked away in her safe.

She nodded. "There has *definitely* been a *major* mistake. I need to speak to your father right away."

"Tell ya what," he said with a big horny smirk. "After we done with the wild thangin', ya can say all the shit thass in yo' pretty white head."

He dropped his pants. She looked down and saw a big flabby stomach and a small, uncircumcised, erect penis.

Although she'd heard a hundred stories from her girls about dates gone bad, Francesca had never personally experienced one. One client, the star of a wildly popular family sitcom, liked to throw punches and strangle women, and nearly killed one of Francesca's girls. There was the guitar hero who wanted to douse a girl with gasoline and set her on fire. She'd listened to their horror stories and nodded with much empathy, but none of those things had ever happened to *her*.

Now, what *was* she supposed to do about Karim and his ugly little erection?

"Suck my cock," he said, pointing at his boner. "Suck it till I squirt."

"No," she said with a vehement shake of her head as she got off the sofa. "No fuckin' way."

"*Yes* fuckin' way!" He jumped on top her and

52

shoved his erection into her mouth. He ripped her dress and grabbed her breasts.

She gagged on his ugly little cock. She tried to scream or vomit but could do neither.

Karim was getting what he was there for, and the fun, at least as far as he was concerned, was just beginning.

Chapter 6
Kayce

Seeing Saul Rofstein again was no great thrill for me, and I was glad that he didn't seem to remember me at all. After all, why would Saul Rofstein, in many ways the king of primetime TV, remember some skinny little chick who'd hung out with his daughter years earlier?

"I'm very sorry for your loss," I murmured, then pursed my lips. That was my way of saying, 'I assume you didn't do it.'

"Thank you," he said as he looked over at Frosty. "Who is she? Your secretary?"

"Kayce White. She's my colleague, an outstanding and accomplished associate who has done fine work for our firm. She's got a brilliant legal mind."

"Brilliant"! I stood up a bit straighter and took a deep breath. Did Frosty really think so highly of me, or was he just bullshitting a new client?

Saul looked in my direction. "She looks very young." He looked much too emotionally together for a man whose wife had just been shot to death. "And what kind of name is 'Kayce'?"

It's my *name, cockwad. Don't like it? Too fuckin' bad.*

Rofstein said nothing more about my name, and Frosty kept quiet about it, too. Not long after I started working for him, Frosty told me, "Maybe you should change your name. I've never met anyone named 'Kayce' before. It's kind of weird."

"Weird"? I'd never considered my name weird. Different, maybe, but not weird. I was totally O.K. with going through life as Kayce.

The two detectives had left us along but were still somewhere in the mansion, trying to decide what they had and what they could do with it. Were they going to arrest Saul Rofstein even though he had two lawyers with him at that moment? If so, what would be the charge? No weapon, no apparent weapon, no witnesses, Not much to go on.

I supposed that they would leave their suspect alone for now. Saul Rofstein was a famous man; he had what in Hollywood they called "juice." He knew everyone worth knowing, and in Beverly Hills that meant plenty.

"Being young is a good thing," I said, which was the wrong thing to say, because from that point on Saul Rofstein looked only at Frosty when he spoke, even when answering one of my questions.

I have always hated men who hated women simply based on our having vaginas, and Saul Rofstein was certainly a vagina-hater.

I wondered if he'd done it. Killed Gina, shot her in the head.

You're not my problem anymore, bitch.

I knew that Rofstein loved guns. Frances had shown me his gun collection. She had picked the lock with ease; throughout her life, she had done as she pleased and always with impunity. On that day she wanted to show me her father's collection of firearms.

I decided to refresh Saul's memory about who I was and why I was there.

"Mr. Rofstein," I said, "may we see your gun collection?"

"What?" Frosty asked, startled.

"Excuse me?" said Rofstein.

"We'd like to see your gun room," I said.

"What gun room?" Rofstein narrowed his eyes, as if wondering just who the fuck I thought I was. "What do you know about it?"

"Your daughter Frances and I used to know each other well," I told him. "She showed me the gun room."

Frosty shot me a look that said, *Why the hell didn't you tell me before we got here that you knew Frances Rofstein?*

"You and Fran were friends?" Rofstein shook his head in disbelief. "I thought I knew all her friends."

I nodded. "We hung out together. She brought me here to watch TV and have girl-talks."

"And she brought you *here*? To *my* house?"

I shrugged. "*You* didn't seem to mind."

"So you're telling me that my daughter brought you home and took you into my gun room?" His face was red with rage, as if he'd just said, *My daughter took you into my living room and let you take a dump on my priceless Persian rug?*

"She probably didn't think she was doing anything wrong."

He shook his head some more.

I took a moment to study his face. He didn't look as old or worried as I would have thought, considering how many million-dollar decisions he'd had to make over the decades—probably because he knew what he was doing most of the time. He was handsome in that way a person can be after a plastic surgeon gets done with the treatments. He'd stayed lean and tanned and dressed in the most flattering way. A fabulously wealthy, outrageously successful and powerful older man. Many women grooved on such dudes. I did not. I liked my men young and hot, buff and cut.

"She showed me your guns because she knew you were proud of them and she wanted to show them off. You know how kids can be sometimes."

"No," he said, "I don't know at all. Tell me about how they are."

Saul Rofstein was just putting me on. His wife was dead upstairs and he was standing there with Frosty and me, being a total douche bag because many years ago a couple of kids went poking into his gun collection.

I kept my yap shut, because to do otherwise would have cost me my involvement in this case, and I *really* wanted to be in on it. This case looked way too tasty.

Later on, the media arrived. We watched them on surveillance cameras. They couldn't get very far up the long and winding driveway, but they made themselves at home on the street below. They had their satellite vans and TV camera trucks, their reporters with hand-held microphones and plenty of attitude.

As the old saying in journalism goes, "If it bleeds, it leads." And this story bled like a hemophiliac. The brutal shooting of a beautiful woman who happened to be the wife of a legendary movie/TV producer.

Money, fame and Hollywood—one of the biggest stories of the year, maybe even the decade.

I need to remember to call Mitch folks. They hate seeing me on TV when it's unexpected. My father felt disgusted when I became a wonderfully overpaid defense attorney who was instrumental in gaining acquittals for defendants who were probably guilty. He probably wanted to say, 'If you're that good, you should be a prosecutor who's putting all that riff raff behind bars.'

Well, I had other ideas.

Being a defense lawyer is a hell of a challenge, and challenges always turn me on. My father is a prosecutor—one of the very best—and I didn't want to spend my career listening to people as they compared me to him. That would have been a monkey on my back I didn't want to deal with.

I love my father a great deal, but doing the same thing he does? Nix to that.

Frosty and I walked down Rofstein's long and winding driveway. I asked myself if, as a young criminal-defense lawyer I wanted a spread like Saul's for myself one day, I told myself that it might not be such a bad thing.

"Well?" said Frosty.

"Talk to me."

"Do you think he did it?"

"Dunno." I might have added, *Don't mean shit anyway, boss man. We're the defense team; our job is to get him acquitted, even if he's as guilty as sin.*

"He sure doesn't seem all busted up about it," I added.

"The cops didn't bust him. He's too important."

"And he had two badass lawyers standing next

to him," I said. "She was important, too."

"But *she's* dead."

No fuckin' shit.

"He may need us yet."

The media people all knew who Bryan Forst was. He had been a prominent Los Angeles criminal lawyer for some time. I was becoming a prominent Los Angeles attorney, too. However, I knew enough to let my boss handle things, so I kept my yap shut as he held up a hand and said, "No comment. Please step back and let us pass."

The photographers snapped our pictures. I knew I would be online all over the world. I kind of liked that. I keep forgetting how cute I am.

"Hey, Kayce," shouted a reporter, "do *you* have a comment?"

I looked at him right away. I'd been checking him out on TV. I'd also been masturbating to his image. He was relatively new to the L.A. market; they'd hired him away from Seattle. Now he was here, and living in my head as I kept my fingers between my thighs. I was much too horny these days and on the heaviest day of my period. He's Cuban or something, with buff shoulders, a full head of black hair and a big blond smile. Even better, he knew my name and used it. He knew that I existed. Way too flattering.

I concluded that he was a major hottie who could probably fuck me senseless. Cuban men are great lovers, I've been told.

I hoped this hunk would chase me, call me, date me, screw me.

"Sorry," I told him, "I have no comment."

Frosty shot me a dirty look. The best way of

declining to comment was by ignoring the question. By apologizing, I was paying him an unnecessary courtesy. Frosty clearly felt I should have known better. Which I did—but I wasn't sorry that I apologized.

The reporter handed me his business card. "When you do have a comment, please call me."

I snatched his card and stuffed it into my pocket. Frosty shot me another nasty look for accepting the card. When we reached his black Cadillac, he just got in and drove off.

I walked over to my red Mustang, a five-year-old gift from Mom and Dad.

"Thank you for accepting my card," said the reporter, who'd followed us unseen.

"You're welcome." I took out the card and looked at his name. "José Benitez."

He was checking me out and I was lubricating in my underpants, lonely and horny and delighted that this handsome man seemed in no hurry to walk away.

I've always had a sort of anxiety disorder that manifests in an embarrassing way. Whenever I'm overcome with nervousness or uncertainly, I smile—a big, huge, all-teeth-displayed smile. A smile can mean many things, especially things you didn't mean.

I smiled big-time. He smiled back. I got the impression that women smiled at him all the time.

"Want to join me for a drink later on?" he asked, stepping closer and clearly confident that I was *not* going to say, 'No thanks. You're not my type.'

Hmm, I thought. *Is that just a 'drink' invitation or does he actually have something different in mind?*

Yes, that was a 'let's fuck' invitation. And I was ready to jump his bones, mainly because my last boyfriend had taken off.

O.K., my new Cuban friend, let's pursue this matter. Bring it on, big man.

I nodded. "Let's have that drink."

I checked his finger. No wedding band.

Give it to me, baby.

Chapter 7
Hayley

Hayley Coleman drove home all smiles, congratulating herself for having her courage to sit down and tell him, really tell him, about what was on her mind and what she wanted from him.

She felt such relief, especially when he nodded and agreed that it would be best for all involved if she told his wife of their affair and they divorced. Then Hayley would end up with the man and they would get married. How cool was that?

Well, he hadn't really specified all that, but how could it turn out any other way? After his divorce he would be the proud father of a bouncing newborn baby. Of *course* he would want to marry her so they could live together and raise their child.

She smiled and smiled and smiled.

She was so excited! She had been intimate with this man for about a year, and all the while he had been promising her he would leave his wife. Well, after all, he was a career politician, and his job was to get elected and stay in power. The way to get elected was by getting people to vote for you, and the way to get those votes was by telling those voters whatever they seemed to want to hear, and to promise things they knew they could never deliver

Hayley, not altogether naïve, knew she shouldn't count on marrying this man till they were at the altar and the preacher pronounced them husband and wife.

But right now she was having the easiest time convincing herself that their life together was a done deal, now that they were about to become parents. That made all the difference.

Hayley, she said to herself, *you've got it made.*   .

"You retarded cunt!" Senator Strom Greggins muttered as he got into his tan Volvo for the drive home. Did Hayley really believe that he would leave his wife Joanie for a *nobody*, a *nothing* like Hayley? True, Hayley was cute a button, a great kisser, had a gorgeous bod and worked her butt off for him. But Hayley was a humble girl from somewhere out west—she'd told him all about herself countless times but he'd never cared enough to remember the details—whereas Joni Drake, an American blueblood, was cultured, stylish, chic, eloquent, erudite, possessed of true *savoir vivre*. Her family was rich and she was considered the most charming of Washington hostesses.

Joni's father was s Supreme Court justice; her mother the heiress to a Wall Street fortune. The Drakes were direct descendants of Sir Francis. Had Hayley come from that kind of stock? *Uh, no,* Strom thought, *I don't think so.*

Despite what he'd promised to Hayley, Strom would never give up the good deal he'd already gotten as a result of marrying into the Drake family. He had grown up a humble young man. His father was a car salesman—the best one for a hundred miles in every direction, but a car salesman just the same—and his mother had worked as a nurse's aide till she retired when her children were born. Strom had grown up deeply ashamed of his family and contacted them as infrequently as possible.

Upon coming of age, he had perceived himself as having looks, brains and ambition in excess. What he lacked was a beautiful girlfriend from a good family. In Joni he found such a person. By marrying her, he came a Drake of sorts himself and suddenly became a viable political candidate and someone envied and admired by all.

While Joni had never been exactly the fuck of the century, he'd been most eager to father two children by her—Francis, eleven and Nanci, seven. Both kids were cute and obedient most of the time. With them in his life, he knew he would always be considered a Drake, and to him, that was a shitload better than being a Greggins. He was reasonably content with things—he'd done well as a senator, and he wanted to run for president—until that workaholic from California came along with her gorgeous titties and gave him a boner that refused to go to sleep.

"I'm pregnant," she'd said, the two words no married man wants to hear from his girlfriend. Especially when that married man has an entire career to lose over such a scandal.

There was also his marriage that would certainly crumble…

What can I do about this mess?

Offer her lots of money if she'll get an abortion?

Nix to that. Hayley would never go for it.

Get her an apartment, wait till the kid is born, then give it up for adoption.

Strom shook his head. She would say no to *that*, too.

He shook his head, chastising himself for considering his own wants and needs, when she had made her own perfectly clear. She wanted *him* to marry *her* and *they* would raise *their* child together.

Strom could be thick-headed when someone was telling him things he didn't want to hear. It took a little while for those things to sink in.

He pondered his options. *Did* he have options? He was going to do just as Hayley wanted, right?

Not necessarily…

"Hey!" Rikki Holyfield called out as Hayley Coleman walked on by towards her apartment.

Hayley, lost in her own thoughts, spun around in the hallway and smiled at her neighbor. Rikki was a light-skinned black, pretty and vivacious, in her late twenties, just now starting to get soft in the middle. She worked as a secretary somewhere and went online nightly, picking up and discarding men by the dozen.

Rikki smiled back. "You look very happy, Hayley. Either you've just won the Powerball or you just got a power-ball."

Hayley smiled some more. She thought of what to say to Rikki. They were friendly but not exactly friends. They'd had dinner a few times, gone out to singles' bars, freaked out each other with tales of being a young single woman in L.A.

"Did I git me some last night?" Hayley said. "Nix. Wish I had. Coulda used some."

"No man you're in love with right now?" Rikki asked, folding her arms. "Because you look like a

66

woman in love."

"I'm in love with life," Hayley retorted. "Only man in my life is Jesus."

Rikki giggled. "You can have him. Jewish men just don't do it for me. Especially when they're two thousand years old."

"Whatever turns you on."

"Call me later," said Rikki, walking away. "Maybe we'll hang out."

"O.K." Hayley entered her apartment.

Wow! This was the most exciting day of her life! She needed to speak to someone about it. Her parents wouldn't approve. Hayley wasn't totally convinced that she herself approved, either.

Why not Kayce, her best bud since high school?

Kayce was tactful and discreet, which made her very different from most of the people Hayley had ever known. Kayce would be delighted, since her whole attitude towards Hayley had always been, 'If you're thrilled, I'm thrilled for you.' Kayce would also be freaked out because Hayley had never said, 'Oh, by the way, I'm bumping uglies with Senator Greggins.'

Double wow! Triple wow! I can't keep this to myself any longer. I'm going to call Kayce and tell her all about it tonight!

"Daddy's home!" Nanci cried out, throwing herself into her father's arms.

"My girl's getting bigger every day!" Strom said, kissing his adorable daughter on the forehead.

"I had a good day. Did *you*, Daddy?"

I had a perfectly shitty day, he wanted to shout at his child. He wanted to throw her against the wall and smack her across the face, too. But he had to admit that the blow job Hayley had given him felt very nice, very nice indeed. He now regretted it, although he did not regret ending their relationship. Hayley did not know they were through; she thought they were just getting started.

Joni sauntered out of their living room into the front hallway of their not exactly magnificent but still very comfortable house. She was always immaculate and impeccable, her blonde hair perfect, her body slim and toned. A very attractive woman of forty, she had long stopped being someone her husband craved for sex; he liked the young ones who would blow him till his cock exploded. The same cutie he'd married years earlier wouldn't consider giving him head now.

"How did it go today?" she asked in a distracted tone, as if not giving a shit. She added that they had a fundraiser to attend, so he'd better get ready.

He interacted with Joni as if she were his business partner, not his wife. They were rarely intimate, which surprised him because he didn't think they were terribly old yet. They did it maybe twice per month, and when it did happen, she lay spread-eagled on their bed, waiting for him to stick it to her.

She didn't climax.

She considered fellatio immoral.

She thought penises were ugly, even his. She didn't want to touch his blue-veined phallus.

His wife was one of those women who hated sex, so what was he to do except get his satisfaction from another woman?

So that's what he did.

Hayley put on some rock music and danced around

her apartment, she was so thrilled about her upcoming marriage and motherhood. How she loved it when things went her way! Too bad it happened so infrequently.

Today is the best day of my life. Today is the first day of my new life. Life can be so beautiful and wonderful when you actually get the things you want. I love Strom and he loves me and we will have so many happy years together.

Beaming, she picked up the telephone and dialed Kayce's number in Los Angeles.

She frowned at the sound of the recorded greeting. She said, "Kayce, it's Hayley. I have some amazing news, so call me when you get in."

She put down the telephone and beamed some more. Strom wouldn't mind that she'd told Kayce, and Strom surely wouldn't find out anyway.

Chapter 8
Nelson

De Vito said he wanted to go to a striptease club. Nelson said nix to that. Artie Jay said he would do whatever the other guys decided on.

"Why go see those chick in a strip club when you live with the finest fox around?" Nelson asked. Frances, he thought, was just too damned gorgeous. De Vito was so lucky to be with her.

De Vito had completely pushed Frances out of his mind. To hell with her and her recently slain mother. He was gonna have himself a good time tonight and not think of anyone or anything else.

"Shit, Nelson, why don't you mind your own fuckin' business?" said De Vito.

"Kiss my ass, crackhead," retorted Nelson.

"What did you just say to me? Did I hear you right?" De Vito scowled. He had a bad temper and would throw punches if provoked. Nelson was pretty sure he could take De Vito if it came down to a fight. De Vito was a decent size, but so was Nelson. Plus, Nelson figured that, deep down inside, Dc Vito was a coward who would back off if Nelson squared off to fight him.

"Gentlemen," said Artie Jay, "let's go chow down. I'm famished. You can kick the shit out of each other after we're done eating."

"Steak," said Nelson. "It's a great way to get lots of energy fast. I'll need it if I'm gonna fight numb-nuts over here, especially if he takes a few hits off the pipe before we mix it up. Nothin' more dangerous than a crackhead who wants to kick your ass because you've insulted him."

They ended up in a steak house in which several young women took turns staring at them. Artie Jay, De Vito and Nelson knew they were uncommonly handsome, and Artie Jay and Nelson knew it helped being handsome *and* rich. De Vito resented Nelson, Frances and Artie Jay for being born into rich families. He resented Artie Jay less because Artie Jay was a black man living in a white man's world.

Their waitress was a pretty woman who had probably come to Atlantic City to try her luck in show business in nearby Manhattan. She smiled at her three handsome guests, and particularly at De Vito, who smiled back.

Hitting on waitresses was usually something De Vito considered beneath him, mainly because he felt they were no better than he was, but this one really *was* cute enough to be an aspiring actress or something and probably vulnerable to seduction. Frances was off entertaining some guy, so why shouldn't *he* show *himself* a good time?

"Hey, beautiful girl, what's your name?" De Vito asked.

She pointed at her name tag, which said Doris. "Remember my name. It will be in lights one day."

"I'm sure it will. So you're an actress who's doing this to pay the bills for the time being. Am I right?"

She nodded. "And I hope my big break comes soon."

Artie Jay and Nelson smirked at each other, knowing that De Vito was about to make her an offer she probably wouldn't refuse.

"Maybe I can help you with that," said De Vito.

"Seriously?" Doris brightened. So many guys came in, full of promises because they wanted to get into her pants. But maybe this one was different.

"I'm very serious. I know people in the biz."

Artie Jay put a hand over his mouth as he smirked, thinking, *What would Doris say if she knew De Vito was a crackhead with a sexy girlfriend?*

"When does your shift end?" De Vito asked Doris.

She looked at him. Handsome man, longish hair, full of himself. It never hurt to know people who knew people. "I'm off at eleven."

"See you then," De Vito.

Doris walked off, smiling. Nelson leaned over and said, "Who do you know 'in the biz'?"

"I live with Frances. Her father is Saul. He knows Hollywood. He *is* Hollywood."

Nelson guffawed. "Saul won't do jackshit for his own daughter, so why would he do anything for that waitress chick?"

De Vito shrugged. "I can make that girl some big money."

"How?" Nelson asked. "By making her another one of the chicks you and Frances send all over Manhattan?"

De Vito's eyes narrowed. "Who told you about that?"

"Uh, just about everyone. It's the worst-kept

secret in New York. You better be careful."

"Why?"

"Because it is illegal," said Nelson.

"We won't get caught."

"And why not?" asked Artie Jay.

"Because we're too well organized. It's all cash, no checks, no credit cards. We won't get busted."

"Don't call *me* at three in the morning to bail you out," said Nelson. "It'll be all over the news. Frances will get busted, too. Saul will shit a brick when he finds out what she's been up to. You've made enough money to buy that fancy car, so you should get out of that business *tout de suite*."

De Vito shook his head, scowling. "Absolutely not. No fuckin' way. You're a fool to think we'll get busted."

"*You're* a fool to think you won't," said Artie Jay. "You're a pimp. Pimps get busted. That's kind of how these things work."

"Thank you, counsel."

"You're welcome, pimp."

De Vito stood up. "I'm goin' for a walk. See ya when I see ya."

As he left, Nelson muttered, "That went better than expected."

"De Vito's a douche," said Artie Jay, "and we *know* he's a douche, so why do we hang out with him?"

"Because he's our friend and we have history."

"You're a loyal friend."

Nelson nodded. "Damn straight. Loyalty is one of the things I value most in life." Then, "He's sucking on the glass dick too much. It's becoming a problem. *He's* becoming a problem."

"We could get him into rehab. Would he go?"

"Maybe."

"And his, uh, 'business enterprise' is a very bad idea. He needs to end it and pretend it didn't happen."

Nelson shook his head. "De Vito doesn't listen to anyone—except himself, sometimes."

"Then maybe we should have a little heart-to-heart with Frances and say, 'We're concerned about your boy De Vito. We think we can help him.'"

Nelson waved this off. "Not gonna happen. She's more stubborn than he is."

Just then Doris returned with their orders. "Where's he gone? To the restroom?"

"He'll be back," said Artie Jay.

"Mind if I ask you a question?"

"Ask," said Nelson.

"Well, in this place," she said, her eyes darting this way and that, "we get lots of horny guys who are on the make. They're away from their wives or girlfriends for the weekend, and it's like they want to get me into bed and then forget we've ever met."

"Ask your question," Artie Jay said, stuffing a mouthful of steak into his face.

"Does he have the juice to help me in my career, or was that just a load of crap? Because I've met customers who've offered me help but *they* were full of crap."

"You're a bright young lady," said Nelson. "Figure it out for yourself."

"So he's full of crap."

"That depends on what you think he can do for you," said Artie Jay.

Doris nodded. "Then I guess I can trust him."

Sure, you can trust him, Nelson thought. *You can trust him to get you into bed and bang you silly, then turn you out so you can start making him some money so he can buy himself more crack. Yeah, you can sure trust him to do that.*

When Doris came by with the check, Nelson handed her his credit card. She stuck it into the handheld reader and he punched in his PIN and a very generous tip.

"It's sure too bad about Gina Roff" Doris said, concluding that they were all friends now and she could mention such a matter to them. She started to think that the black guy was the one she should flirt with because of his big eyes, muscular body and big sunny smile.

"The cops are thinking that maybe Saul Rofstein might have killed her," Margot added.

Nelson swallowed hard. "Gina Roff is dead?"

Artie Jay shook his head. "Unreal. Tragic. I had no idea."

"CNN has been all over it for the past while," Doris said. "Everyone is talking about it."

Nelson put his credit card back into his wallet. "We better go get De Vito and tell him. He needs to get back to Frances right away."

"Frances? Who's she?" Doris asked, in a voice that suggested she didn't really want to know.

"Gotta split," Nelson said. He and Artie Jay got to their feet.

"So your friend De Vito can give me a career boost?" Doris asked, smiling. "Do you have his business card? May I have it?"

"Better find another mentor," Nelson told her. "I have a hunch you're not going to be his top priority for the next while."

Chapter 9

Frances

Frances wrapped her coat around her torso to conceal her ripped dress as she ran out of Karim's suite after being slapped around, raped, degraded and humiliated for very nearly two hours. She had screamed, *"No! Stop! Fuck off!"* but he'd merely laughed in her face and abused her some more.

Once done with her, he'd backed off a few steps, letting her gather her coat and handbag and bolt away, cackling as she wiped tears from her face. Down in the lobby, she snatched out her iPhone with shaking hands and called Chick.

"You there? I'm on my way out now."

"Fuckin' doorman shooed me away," he replied. "I thought you said this gig would be, like, half an hour."

"Doesn't matter what I said. Get your ass here *now!*"

She stood just inside the lobby's huge glass doors, shuddering at the memory of Karim's huge hands all over her breasts, buttocks, vagina.

Well, I'm going to get even with that fat sack of shit. Not sure how, but I will retaliate. Wait till I tell his old man about our session. Either discipline the boy or I will never send another of my girls to you.

By and by the Rolls driven by Chick appeared. She slid into the back seat and said, "Where the hell were you?"

"Down the block. Manhattan traffic is impossible. My boss says half an hour, so I figure it'll be thirty minutes."

"You're fired," Frances said.

"You don't mean that." Then, "That gig go O.K.? You took like someone took a few punches at you."

"Shut up and drive."

The sheikh was in a meeting when his cell phone rang. He left the room and realized the call was from that madam, Francesca Roff. He had a very beautiful young wife who wouldn't understand about why Francesca was in his life, and he had many business associates who would love something like a marital indiscretion to use against him.

Francesca fuckin' Roff. Why was she calling *him*?

"Yes?" he said into the cell phone.

"Abdul?" she asked in a thin, tiny voice.

"What you want?"

"I want to know why you did that to me."

"What do you want?"

She realized that she didn't know what she wanted with him. She wanted an apology, from him and his brute of a son.

"Karim is a pig! He slapped and punched me! He ripped my clothes! You told me he was a fifteen-year-old virgin!"

She said more, then waited for a response. Only

then did she figure out that he had hung up on her.

She imagined his voice in her ear, saying things like, *"Hooker. Tramp. Whore. Trash."*

Frances shook those words out of her head. She was a hip, stylish New Yorker who'd found success on her own terms, without any assistance from her filthy rich parents.

She wiped tears from her cheeks. Where was that goddamn De Vito when she needed a hug?

De Vito sat in a strip club getting a lap dance from a voluptuous brunette who probably could see that she did not have his undivided attention. He decided that getting mad at Nelson and Artie Jay wasn't the best idea he had ever had. They were just envious of him because he was the very best disc jockey around, plus he'd gotten into this other business that paid megabucks. Nelson and Artie Jay had parents who had always given them whatever they asked for. They were spoiled brats.

De Vito Silvera saw himself as a true survivor. He'd come up the hardest way possible and made it on his own. He was still young enough to enjoy all the pussy and money and drugs that went with being successful.

Alas, there were some things he had said and done along the way. Things he considered most regrettable and that he would forget about if he could.

Smoking crack helped put him in an ideal frame of mind. He temporarily forgot about the bad stuff and focused on the good stuff. Too bad it was so damned expensive.

He liked to smoke crack. Everyone had his own

thing. Crack was De Vito's thing. If some people didn't approve, too fuckin' bad.

The stripper kept at him. He just wasn't responding. She knew the old saying: The bigger the thrill, the bigger the bill. She was after a big tip and decided to keep stimulating him so that the big tip would happen.

De Vito was tired of her. He got up and pushed her off him. Then he reached into his pocket, pulled out a few twenties and tossed them at her. "You're a very pretty lady," he told her. "Buy yourself something nice."

Since De Vito was temporarily unavailable, Frances called Allyn, one of the girls who occasionally worked for her. "Would you come over? I can't reach De Vito and I'm all alone here."

"I'm already there." Click.

Presently Allyn, a thirty-year-old singer who did not know her voice was mediocre, arrived with a bottle of champagne and a jug of orange juice.

"The best things to drink on a bad day," she said, mixing the two beverages.

As they drank, Allyn said, "You go out on a bad date?"

"The fucking worst," Frances said, sipping her Mimosa.

"Your kitchen looks as if you've never used it," said Allyn.

"We never cook. We had a cook when I was growing up. De Vito doesn't cook, either."

"So, what's the deal? You and De Vito having problems? He's a handsome man, but I don't guess he's the easiest roommate—"

"De Vito's not the problem," Frances said, shaking her head. "Why would you say such a thing?"

"Because if you're a woman who's having problems in life, it's usually due to a man. They're all such douches. They eat, sleep, fart and not much else. They take us for granted. My right hand can show me a better time."

My man De Vito would make you scream, Frances thought.

"Know what?" Allyn continued. "I've sworn off men unless I'm being paid to go out with them. But I will date them if the price is right. Aside from that, I'm putting all my resources into my singing career."

"As we've established," Frances said, "I've just returned from a bad date."

"I didn't think you even *went* on dates anymore."

"Well, this one was special. Or at least it was supposed to be special."

"What went wrong?"

"He abused me. Practically raped me."

"Had you already been paid?"

Frances nodded.

"Not sure if you can call it rape if he paid you for sex. You can't exactly pocket his money and say, 'You can't do this or that.' You took his money, so you have to submit to him."

They spoke of other things for an hour, then Frances, cranky and bruised, got rid of Allyn, who was slurping down Mimosas. Frances realized she would be happier sitting there alone, watching TV.

Presently Frances got a throbbing headache, so she took a couple of codeine tablets and went to bed.

What if that fat fuck had given her herpes or

H.I.V.? Or gotten her pregnant?

She could sue the sheikh for millions. Sue him and his family. Didn't he have two dozen children by as many women? Didn't Arab oil guys do things that way?

If she did sue, wouldn't she have to admit that she was a prostitute, and he a trick, and that he had roughed her up during a date? That would make the six-o'clock news and Mommy and Daddy would get an unwanted update of their daughter's comings and goings and doings.

After a while she closed her eyes and dozed off. She told herself, *De Vito will be home soon. He will put things right. He always does.*

Chapter 10

Kayce

José Benitez is way too hot. He should be ashamed of himself. He should have a warning label covering his ass: *This could be hazardous to your health.*

We went from a drink at a bar to sex in his apartment. His place was small but tidy. We fucked like minks. I had been told by other guys that I wasn't the best lay around; I think all I needed was the right partner.

Now he's asleep, and I can't believe just how handsome he is. I'm looking at him all over; later I'll look at his apartment. I love looking at him when he's naked because he's got it all hanging out and isn't embarrassed or anything—not that this one has anything to be shy about. I poked around in his home as he woke up.

"Het! Where are you?" he called from the bedroom.

"Ripping you off," I said. "Trouble is, you have nothing worth stealing."

He emerged from his bedroom, naked and with a raging boner. "Back to bed, baby girl. I want to get something straight between us."

I looked and smirked. "So I see."

Just then my iPhone rang. Stupidly I answered it.

Saul Rofstein. At two in the morning! What the fuck?

I answered my telephone because Frosty had given him my number so that I, not Frosty, would have to put up with Saul's ridiculous bullshit at the most impossible hours.

"Hi," I said.

"I need to speak to you," he said.

"I'm listening."

"I need to speak to you in person."

"It's two in the morning."

"So what? Put your panties on and get over here." Click.

"Who was that?" asked José.

"Some guy who says that if I don't go see him right away, he's gonna do something desperate."

José frowned. "So you're leaving me at this hour to go to him?"

"Looks like."

"Call me. Or I'll call you. We'll fuck again."

I smiled. "Sounds like a plan."

Presently I was on the freeway, driving out to see Saul Rofstein in nonexistent traffic.

When I reached his house, Saul Rofstein sat smoking a cigar in his bathrobe, looking nothing like a man who'd just lost his wife in a brutal murder. He glanced up and said, "You look like you just got laid."

"How may I help you?"

"You can go to LAX and fly out to New York."

"Why would I do such a thing?" In my brief career as a lawyer, I've always tried not to be surprised by clients and their requests, but being asked—

told?—to fly out to New York at two in the morning seemed a bit much.

"I need you to fly out there and fetch my daughter because I can't seem to reach her and you know her."

"You need me to do *what?*"

"Are you hard of hearing?" Then, "I'm not asking you to fly to Mars and bring me some rock samples. I just want to you bring my daughter to me and I'm thinking you're the only who can do it."

"I haven't said a word to Frances in years. I probably wouldn't know her if I saw her on the sidewalk."

"I'm not asking you, I'm telling you. Bryan Forst and I have already spoken of this matter, and we agreed that you should collect Frances and bring her to me."

"But—"

"There's an e-ticket in your laptop's mailbox. Your flight leaves at seven. I have a computer printout here with Frances' address and telephone number. I've left a message on her machine saying that she should expect you today. Good luck."

I boiled with rage as I got back into my car. Who did Saul Rofstein think I was, his personal flunkie?

"Fuck you, Frosty Forst, for thinking it was O.K. for Saul Rofstein to treat me this way!" I said aloud. "How come I have to bring Frances Rofstein home for her mother's funeral? How come it has to be *me?*"

Chapter 11
Hayley

After calling Kayce and leaving a message. Hayley regretted not finding out where Rikki was going and inviting herself along. She felt all pumped up with adrenalin and didn't want to spend Saturday night alone in her cramped apartment.

What's Strom doing right now? Is he thinking of me and our baby? Is he as thrilled as I am about our life together?

Hayley just couldn't wait for the two of them to go public about their relationship. She tried to imagine the look on Joni's face when he told her they were through, but from what he'd told Hayley, Joni didn't care about their marriage, so maybe she'd just shrugged and said, 'O.K., do what you want.'

Strom had told Hayley, 'Joni and I never have sex. We have nothing in common except our children. They're the only reason we're still together.'

Hayley believed him and loved him without judging him. She considered him the best thing that had ever happened to her and wanted to be the best wife to him any man had ever had.

Looking back on it, she regretted having yelled at and threatened him. But a pregnancy was a serious matter and she needed him to be aware of what was happening in the lives and act accordingly.

He now knew what he needed to know and was aware of what he needed to do.

Now she just needed to hang back and be cool.

"Joni," Strom whispered into his wife's ear, "who the hell *are* these people?"

"They're reformed criminals who are doing their best to make our city much safer."

"Meaning…?"

"See that longhaired guy over there?" She pointed to a Hispanic man with a tidy ponytail, a goatee and a gold stud in his ear.

"Yeah? What about him?"

"He's a former Satan's Slave who is now a law-abiding citizen. He now spends his days with young groups, talking about the 'gangbanging' life and how to avoid it."

Strom frowned as his wife spoke. What the hell did she know about 'gangbanging' and its hazards? She was the most sheltered person he had ever met. She always had a cause and seemed to consider herself superior to everyone else.

"Let me introduce you to him," Joni said.

"No thanks." He had other things on his mind, like what to do about Hayley. Pretty, wholesome, pregnant Hayley with her blow jobs.

"You must meet him." They went over to meet the reformed biker. In her most ladylike voice, Joni said, "Eduardo, I would like you to meet my husband, Senator Strom Greggins."

Eduardo eyeballed him, and Strom could see right away that this was no reformed biker—he was a criminal making some friends in the straight world.

"Pleased to meet you," said Strom in his best bullshit-artist voice. "My wife tells me you're doing good work for the kids."

Eduardo shrugged. "Doin' what I can. Not always easy, pretty often hard, but I'm doin' what I can."

"I'm sure you're making a big difference," Strom said, waving at the waiter for another drink.

"Eduardo never gives up," said Joni, nodding. "We need funding for all of the youth centers he wants to open across the country. Unfortunately, right now we have only one. When we have the kids in centers instead of on the streets, it can make all the difference. I want to put together a special concert to raise money. Eduardo thinks it would be a great idea to get some of the local rap guys involved."

Strom winced. *Rap guys!* She was such a square white girl! Even he knew that the term was *rappers.*

"I appreciate whatever you can do to help," Eduardo said. "Maybe tomorrow you can come by, check us out, see what we're doin'."

Good deal, thought Strom. *That's exactly how I'd love to spend my Sunday.*

"Maybe I'll do that," he said. *But don't be too heartbroken if I'm a no-show.*

Eduardo licked his lips as he stared at Joni's breasts.

Shit! Strom thought. *I sure hope Joni hasn't given him our address or telephone number.*

Norma Norgard had the apartment next to Hayley's.

Norma was pushing ninety and everyone she knew had died. No relatives or friends; nobody really seemed to give a shit about her.

Many, many years earlier, and quite far away, she, a splendidly beautiful young woman who, on her best day, was a moderately competent actor, resided in a Hollywood mansion with an old man who also happened to be a millionaire movie producer. Back then, being a millionaire was tantamount to being a billionaire today. At least that's what Norma said— she had plenty to say to those few who cared to listen.

Hayley made a point of stopping by Norma's suite every couple of days, mainly to make sure that the old girl was still alive. Hayley also fed Norma's emaciated cat, Cary. Norma said—and Hayley had no reason to doubt her—that she had been the lover of many major stars, including Cary Grant.

"That man was meant to be 'The Man from Dream City' since he was born." Norma closed her eyes and sighed. She remembered old Hollywood to Hayley, leaving the younger woman feeling as if she'd actually been there and done that herself.

"The movie stars today aren't sexy or glamorous anymore," Norma said. "Now, in my area, we *knew* about being chic and stylish…"

With Strom on her mind, Hayley knocked on Norma's door, always relieved to discover that the old lady had lived to see another day.

"Just saying hi. Can't stay," Hayley said.

"You look so pretty today. You're just radiant with happiness. Looks like someone has a new beau."

Hayley blushed and smiled. "Well, it's complicated."

Cary the cat wandered on by and began rubbing

against her legs. She bent down to scratch him and he turned his face up towards her, eyes closed. He started purring.

"Not so complicated," said Norma. "It's your fella, Mark, isn't it? He has proposed marriage."

"Mark and I broke up."

"But there's someone new."

Hayley wished she could talk about it. Wished she could go on CNN and say, 'I'm pregnant with Senator Strom Greggins' baby. He's married but I want him to divorce his wife and marry me.'

"I'm keeping company with an old friend," was what she said.

"Old friends." Norma nodded. "Had my share of those." Then, "Well, thank you for coming by. As always, I certainly appreciate it."

"Glad to do it." As she walked away, she thought of inviting Norma to her wedding: *Senator Strom Greggins and Ms. Hayley Coleman request the honor of your presence*…Yes. Yes! *Yes!*

"No!" Strom shook his head with the utmost vehemence as he and Joni drove home. "I will not go to Eduardo's 'youth center' just because you say I should. It's probably filled with gangbangers, anyway."

"Strom," she said in the coolest, calmest voice, "visiting Eduardo would be a terrific idea. It would show your constituents, and everyone else, that while you may not have much in common with the Eduardos of this world, you certainly have empathy and are eager to see them improve in life. Call your assistant and have her alert the media. I would make for a first-rate photo opportunity."

Why did Joni always refer to Hayley as "your assistant"? The two women had met at least a dozen times; surely Joni could remember Hayley's name by now? Maybe that was just Joni's way of putting her down. Joni, overprivileged in every way from birth, had been brought up to believe it was O.K. to look down on everyone who was not as fortunate as herself. Josie also felt it important to pretend that she was the biggest-hearted of all liberals.

In reality, Joni had gone through life considering herself inherently superior to all others. She had married Strom because he seemed to be destined for a powerful political career, and she knew that she, as his wife, would be the envy of everyone else. Did she love him? Probably not; but did she love anyone, including herself?

But Joni seemed content with their life together, so long as their children stayed cute and healthy and their father's career went from the senate to the White House. Still, there was this problem called *Hayley Coleman* that just would not go away.

What was he to do about her? He didn't know, but he needed to something immediately.

Chapter 12
Nelson

Back in their deluxe hotel suite, Artie Jay hurried as he threw items into their overnight bags. Nelson tried to contact De Vito on his iPhone but it didn't work; when he called Frances on hers, she didn't answer it.

By then, Artie Jay had turned on the TV and they had gotten the full awful story about Gina Rofstein's murder.

"It's weird that we're just now hearing about it," said Nelson. "Poor Frances. That's all I can say."

"Maybe," Artie Jay said, "the husband did it. That old dude always freaked me out."

"That dude's a self-made billionaire," Nelson retorted. "I think he's got enough brains *not* to do something like that."

"Or maybe he's got so much *chutzpah* or conceit that he's like, 'I can do this and get away with this because I have the money to get the best lawyers like O.J. did.'"

"The media will love this one. 'Legendary movie and TV producer shoots own wife in the head while she sleeps.' Unreal, surreal, outrageous."

Nelson had wondered if he should call his mother. Lovey had run Sappho Pictures and Gina Rofstein had appeared in a few Lovey-Rofstein co-productions. She must have known Gina; maybe the two had been friends. She probably didn't have much use for Saul.

De Vito burst into their suite, running a hand through his long hair. "You fuckers had me paged! Anyone want to explain what *that* was about? I was all set to make a fortune at the baccarat table."

"I guess you haven't heard," said Nelson.

"Heard what?" De Vito thought, *Shit, man. Now they know. They want me to go back to Frances and call off our fun weekend.*

"Gina Rofstein," Nelson said.

"Frances' mom," said De Vito, nodding.

"She's been shot," said Nelson.

De Vito closed his eyes. "Oh, wow," he murmured.

"She's dead, De Vito," said Artie Jay. "You need to call Frances now."

"Plus," said Nelson, "you need to go back to New York."

"Frances never carries a cell phone." De Vito felt hugely disappointed with his friends and their do-the-right-thing bullshit. He knew he would have to follow their advice if he wished to continue being their friend.

"They're saying that Saul probably did it," Artie Jay told him. "Brutal, nasty shit, man."

De Vito shrugged. "Never met the folks. Frances didn't have much use for them. She called and said, 'How about some startup cash? I'm trying to begin my career,' and they said, 'Not gonna happen.' So they rarely spoke afterwards."

"All the more reason you should be at her side right now," Nelson said. "We're all packed. Let's roll."

"O.K.," said De Vito. Thinking, *Goodbye, liaison with the sexy waitress at the steakhouse. I would have banged her silly, then made her one of my whores.*

A few hours later, Nelson cruised up in his BMW to De Vito and Frances' building.

De Vito eased himself out of the car, dreading what lay ahead of him upstairs. The time was well past midnight, and as soon as he got up there he would have to listen to Frances bitch like a motherfucker about her parents. She had done so a zillion times already, and that was her favorite thing to do once her anger built up enough—just blame everything on Mommy and Daddy. Usually he simply said, 'Your life is good, *our* life is good, so quit pissing and moaning about your parents.' But this was different, and he knew that he would have to sit there and listen to her *kvetch* till the sun came up.

"Should we go up with you?" asked Nelson, certainly hoping the answer would be no.

"Yes, please."

Nelson reached over to unbuckle his seat belt.

"Just kidding. I can deal with her shit myself. Goodnight."

He got out of the car, and once he was out of sight, Nelson said to Artie Jay, "You tired?"

"Not at all. What you have in mind?"

"Go over to the club."

"Let's do it."

Nelson wondered if Ria would be there, surrounded by a dozen butt-kissers. He hoped she would be there but knew that he would have a panic attack if he saw her. His infatuation with her was simply ludicrous. He could have five hundred women if he wanted them, but he had eyes only for that sexy woman and her gorgeous voice. She treated him like shit—no, she treated him worse than that—and he, Nelson Skalbania, wasn't used to being treated that way.

He was Nelson Skalbania, and he deserved to be treated with dignity and respect. And he was going to get it, dammit.

"Another screwdriver," said Ria in her soft European accent.

Her boyfriend of the moment nodded and stood up. A South American model, not quite out of his teens, and Ria showed him off as her newest possession, someone or something she could play with and enjoy till her bored her, at which time she would cast him aside as she had done to all the others. He was handsome, though, and she wasn't ready to part with him just yet.

Ria called him Pet. She called all of her boyfriends Pet. This one didn't mind; he was just too thrilled to be with her.

She looked in the mirror for a moment, smiling at how beautiful she was, and then she noticed that Nelson Skalbania had entered the club.

So handsome. Always trying to say and do the right things. Always with a king-sized boner for her.

She wondered what he would think if he knew that many years earlier, when she was in her middle teens, she'd been deflowered by his father, the great Theodakis Skalbania, on board his yacht in the middle of nowhere.

Ria looked at nothing in particular and smiled. The great Theo. The great lover.

Did the son have his father's virility?

Should she trouble herself to discover if it was so?

Maybe. It might entertain her to find out. But then, it might disappoint her.

Nelson made his way to her table. He was late that evening; usually he entered the nightclub much earlier in the evening. She checked him out, deciding that he did have his own style, his own way of doing and saying things. Style, of course, was nice but it wasn't everything. If they weren't barely legal, somehow preferred men who were older and immensely powerful.

She watched as Nelson went from table, his arms grabbed by females who wanted him to sit with them. He shook his head, smiled and moved on. By and by he reached Ria's table.

"Ria," he said, as suave as a movie star. "Lovely to see you. Is there anything you need? Can I do anything for you?"

"If I desire or require anything, Nelson," she replied, stroking Pet's hair, "I will get a waiter."

"Just so," he said, smiling. Thinking, *Well, at least she remembered my name tonight.* "May I send over a bottle of Cristal for you to enjoy."

"Bring a few. We get thirsty."

Shit! What an attitude! Gimme, gimme, gimme.

"A few," he said.

Pet grinned.

Yeah, punk, Nelson thought, *keep on grinning. You'll be out of her life within a month.*

"Five bottles," said Ria.

"*Five?*"

"Five. We talk and dance. We get thirsty."

Nelson took a deep breath, doing his best not to think of how irresistible she looked with her big dark eyes and wide blonde smile. She was wearing a buff-colored dress that scarcely concealed her breasts. What beautiful breasts she had, he thought as he licked his lips.

"Two bottles on the house," he told her. "The rest you'll have to pay for."

She frowned. "Really? Are you serious?"

"I'm afraid so." He might be crazy in love with her, but he was *damned* if he'd *give* her and her posse five bottles of his most popular bubbly. "We have bills to pay."

"Nelson," she said with a little pout, "are you aware that I can go to places all over the world and everything is complimentary?"

"How nice for you," he said.

"Yes, it is nice to be me. How about you, Nelson? Is it nice being *you?*"

He looked from her to Pet to her again. Pet was scowling at him, but he wasn't sure why, because he was pretty certain that Pet was queer.

"Yes," Nelson said, "it's very nice to be me."

"It's nice being me, too," said Ria, who grabbed Pet's head and gave him the biggest, juiciest French kiss Nelson had ever seen.

Nelson turned around and walked away. To hell with Ria and her freaky friends. She was jerking him around and he didn't like it one bit.

Or maybe he liked it a lot.

Chapter 13

Frances

"Wake up, sweetie! Time to rise and shine!" said De Vito.

Frances rolled over and moaned. Someone was trying to wake her up from the most delicious dream. In her dream she was in bed, being ravished by two very handsome men who wouldn't stop making love to her despite her pleas to cease and desist.

"What the *fuck*?" Frances cried, opening her eyes and seeing De Vito standing over her. "I thought you were in Atlantic City!"

"I know what happened. I came back as soon as I heard," he lied. "You know I wouldn't let you go through something like this all by yourself."

Frances blinked away the last remnants of her sexy dream, reluctant to let it go. She wondered how De Vito had learned of her awful date with Karim but decided it was kind of him to cut short his weekend with the boys and rush home to her.

She shook her head. "De Vito, it was just *too* awful…"

He nodded and stroked her hair. "Yes, sweetie. It was a terrible thing, but life goes on."

She thrust out her chin. "Fuckin' easy for you to say. What time is it? Whatever time it is, you got to get on that phone and call that bastard and give him what-for. That cockwad actually hung up the phone on me! Can you believe it?"

De Vito frowned. Had Saul Rofstein really hung up on his daughter? Weird. Maybe the nasty old due had shot his wife, too, and now was ravaged by guilt. After all, they were showbiz people—who knew what kind of atrocities they were capable of?

The young man got to thinking: *If Rofstein had offed his missus and he goes to prison and another inmate whacks him, who would get the old guy's money?*

Frances, of course. This whole tragedy could turn out very well for a certain young couple in New York.

De Vito pictured himself moving into the Rofsteins' L.A. mansions, throwing the biggest parties imaginable, *schmoozing* with the biggest stars from movies, TV, music, sports...people he had always yearned to have as his "friends."

He'd gotten pissed at Frances for saying, 'Don't ask me to fly out there. I hate that place. The worst years of my life happened there.'

Now things were just a little bit different.

Frances asked, "So, are you going to call him or not?"

"I don't think I know his number. Plus, I don't know him, so what would I say?"

Frances rolled her eyes. "Just tell him we're never doing business with him again!"

"*What?*" Then they would never get a dollar of his money.

"I hate that bastard," Frances said. "I don't care how much money we'll lose out on. We do a good business. We'll get by."

De Vito swallowed hard. The trade papers all

agreed that Saul Rofstein was worth at least a billion. Was Frances really O.K. with losing out on a billion-dollar inheritance? *He* sure as fuck wasn't.

Concluding that Frances was delirious, De Vito said, "Look, sweetie, I know this has been difficult for you—"

"*Difficult?* Want to see my bruises?"

"*Bruises?*" De Vito thought she had totally lost her mind. Maybe he needed to call an ambulance and have her rushed to Bellevue.

"Just what I said. I got bruises all over, De Vito. You know that sheikh who fucks our girls every week? Well, he put in that special request for *me* to date his fifteen-year-old son? So what happens? I show up and there's no fifteen-year-old virgin, just this big fat creep who bit me and slapped me around."

Oh, fuck! Frances wasn't even talking about her mother's murder. She was going on and on about her bad date with Adel Nasrallah's son. Did she even know *about her mother's murder? How could she* not *know by now?*

"Haven't you heard yet?" he asked her.

"Heard what?" she replied, frowning. Then, "It couldn't be more important than the text message I sent you about being beaten and raped."

"I'm here with you now," he murmured. He hadn't checked his cell phone for text messages. He had been too busy losing a small fortune at the casino, trying to boff a pretty steakhouse waitress and having a lap dancer stick her perfumed crotch in his face.

"Sweetie," he said, "I have some bad news for you."

"I hate bad news. What is it?" She snarled, angry

that he was less outraged by her bad date than she was.

"Something's happened to your mother. She's dead. Murdered. Shot in the face."

She stared at him as if he'd spoken to her in an unknown language.

"I'm just so sorry. So, so sorry."

She swallowed hard a few times, the her eyes darted every which way. "When? When did it happen?" she asked in a hoarse voice.

"This morning in L.A. I didn't know about it till later on. When I heard, I hurried over."

"Why didn't anyone contact me sooner?" Her voice was scarcely more than a whisper.

"I'm sure someone tried to. Have you checked your messages?"

She shook her head. Suddenly she felt as if she were a character in a freaky movie. Her mother had been murdered, a spectacular beauty no more. The woman every woman admired and every man lusted after. The star of many movies, the winner of three Oscars.

Her mother. The incomparable Gina Roff. A woman who'd never cuddled nor sung to her. A mother who'd hired a succession of efficient, bloodless nannies to care for her. A mother who had spent her daughter's youngest years away on movie shoots. Her parents took her along and sat with her only when one of the magazines wanted a picture of the mother or father with their daughter. But that ended once Frances reached puberty.

For her, puberty seemed to be a time when her folks said, 'Your body is changing. We're ashamed of you.' Her European nanny taught her about masturbation and menstruation. Her mother said, 'You're fourteen. Your nose is ugly but we can fix that.' One afternoon a young Haitian groundskeeper took the Rofsteins' only child into the bushes and instructed her on how to give a great blow job.

At school she became the local expert on fellatio. The boys wanted her to give them head and the girls wanted to watch so they could learn. Sex was a great way to get attention. She got as much as she wanted.

She also became an accomplished shopper. Her parents made more money than they could have spent in a dozen lifetimes, so they stuffed her pockets with greenbacks and sent her off to Melrose Avenue or Rodeo Drive so they wouldn't have to spend time with her.

So there she was, Frances Rofstein—popular, rich spoiled rotten—a girl who had nobody around to tell her no or stop her from acting on whichever impulse was firing through her brain at any moment.

What she wanted, which was more than a mere impulse, was to get away from her self-obsessed, filthy rich parents. To stop being who she was—*"This is Frances. Her mother is Gina Roff and her father is Saul Rofstein."*

Moving to New York turned out to be a great idea. Everyone seemed unaware of who her family was and most, if they did know, were quite indifferent. She liked that just fine.

Gina Roff. Mother. Murdered. *Who were you, Ma? I hardly knew ya.*

Frances sighed. "Check the messages on the SoHo phone. That was the only number Saul had."

De Vito did as told, and heard many messages, one of which was from Saul himself.

"Saul said, 'I'm sending someone out to New York to bring Frances home,'" De Vito told Frances.

She made a face. "He's doing what? Bullshit! I'm a grown woman! He doesn't tell me what to do!"

"Well, this matter is kind of different. Your mom's dead and he needs you because there's going to be a funeral. It's a family thing. You have to do it. I'll go out there with you. We'll get through it together."

Chapter 14
Kayce

My flight to New York was boring except for the fact that one of my fellow passengers was Bruce Springsteen. I have been a Bruce fan since birth, and might have gone up to tell him that I thought he was the most amazing musician ever, but I didn't do it because I figured he already knew how great he was. So I just sat there and tapped on my iPad, reading about the brutal murder of Gina Roff.

It occurred to me as I read about the murder that Frances would already know about it and likely would be on her way to Los Angeles as I flew to New York, thereby making my trip completely useless.

I asked myself how Frances was taking the news of her mother's death. Bad enough to lose a parent, but to have one murdered by being shot in the face? Too much to comprehend.

I decided that such a murder was too awful to think about, so I started grooving on José. Should I call him or something and tell him I'm out of town? Would he give a shit? If not, why should he? After all, he isn't my boyfriend and I'm not his girlfriend. I want to keep it that way, too. I think.

Of course, I do miss all that cuddling and snuggling you get with a boyfriend when you're in like with each other.

Once my flight landed I checked my cell phone and found a message from my father. He wanted to know why they had chosen me to defend Saul Rofstein and did I think he did it? Frosty left a voice message reminding me that I should get Frances on the next flight back to Los Angeles (as if I needed such a reminder). Best of all, I got one from Hayley, telling me she had some big news.

Hayley has been my best bud for the longest time. I hope she has something great to tell me, like she and Mark have reconnected and gotten engaged. She should be married, and her husband should be a man who's worthy of her.

I am not the kind of woman who will ever marry. Be with the same man till I or he dies? No thanks. I don't want children, either, though I do adore other people's kids. I am nobody's idea of a nurturing woman, and I'll be the first to admit that my career is my main thing in life. That is why I am in New York right now instead of riding José's dick.

Hayley and I haven't seen each other in the longest time and I truly miss her. I am so eager for our reunion in Los Angeles, even if it's a brief one. She says she's going to be around for a week and a half, and I have plans for us. I'm thinking we might sneak off to Vegas for a few days and go to a spa for a couple of days. After all the hard work we do, we need to close our eyes, relax and decompress. I've already told Frosty that my Christmas vacation will be a little bit longer than usual. If he doesn't like it, too fuckin' bad.

As I exited the airport terminal and stood outside waving at taxis, I wondered if sex with José really had been all that good, or if my problem was just that I hadn't done it in some time. Or maybe José seemed great because Mark had been a lousy lover.

I waved at a driver and he waved back. He pulled over and I slid inside.

"Where you going?" he asked.

I gave him the address Saul had given me. I also took out my iPhone and dialed the number he had provided me. I got a recorded greeting and said, "Hi. My name is Kayce White and I'm a lawyer who's been asked to accompany you back to L.A. so you can attend your mother's funeral. I'm very sorry for your loss." Click.

I wondered for a moment if she might remember me. I suspected that Frances Rofstein had had relatively few friends in her life—often by choice—and Kayce White was not the world's most common name. We'd had many fun girl talks and laughed our asses off before she decided we had too little in common—she had money and designer clothes and I had neither—and terminated our friendship (if, indeed, we'd *had* a "friendship"). But that was years ago, and I felt confident that she was a more likable person now.

I dialed José's number. I probably shouldn't have, but what the fuck. You only live once.

"That you?" he asked.

"Yeah. Guess where I am right now?"

"Not with me. Unfortunately."

I giggled. "Right now I'm in New York."

"Why?"

"Have some things and stuff to take care of

107

here."

"Does that have anything to do with the Gina Roff case?"

You're too smart for your own good. "My firm is involved with that, as you know. But my trip to New York has nothing to do with that."

"You'll get very busy very soon is Saul Rofstein gets busted."

"Why would he get busted?"

"Because the cops think he did it."

"Ridiculous!"

"Is it?"

"Gotta go," I said, eager to hang up.

"When are you coming back?"

"Maybe tomorrow. Probably."

"All that way and you're getting back on a flight tomorrow."

"Yeah, and I hate flying, period."

"Dinner as soon as you get back. Promise?"

"O.K." Click.

José Benitez could be a problem for me. I was an attorney involved in what would probably become a high-profile case, and he was a TV reporter. I was riding his dick. He would ask me questions I shouldn't answer, and I would tell him all I knew, because I was too much in love with riding his dick.

The traffic was very bad and so was my hackie. But by and by he got me to my destination, a building in SoHo.

The local time was just before five. I pulled my lightweight jacket around me because the city was as cold as ice. I pushed the button for F. Rofstein and waited for the longest time.

No answer. I stood shivering in the brutal Manhattan cold. Just then a tall blond guy all dressed for inclement weather came bounding out of the building.

I jumped in front of him. "Excuse me, but do you know if Frances Rofstein lives here?"

"Who?"

"Frances Rofstein. The directory says F. Rofstein."

He nodded. "Oh, the tall, swarthy chick upstairs. She doesn't come by much."

"But she *lives* here."

He shook his head. "Sort of, but not really. Her boyfriend has a crib uptown. She stays there most of the time."

"Got an address for me?"

"Can't help you. In a hurry. Later." He took off, but he didn't wait to make sure the door was shut and I let myself in. So nice and warm in there. The mailboxes were in the lobby, and since hers was unlocked, I went through its many contents to see what I might find. Soon I came across an envelope addressed to De Vito Silvera; I assumed he was her boyfriend.

Unsure of what to do next, I took out my iPhone and called Saul Rofstein. The bitchy woman on the other end told me he was taking no calls, and when I assured her that he was waiting to hear from me, she hung up the telephone.

Way to go, Saul!

Then I dialed Frosty and told him what was going on.

"Hold your position," he said. "I'll find out

where she is and call you back."

"Hold your position"? I guess he didn't know that Manhattan was in the middle of a cold snap.

I sighed and left the building, turned left and headed down the street till I reached a dingy little coffee shop, the kind of family place I thought no longer existed in Manhattan. There I found the young guy in Frances' building who'd blown me off minutes earlier. He clicked away on his MacBook as I strode by.

"Hey," I said.

He sort of nodded.

I ordered an espresso and a slice of apple pie from a big, bald man. "Do you know someone named De Vito Silvera?"

He frowned. "De Vito? Yeah. Haven't seen that guy in quite some time."

"Got any idea where I might find him?"

"He's a hotshot. Plays music in all the best nightclubs. Used to work all night, come in here first thing in the morning, then go home and sleep all day. Nice work if you can get it."

"Got any idea how I can locate him?"

"Why? He knock you up or somethin'?" The man howled. "Jeez, I crack myself up sometimes."

I looked over my shoulder and noticed that Frances' neighbor had taken off his beanie, revealing a head of dirty blond hair.

"The deal is," I said, "that De Vito has inherited money. I need to give him the good news."

"I'm sure he'll like that." He yelled into the distance behind him, "Hey, Sylvia! Get the hell out here!"

A heavyset woman appeared. "What you want?"

"This kid here is lookin' for De Vito Silveri. Didn't he give us his card once?"

She scowled. "Threw it away. He wanted way too much money for a few hours' work."

I gathered up my espresso and pie and headed over to a seat in the corner. Presently I looked up to see Frances' neighbor leaning over, handing me a piece of paper.

"What's this?"

"De Vito Silveri's contact info."

"How did you get it?" I asked, accepting the paper.

"Wasn't hard. I overheard you and looked him up online. A self-employed person without a Website is an unemployed person."

"Wow. Thanks."

"You're not a New Yorker, are you?" he asked.

"How could you tell?"

"Because you speak with a funny accent."

"I flew here on business. Just got in, as a matter of fact."

"From where?"

"L.A. Isn't it obvious?"

"Not at all."

"Really?"

"Really."

"Why isn't it obvious I'm an Angeleno?"

"Because of the salon tan you don't have." He smiled and offered his hand. "My name is Mac, and who are you?"

"Kayce," I replied, shaking his hand.

"Is that C-a-s-e-y?"

"No, it's K-a-y-c-e."

"Unusual spelling."

"Tell me about it."

"So, Kayce, why are you here? For real."

"Business."

"What kind of business?"

"Wow, Mac! You sure ask lots of questions!"

He grinned. "That's because I'm a writer. If you don't ask questions, you don't get information."

"A writer, huh? What do you write?"

"Screenplays. And what kind of business do you do that makes you fly out to New York and get into coffee-shop conversations?"

"I'm a lawyer working for a firm in L.A." I nibbled at my apple pie, thinking, *You're in the wrong town, pal. The screenplays are bing bought and produced in L.A., not New York. You could grow old and die trying to make your first sale out here.*

"So, Kayce," Mac asked, leaning forward again, "why are you really looking for De Vito?"

"He's inherited money," I repeated. "I'm here to make sure he knows about it so he can go get it."

"I'm sure," Mac murmured.

"I wonder where the ladies' room is." I'd had enough of Mac and his bullshit.

Soon I found a sign saying RESTROOM and ducked in. The truth was, I felt no need to relieve myself; what I did need was to dial this De Vito Silvera and ask if he knew where Frances was so I could hustle her on back to the Coast.

I took out my iPhone and made that call.

Chapter 15
Hayley

On Sunday morning, Hayley got up late. She lolled about in bed for as long as she damn well pleased. Such a shame that Strom could spoon her or hold her and cover her with kisses, but there would be time enough for that when they slept as husband and wife.

She tried to picture their domestic bliss once they were together permanently. She would fix breakfast for them while he read about the world's news on his iPad and watched the today-in-politics shows on TV. She knew what he liked to do because not too long ago they had flown up to New York so that he could do some business, and their entire weekend together had been too much fun. Well, she thought, there was just one little problem: sexually, he was a little too selfish. He loved fellatio and assured her that she gave the best head around. But she herself had a very sensitive vagina and would have appreciated a few kisses down there that did not happen.

She assured herself that once they were sharing a bed every night she would tell him, in the most diplomatic way possible, what she wanted and needed and he would do his very best to satisfy her. Of course he would do that. Why wouldn't he?

Sprawled underneath the covers, she wished she

could dial his number and say good morning, just to hear the sound of the voice she so adored.

But he had said nix to that. "Never call me at home on a Sunday. I spend the entire day with my children. Call only if it's an absolute emergency."

So she called Rikki instead and said yea to a trip to the mall. They agreed to meet at noon.

At long last she got out of bed, inhaled her own stink, grimaced and took a shower. Afterwards she stood in front of the full-length mirror and checked herself out. Strom was lucky to have her—she was a pretty woman. Nice and tall, delicate features, smooth clear skin. Her tummy was still tight; why couldn't she see a baby bump yet? Still, she felt sure she would show soon.

Pregnant! By Senator Strom Greggins! Could life *possibly* get more exciting?

My wife, Strom told himself, *is the world's biggest pain in the butt*. Today he wanted, more than anything, to get away from Joni for a little while.

He sat back in his big leather reclining chair and thought of calling Liz, that Canadian correspondent he'd met. She was young, eager to get ahead and she'd emitted all the right signals.

Strom wanted to call her even though it was Sunday, then decided it wouldn't hurt to wait till Monday and have a lunch appointment set up for them. Liz said she wanted to interview him. Well, she would get her interview, all right.

He still has the issue of what to do on this boring Sunday. His children were staying with Joni's parents, so he was stuck with his missus for the entire day.

But then Eduardo called on his private line, the line whose number was known to maybe half a dozen people in the world.

How the hell had Eduardo gotten his private number?

Joni had given it to him, of course.

"Hey, Senator," Eduardo said. "Me again. Thought I would follow up on our conversation about the concert in the center. If you can make it over here today, we would be delighted to see you."

Strom started to think of some excuse, but Eduardo started giving him directions. He jotted down the information and told himself it was a good thing, because at least now he could get away from Joni. His wife had no intention whatsoever of attending any rap concert in a community center that served the underprivileged.

Strom told Joni he was going to that concert. She said, "Have you told *Hayley* to alert the media?"

Fuck you, Joni, he thought.

Strom now thought of calling Liz and inviting her to that rap concert. Good idea; but what was he supposed to do about Hayley and her pregnancy? He certainly wasn't going to leave Joni and move in with Hayley, then marry her, or whatever the hell Hayley wanted him to do. If Joni found out about his affair with Hayley and her pregnancy, she would divorce him, get sole custody of their children and destroy him professionally.

He needed to get Hayley out of his life. If he could do such a thing, his life would return to normal. But how would he do such a thing?

Fuck Hayley, fuck Joni. Women are all fucked,

no matter how you look at it.

Rikki loved shopping and malls. She knew her way around those places, literally and physically. Hayley hated shopping and malls. The merchandise all looked alike to her.

Rikki dashed from store to store like a kid on Christmas morning. Hayley traipsed along at her own speed.

"This is *way* too much fun," Rikki sang out as she tried on boots that came in many colors. "Don't you think so, Hayley? Isn't this just way too much fun?"

"You should maybe think of buying footwear in beige and black."

"Way too boring. If there's one thing Rikki ain't, it's boring."

Hayley nodded. Rikki never shut the fuck up, and much of what she said was almost worth hearing. Lately Rikki spoke of her (mis)adventures on the Internet.

"There are some sites," she said to Hayley with a broad wink, "that will freak you out. Just post a picture of yourself and a brief description. Then wait a couple of days and you'll have *zillions* of male admirers!"

"That many, huh?" Hayley could scarcely imagine anything more pathetic—or potentially hazardous to one's health—than going online looking for love and *agreeing to meet* the losers who visited one's profile. No, she had already met the man she wanted, and his name was Strom Greggins.

Just as Strom suspected, Eduardo's community center sat in the middle of a ghetto. Strom's car was expensive and immaculate, and so he looked for somewhere to park so that the desperadoes wouldn't steal or strip it. He thought Joni should have warned him that his destination anyway in a rough neighborhood, but then he figured that she didn't know about it either.

The good thing was, Liz had agreed to attend the concert, too. He liked Liz and her blonde smile and lovely, firm young breasts. He had called her, told her where he would be and invited her to join him. She'd practically squealed in delight at the prospect of hanging out with him.

"I'll need to bring my photographer," she'd said.

"Go right ahead."

He believed that screwing Liz would be very easy to do. He was angry at Hayley for being such a bitch and wanted to be rid of her immediately. Just thinking of banging that cute young reporter gave him a boner that refused to go down.

He found a parking space by an empty lot and left his vehicle there, only half-believing that it would still be intact when he returned to it.

Strom hurried to the center a block or so away, passing by a couple of brown winos who took turns pulling at a bottle of something called Wild Irish Rose. Then he encountered a couple of skinny Latino boys who snarled at him as he entered the center, which turned out to be an abandoned warehouse.

He found Eduardo and approached him.

"You made it after all."

"Did you think I would stand you up?"

"Yes, I did. You're a politician. You tell the

people what you think they want to hear, then do whatever is convenient for you."

"Well, I'm here. What can I do for you?" he asked, the question that had come out of his mouth a zillion times. Usually they asked him for things he couldn't deliver. The main thing was never to tell them that.

"Funding," said Eduardo. "We need bucks, lots of them, to make this place a great hangout for kids so they don't roam the streets and make trouble."

"My wife is the one who beats the bushes for big money. You should take that up with her."

Eduardo grinned. "Oh, I'm sure you can help us. You know all the right people who can get us grants."

Strom shrugged. "See what I can do." That was another thing he'd said a zillion times to as many people. He thought, *When is Liz going to get here? I'm not staying that long.*

"But you're the one who works for Uncle Sam personally," Eduardo was saying. "You know all the right people. Look, I want you to meet some great people who have worked hard to make this center a reality."

"Lead the way," Strom said, because he knew there was nowhere else for him to go and nothing else for him to do.

Hayley sat with Rikki in the mall's food court, eating Chinese food out of cartons. Rikki had a particularly severe case of verbal diarrhea.

"I dated this one dude," Rikki was saying between shoveling forkfuls of noodles and meat into her yap, "and at first he seemed as normal as the next

118

dude, you know? Not exactly *GQ* material, but totally acceptable nevertheless."

Hayley nodded and smiled, bored shitless.

"Well, we went out on a few dates." Rikki munched away for a few minutes and swallowed. "Then he was sort of, 'Well, I've taken you out and put our evening on my American Express, so I think I'm entitled to a night of sex.' Can you believe that? Not shy about saying what he wants."

"Awful," said Hayley.

"Oh, it gets worse."

"Continue." Hayley stifled a yawn.

"He wanted a *ménage a trois* with me and his ex! She was waiting at her apartment for us to come by and join her in the sack. How yucky is that?"

"So you said nix to that."

"Damn straight I did, girlfriend," Rikki said, her eyes wide.

Hayley checked her watch.

"That a Rolex?" Rikki asked, raising her eyebrows.

Hayley shook her head. "Seiko."

"Looks like a Rolex. Wish I had one."

"Seiko's good enough for me," said Hayley. "Anyway, I got to go."

Rikki pouted. "But we haven't visited all the stores."

"I've got some work to do, and I promised Norma I'd come by and say hi. She doesn't have anyone, you know."

Rikki nodded as she devoured more food. "You're just too kind to do that for her. I've been promising myself to reach out to her but somehow I just never find the time. I do pick up her prescriptions for her, though."

"I guess you're just too busy with boyfriends and dating sites. How many sites are you on?"

Rikki rolled her eyes. "Too many! And we got to sign you up, too. You'll have *way* too much fun."

Hayley smiled. *No, I will not go online looking for love. I have already found love, and his name is Strom Greggins. Someday soon we will be together and we will love forever.*

Chapter 16
Nelson

Nelson belonged to a group of guys who played touch football every Sunday morning in Central Park. Nearly a dozen guys would show up, and after their football game one of them would invite the others back to this apartment. The host would make sure he had plenty of delicatessen food and snacks plus many bottles of imported beer on ice. They would spend the afternoon watching ESPN and indulging in guy-talk.

They dubbed themselves "The Central Park Sunday Dozen." Nelson and Artie Jay were the group's founders.

In many ways, Nelson considered these Sunday get-togethers the highlights of his week. No women; just the guys and whatever was on their minds. De Vito, much by choice, was absent—male bonding held little appeal for him. He preferred hanging out with Frances or catching whichever movie was doing huge business. He also enjoyed shooting pool and playing cards.

Nelson and Artie Jay felt relieved about De Vito's absence on Sunday, because while they accepted their friend's cocaine use, the other Sunday guys probably would not. Many of those friends thought that sticking a crack pipe into your mouth was beyond stupid. Whenever Nelson tried to talk to De Vito about his drug use, the druggie would simply nod and mutter, so Nelson finally gave up and said nothing more.

The Sunday bunch consisted of unmarried guys between twenty-three and thirty. All of them had great jobs, made good money and agreed that being a guy was lots of fun.

Nelson hosted the gang on this day but was worried about De Vito and Frances. He thought about leaving his apartment for the day and letting the guys have their fun while he checked on De Vito and Frances. Mostly he found her a pain in the butt but they had known each other forever and he pitied her.

He called De Vito, who muttered something about being far too sleepy for conversation and would call him back later, when he had his shit together more.

"Frances O.K.?"

"Who?" Yawn. Click.

You clearly don't need my help, Nelson thought as he hung up his phone.

Central Park was cold and hard, but Nelson played his best and felt terrific once their game ended. He got back to his apartment and looked forward to a fun session with his friends.

As he readied the cold cuts, potato salad and coleslaw to be devoured, Nelson thought it might be helpful to have a girlfriend who could do this work with him. He had never met that someone special; his girlfriends had rarely lasted more than a few months. He simply was not especially taken by the girls he knew—the aspiring models and actresses, the party monsters and society belles—most of them looking for rich husbands and quite aware that Nelson Skalbania had huge money he had inherited from his father. The girl he had dated were as horny as he was, and they fucked each other silly for a while but then went their separate ways.

He was hardly worried about his single status. Nelson, in his mid-twenties, thought himself far too young to marry just yet; still, a steady girlfriend might be just the thing for him at this stage in his life.

De Vito had Frances, but he kept screwing other girls, and Nelson didn't see the point in having a relationship if you were going to cheat.

Nelson thought of Lovey and Sid as the perfect example of how great a relationship could be. While both were remarkably independent, they cared deeply for each other with a passionate volatility. They were still crazy for each other after many years of marriage. That's what Nelson wanted—a hot, fiery romance that lasted for decades.

Ria had that heat and fire he craved. He knew she was somewhat older than himself, but so what? If he spent the rest of his life with her, things would always be unpredictable and exciting.

Was age such a big deal, anyway? Nelson knew of many older women who still looked great and had taken up with younger women.

Fuck it all, he told himself. The next time he saw Ria, he would get busy letting her know how he felt and what he wanted.

That next time came fast. As he stood in his

apartment cleaning up after the Central Park Dozen, his doorbell rang and there stood Ria.

"Nelson," she practically whispered, slinking past him into his living room as if she'd visited him a hundred times. "I was in the neighborhood and thought, 'Maybe I should go see how the heir to a billion dollars lives.'"

Nelson winced. He hated to be reminded of how the whole world knew of his father's success and his own huge inheritance. Still, he was glad she had come. She was wearing nothing but black leather. He wondered what passersby thought as they watched her stride down the street.

You want somethin' with me? he wanted to ask. Instead, he said nothing.

She surveyed his apartment, her face expressionless. Not a good sign. She usually smiled at things and places and people that pleased her.

"So," she said, "now we are alone together. Isn't this what you've been wanting, Nelson?"

"No pretty-boy faggot on your arm today?" he asked. "Where is he?"

"Did you want me to bring him along? I thought you didn't like him. Or maybe you like him too much. Maybe you're gay. You're too beautiful to be a man, Nelson. *Are* you gay?"

Damn! How she reminded him of Charisma! All that bitchiness and attitude, her backtalk coming out of a mouth he yearned to kiss.

Was Ria's sassiness the thing that turned him on?

He guessed it was, because he felt his cock spring erect and felt an overwhelming urge to walk over to Ria and give her the longest, hottest kiss of her life.

That's what he should do, and he should do it

because that's why she came to his place—to be kissed or whatever else he had in mind.

Chapter 17
Frances

Some bad shit had built up between De Vito and Frances on early Sunday morning and culminated in the worst fight they'd ever had.

In the middle of their row, she had picked up a bottle of Smirnoff vodka and begun chugging it down. Since she had a low inebriation threshold, she soon became falling-down drunk.

In a strange variation of two-can-play-that-game, De Vito took out his crack pipe and had took half a dozen hits. Ordinarily he did not use street drugs in front of her because they freaked her out. But the cocaine reached his brain immediately and he wished everyone could feel as great as he did when he was high on crack.

They yelled and screamed at each other. She'd accused him of being a cowardly dopefiend.

He'd called her a spoiled Jewish cunt who cared about Number One and nobody else.

She'd screamed that he was just a no-class pimp who would be dead or in prison if not for her.

Their pissing contest dragged on for an hour.

By and by Frances groped her way into their bedroom, still clutching the bottle of vodka. After collapsing onto their bed in an alcoholic haze, he reminded herself that her mother had just been murdered, and that she hadn't had a really good cry in quite some time. She burst into tears and after a while fell asleep.

De Vito, tempted to storm out, realized that he really had nowhere else to go, so he curled up on the sofa and stared at the TV with the sound turned off.

Both members of the household had snored themselves into early Sunday afternoon. Frances woke up just before dinnertime with the worst hangover she'd had in years.

She lay prostrate in bed for several minutes, recalling her fight with De Vito and the events prior to that. An image flashed in her mind of her dead mother, face blown away, and Frances cried again, her body wracked by horrible heaving sobs.

Her cries woke De Vito from a dreamless sleep, and, forgetting the fight they'd had and the vicious verbal blows traded, he rushed into their bedroom to comfort her. The sight and sound of a crying female always made him think back to when his father beat the bejesus out of his mother and De Vito's job was to provide succor.

He had always been reluctant to leave town, because once he was gone, who would comfort his mother after one of those thrashings?

Only him. Nobody else.

De Vito said goodbye to Chicago and was in New York, trying to make a new life for himself.

He gathered Frances into his arms and whispered into her ear, "Sweetie, it's O.K. Everything's gonna be just fine."

She shook her head. "Wrong. My mother's dead—and you know what, De Vito? I hardly knew her."

"Don't blame yourself." He stroked her hair.

"Maybe I should." She grabbed a tissue and blew her nose. "Maybe I should have *forced* her to pay attention to me."

"Dream on. She lived for Number One and nobody else. She said, 'Frances, this is so-and-so, and she's going to be looking after you while I go off and make a movie.'"

"I should have been there for her," Frances muttered.

"She didn't want you there. You did all you could for her. You did all she would let you do."

"Do you really think so?"

He nodded. "I *know* so. You were as good a daughter to her as she would let you be."

Frances spent the rest of the afternoon in front of the TV set, watching the coverage of her mother's death, as if she'd finally accepted it and was eager to learn all she could about it.

De Vito suggested that she call Sault, but she just shook her head and kept watching TV. He felt relieved that she was longer whining about being brutalized by Adel Nasrallah's son. Adel was a huge spender, and losing him would be a catastrophe for them.

As soon as Frances had fallen silent and bemused for an adequate amount of time, De Vito fed her some unsweetened iced tea—her favorite—and a couple of Tylenol 3s, which always mellowed her out. He persuaded her to crawl into bed and stretch out till she fell asleep. Then he called Barbara Tonucci, their assistant, and asked her to check on things.

Barbara did not come to the office on weekends; instead, she did her work on the MacBook De Vito had given her.

"I'm *so* sorry for your loss," Barbara said, fighting back sobs. "How are you guys holding up?"

Barbara was one of the few people who knew that "Francesca Roff" was actually Frances Rofstein, daughter of mogul Saul Rofstein and his wife, Gina Roff. De Vito had said to her early on, 'You have a great gig here, Barb. But if you tell anyone about Frances or our business, you will become *so* unemployed.' Since Barbara was crazy in love with her handsome cousin, she would say nothing to anyone. Barbara's son Chick, who had learned so much about Frances and De Vito from his blabbing mother, kept all that sensitive information in a safe part of his brain in case he needed to use it one day against certain people.

De Vito had never paid much attention to Chick. So far as he was concerned, Chick was around just to make himself useful. He was a decent chauffeur and gofer, qualities that De Vito considered somewhat valuable. Besides, Chick would never do nor say anything to anger his mother.

De Vito said, "Babs, I want you to double-check on everyone who's made an appointment and make sure everything is still running nice and smooth. Frances is gonna need to take some time off, and we may have to fly out to the Coast for a few days. You just make sure it's all business as usual. No fuckups. You'll get a huge bonus if you make Cousin De Vito proud."

"Want me to come in?" Barbara asked, eager to be near her heartthrob for a few hours. "I can hurry

130

over there right now."

"Nix," he said, as eager to hang up as she was to hurry over. "Gotta go now—someone's on my other line."

Chick Tonucci wanted more out of life than days and nights filled with driving bimbos to their dates, doing errands for fuckin' De Vito and being the personal flunky of that cunty bitch Frances Rofstein.

Yeah, baby, he knew who she was. She'd moved to New York to get away from L.A. and her old man who had produced all those TV shows everyone loved to hate and hated to love. Chick had figured that out soon enough, and he pelted his mom with questions until she explained all about Frances' and De Vito's business.

What did Barbara Tonucci think? That her son Chick was a perfect idiot?

It sure seemed that way.

When his mother thought him a retard, Chick could take advantage of her much more easily.

He still lived with her—why move out and pay rent?—and she did everything for him except wipe his butt. She gave him pocket money and tried not to rag on him too much, although she pleaded with him to get interested in *something*. *Oh, but I* am *interested in something*, he had been tempted to say. *I am interested in sleeping late, watching TV and jerking off.*

When not running his ass ragged for De Vito—a man whom he hated a little bit for having started with zilch and actually made something of himself—he loved beating off to Internet porn, banging whichever girl would put out for him and drink beer

131

till he belched and farted for an hour.

Barbara had no clue that Chick knew all about what was going on in his new job, especially the identities of some of the more prominent women who worked for Frances and De Vito as he drove them to their sordid little trysts. Everyone treated him like Mr. Cellophane, but he was smarter than that. He kept his own records of his comings, goings and general observations.

Gina Roff's murder struck him as something he could use for his own personal profit. The awful story was everywhere in the worldwide media, and Chip believed he could score some colossal bucks off it.

Chick Tonucci believed he could now afford to make big plans for himself, and those plans did not include his obese, garrulous, De Vito-worshipping, semiretarded, pain-in-his-butt mother.

Chapter 18

Kayce

"Whew," I said as the ringing stopped and I knew that Frances' boyfriend was on the other end of the line.

"Is this De Vito Silvera?" I asked.

"Who's askin'?"

"My name's Kayce White. I'm a lawyer working for Saul Rofstein and I'm here in New York trying to contact his daughter, Frances Rofstein."

"What do you want with her?"

I detected a Great Lakes accent, probably Chicago, and a definitely lack of book reading and diction class. I wondered how Frances, snob that she was, had ended up with this street boy. She decided that he must be handsome, well hung and a real heller in the sack.

"I guess you've heard about the death in her family," I said.

"No shit," he muttered.

"So you understand that I am a lawyer who needs to speak to her as soon as possible. Do you have a number where I can reach her?"

"How'd you get *this* number?"

"On the Internet. You have a Website with a phone number—De Vito Silvera, Disc Jockey. You're her boyfriend, right?"

"Who says?"

I sighed. Did he act like such a douche around Frances? I was cold and exhausted and had spent hours trying to reach Frances. I was grateful that her neighbor had invited me back to his apartment to sit down, relax and start calling De Vito, who was acting like *such* a douche. Why had I agreed to this ludicrous assignment when I could still be in José's bed, warm and naked and horny. Instead, I'm in the apartment of this guy—which is not so bad, since he's kind of attractive in a Marjoe Gortner kind of way—freezing my *tuchus* off and worrying about when the next flights for L.A. depart.

"So, *De Vito*, what's the deal? Can you help me find her?"

"Is her old man sending a private plane?"

"*Huh?*"

"He's got to have his own private plane."

"Well, he doesn't." Truth was, I didn't know if he did or didn't. "May I speak to Frances?"

"She's unavailable."

"I *do* know her," I said, hoping he would take me a little more seriously. "Tell her I'm Kayce White from Beverly High. I'm sure she'll remember me."

"I'll have to get back to you."

Click.

Shitfuck! This trip is a joke. I wanna go home! Waaah! Why hasn't Frosty called yet?

"Didn't get what you needed?" my host asked, noticing my scowl.

"Frances has piss-poor taste in men," I said.

By then I'd told my host—his name was Richie—exactly why I was in New York. By the time

134

I sat in his apartment and was blown off over the phone by De Vito, Richie knew all about my mission and why I didn't exactly have the option of returning to the Golden State without Frances by my side.

Richie had turned out to be a most empathic listener. He made me a hot beverage and said, "Drink this."

"What is it?" I asked.

"Hot chocky spiked with a date-rape drug. Just joking."

"I'm a lawyer. Don't joke about those things with me."

I curled up on his sofa, sipping the hot chocolate and wondering when De Vito Silvera would stop jerking me around so I could get on with my task and uphold Frosty's high opinion of me.

But things weren't really so bad at that moment. I just sat there with Richie, who in his long-and-lanky way was a handsome man. We were definitely doing some serious flirting, and I've always loved to flirt.

Was I cheating on José? Absolutely not. He wasn't my boyfriend, nor was I about to jump Richie's bones.

But if Richie were to jump my bones, I wouldn't fight him off.

From lonely days and masturbatory nights to a couple of handsome male acquaintances, I'd had a fun, weird couple of days.

"Are you hungry?" Richie asked. "We could send out for pizza, spaghetti, Chinese, whatever you want."

I frowned. "Why are you being so kind to me?"

"Well, first of all, I'm a gentleman. Second, you're sexy as hell."

I guffawed. I grabbed at my loose-fitting clothes. "Me? Sexy?"

He nodded. "You. Sexy."

"I come from California, land of the beautiful people. Out there, I'm considered nobody's bargain."

"Then they're fools. You can't take a compliment very well, can you?"

I just shrugged.

He smiled. "I just ended an engagement to a woman who expected a hundred compliments a day. What a bitch." He laughed.

"Did you now?" I tucked my feet under my butt on the sofa, relieved that he weren't talking about my dubious good looks.

"I did indeed. So now I'm single and open to new relationships. Are *you* seeing anyone right now?"

"With the hours I work? Are you kidding? I barely have time to pleasure myself."

"So you're in a very committed relationship with your right hand."

We laughed, and I thought, *I could like this guy, with his Marjoe Gortner looks and his sense of humor. Too bad we live three thousand miles apart.*

I don't imagine that Richie has buns of steel like José, but do such buns really matter all that much?

"So," said Richie, "we're hungry, right? What are we going to do about it?"

"*We*?" He seemed to think we were a couple or about to become one. Not gonna happen, dude.

"If we send out for something it will take forever to get here because this is New York. If we have eggs, I can fix them here in just a few minutes."

"Scrambled, please." Then, "As soon as I've finished eating I should start looking for a hotel."

"Got a sofa here you can use. Manhattan hotels are among the most expensive in the world."

"It wouldn't cost me a dime. My boss reimburses me for all business expenses."

He smirked. "Well aren't you the lucky one?"

"Sometimes I wonder."

Just then my iPhone rang. I answered it.

"Tomorrow morning," said De Vito Silvera. "Be at our SoHo apartment. Do you know where that is?"

"Uh, I think I can find it."

"Book us two first-class tickets on the two-o'clock American flight to LAX. Make sure a limo comes to take us to JFK and one is waiting at LAX to take us to the Beverly Wilshire, where we'll need a deluxe suite plus a car and driver with round-the-clock availability. See you at the apartment." Click.

I hoped this was all a done deal. But with De Vito as the boss, who knew?

Chapter 19
Hayley

Hayley was being so kind to Norma the neighbor that Rikki felt obligated to accompany her to the old woman's apartment.

Hayley said, 'I want to check in on her' just as a reason to leave that awful shopping mall. Rikki, apparently eager to continue their afternoon together, insisted on joining her, so the two spent an afternoon listening as Norma went on about the murder of Gina Roff.

Hayley felt relieved many times that Norma had failed to pick up on her young friend's southern California accent and never shown enough interest in Hayley to ask questions and figure out that her neighbor had gone to school with Saul and Gina's daughter Frances. Hayley, a reluctant attendee, had gone, at her mother's insistence, to the Rofsteins' mansion for Frances' birthday parties because she had been invited. Hayley mostly loitered in the background, rolling her eyes while circus clowns did tricks, elephants lumbered across the lawn and a half-dozen ponies gave rides in a circle. A huge tent was laden with hot dogs, cheeseburgers, cookies and cakes, punch and lemonade. Hayley remembered looking at all that food and beverage and thinking it would be enough to sustain Los Angeles' skid row for a year.

Gina Roff had appeared only in front of the cameras. Hayley had not considered Gina the most attentive and available of mothers, but then Frances seemed scarcely the most likable and controllable of daughters. Frances always had to be the center of attention, bragging and making faces, flaunting her family's spectacular wealth and rubbing the other kids' noses in it.

Hayley felt much relief when, at age thirteen, Frances' parties stopped. Or at least the Rofsteins took Hayley's name off their guest lists. Around that time she had gotten chummy with Kayce and formed the greatest of friendships.

Kayce had not returned her call, which disappointed Hayley because the two had so much to talk about.

Damn! Hayley needed to talk to someone and share her exciting news!

"What we got to do," Eduardo said, "is to stop the cycle of fatherless boys getting into gangs." With his sharp features and pockmarked face, he looked like the meanest man alive. "There is no father around, and the mother is messed up on dope or workin' two jobs to pay the bills, their sons are looking for a new family, and the gangs say to them, 'Hang with us and we'll be the only family you'll ever need.' That's when gang involvement starts. I should know, because I was one of the most effective recruiters. I told them just exactly what they wanted to hear."

The group surrounding him nodded and murmured.

"The street gangs have one thing in mind: To ensure their own continuation. So they recruit kids who aren't even teenagers yet. By the time they're old enough to drive cars, they're hardened criminals of sixteen. We *must* work together to stop this insanity, and together we *can* do it."

"Yea! Yea!" said Liz, the Canadian reporter who had arrived just as Strom was about to leave.

He observed that she was petite and perky in her tight jeans and crewneck sweatshirt. He also observed, with some disappointment, that the photographer she'd brought along was her husband.

Strom swore under his breath. First his assistant was knocked up, presumably by himself, and now that pretty Canuck journalist he'd wanted to boff had shown up with her hubby. Shitfuck!

He concluded that Liz wasn't such hot stuff after all. Her breasts were too small, her voice was too high and squeaky, and her very prominent, very goofy Canadian accent would soon make him shudder.

Eduardo said more, and Strom decided that he had to stand there and listen till Eduardo shut up.

Liz listened with eyes blazing and mouth hanging open, while her husband—who got to pork her every night, that lucky bastard—kept taking pictures.

Strom, knowing that many people there took turns glancing at him, struggled to keep his eyes on Eduardo and frowned once in a while when the activist said something that sounded tragic.

Earth to Kayce, texted Hayley. *Where are you, bitch? Got some news for you.*

She also checked her messages to make sure

Strom hadn't contacted her that day, although she knew he would do no such thing on a Sunday.

She knew that Strom was a wonderful father to the two children he'd had with Joni and would doubtless be a doting dad to the boy or girl he was having with Hayley.

Norma talked more than usual that afternoon, but Hayley finally got away as Rikki and Norma jabbered away at each other. She looked forward to Monday, when she could spend the entire day with her beloved Strom. Hayley loved being young, beautiful, smart and in love with a man like Strom Greggins. Life could be so grand sometimes.

After Eduardo finally ended his talk, Strom smiled at the sight of two Latino males who entered the center and, after grabbing a few people and flinging them aside as if they were rag dolls, walked up to Eduardo and started cussing him out in Spanish, flailing their arms and contorting their faces as they eyeballed him.

Eduardo kept his face expressionless and breathing normal, he soon lost his composure and began to sweat and yell back.

What the fuck? Strom thought, shaking his head and watching this confrontation. *Just what the freakin' fuck?*

He shot a glance towards the entrance, wondering if he should just haul ass out of there before someone pulled out a knife or gun and things got heavy. He spoke no Spanish, but his knowledge of human behavior told him that these two newcomers weren't among Eduardo's friends and admirers.

Liz stared open-mouthed at the tough guys, while her husband kept clicking away with his camera until one of the Latinos wheeled around and made an obscene finger gesture at the shutterbug. When the photographer failed to cease and desist, the Latino shouted, "Hey, bitch! Stop takin' pictures or I'll make you eat that fuckin' camera!"

Oh, thought Strom, so they do speak English.

The Latino turned back to Eduardo and their bickering continued.

Liz eased on over to Strom and said in a quiet voice, "Habla Espanol?"

"No," he replied, getting a delicious noseful of her perfume.

"Well, I speak some. They're arguing over a dope deal. This man says that Eduardo must pay up right away or risk getting a broken neck."

"And what's *he* saying?"

"To piss off."

"But they're staying put."

"I think the two mean guys are brothers," she said.

Liz's husband had zipped up his gear. He turned to her and said, "Let's leave immediately. This might become a shootout."

"Leave with us," Liz told Strom, breathless.

"Great idea. Let's do it."

As soon as they got outside, Liz's husband hustled her into their pickup truck and sped off before she could properly gay goodbye to Strom. He stood there on the crumbling sidewalk, swearing under himself breath about wasting a perfectly fine Sunday.

He started walking in the direction of his car, hoping that the vandals had spared his vehicle. Just then he heard a racket, and when he turned around he saw the two Latinos who'd confronted Eduardo come bursting out of the center and start running down the street. A rusted-out sports car appeared, tires squealing.

Strom turned this way and that, trying to understand it all. Shots rang out and he felt a pressure on his skull. Then he closed his eyes and all went black.

Chapter 20
Nelson

"I'm getting the impression," he said to Ria, "that this is all a joke to you. That *I'm* part of the joke."

"A joke?" Ria lay in bed, too beautiful for Nelson to believe.

"Yeah, a joke. But guess what, Ria. I'm not one of your bimbos you can just use and discard."

"Nobody said you were."

"I'm being very serious."

"Maybe that's your problem—you take yourself much too seriously. You're so young, too. *My* problem is that I always pick up the boys instead of the men."

"I resent that. Anyway, what's the age difference between us, fifteen years? That's not such a big deal."

"Let me pay you a compliment: You're more emotionally mature than most of the males whose bones I jump." She paused. "Poor Nellie. You're so rich and handsome but maybe you need to improve your self-esteem. You could also work on your lovemaking technique."

He scowled and shook his head, concluding that she was just like Charisma, a good-looking cunt who loved messing with his head. Ria was the first woman to complain about his sexual prowess. So far as he knew, he was a caring, giving, patient lover, someone who made all the right moves.

"It looked to me like you had an orgasm," he told Ria.

"I did. I always do."

"I made you come."

"I made myself come."

"So you're saying that you did it for yourself? That you didn't need me?"

Ria smirked. "Any woman who says she needs a man to make her come is a fool."

Nelson rolled his eyes. This was *not* his idea of postcoital conversation. "Time to get dressed and go our separate ways."

"Why? Neither of us has anywhere to go or anything to do that can't wait till later," she said. "We should fuck some more. When will you be ready, Nelson? I don't like to be kept waiting."

Later on, he woke up, checked his clock and saw that it was early Monday morning. He had no idea when Ria had left. She had gone without saying goodbye or leaving a note of any kind. She seemed to get off on humiliating him. He needed to remind himself that he, not she, was the male in their relationship. He owned the cock and balls, and she needed to respect that fact.

He decided he didn't want to see her again. He had many other romantic prospects in mind. What made Ria so fucking special that she could treat him with such condescension and he would tolerate it?

His iPhone rang, so he answered it, half-hoping Ria was on the line, wanting to thank him for a wonderful time. Instead, the caller was Artie Jay.

"Talk to me," Nelson muttered.

"We have an eleven-o'clock meeting with some Cubans about expanding the nightclub into some other markets. You remember, right?"

"It's not yet eight. Why you calling so early?"

"I thought it would be a good idea to go and see Frances so we could pay our respects."

"Yeah, let's do that. I'll call De Vito and tell him we're coming."

"You do that. While we're on the subject, what happened to you last night? I thought you were gonna hang out with us all night."

"Shit happened. My plans changed."

"What was her name?"

"Just this chick I used to know."

"Get in her pants?"

"Let's just say we got reacquainted." Click.

Nelson set about cleaning up his apartment. He promised to do his best to forget all about Ria.

Chapter 21
Frances

"We're flying out to LAX tomorrow. Before we do that, we're goin' over to the SoHo apartment to meet with your dad's lawyer," De Vito said.

Frances frowned. "Didn't I say—"

"Don't mean shit to me what you said. *I* say you've gotta be there at your mom's funeral. You'd never forgive yourself if you missed it. That's how it's gonna be. You don't like it? Too fuckin' bad."

Frances opened her mouth to protest some more, then shut it. He had spoken to the lawyer, told her what he and Frances wanted, and gotten it. De Vito was right—she needed to go to her mother's funeral. Also, after watching all those TV programs about her mother's murder, Frances was eager to find out what really happened.

They were saying that her father was a suspect. Could that be true?

Ridiculous. Ludicrous. King Shit Daddy would never harm Gina, the only female he had ever loved and worshipped.

Frances and her father had spent very few times alone together, and during those occasions he had seldom, if ever, paid her any compliments or asked about her hopes and fears in life; indeed, he spent most of their visits rhapsodizing about priceless, exquisite Gina. 'She's someone you should emulate,' he'd told her.

Frances had inferred from his remark that he considered his daughter highly inadequate. He probably always would.

From then on, Frances just wanted to get away from him. Get as far away as possible.

Now she was flying back, at De Vito's insistence. She knew she would hate herself forever if she missed Gina's funeral.

L.A., I'm comin' back once more, she thought with a sneer.

"Tell me again," she said as she decided which clothes to pack, "why we're going to the SoHo place."

"Because," he said, "that's where your California people think you live." Then, "If they find out about your Park Avenue digs, they'll be like, 'How can you afford that lifestyle? What do you two do for a living?' Believe me, you don't want to have to answer all those questions."

"Maybe,' she said with a smirk, "I should tell Daddy about our immensely lucrative new enterprise. Then he'll *have* to pay attention to me."

De Vito shook his head. "Saul can't be as bad as all that."

"Just wait till you meet him. Mister Megabucks is *such* an asshole."

De Vito smiled. "He hasn't met me. I'm De Vito Silvera, a nice professional. A professional nice. He's gonna like me just fine."

"We'll see. But let me repeat: I will *not* stay at the mansion."

"I got the lawyer to book us into the Beverly Wilshire. She's getting us a car and driver, too. T.C.B., sweetie. That should be my middle name."

"Did Saul really agree to all that?"

"His lawyer gave me what I asked for, so, yeah, I assume Saul sort of handed her a blank check."

"I guess he wants me back there for some reason. Also, while we're away, what are we going to do about our business?"

De Vito shrugged. "Let Babs run it."

"Yuck."

"What? She's totally competent. She runs it most of the time anyway."

"No, *we* run it. You recruit the girls and I deal with the horny guys."

"I'll have Babs move in here while we're out west."

"Yeah, she can sleep in our bed and masturbate to pictures of you."

He grimaced. "How come you always raggin' on her? She does the best she can for us."

"I wonder about that. We have a great business going on, but it requires sensitivity and intelligence and sophistication that she doesn't have. We let her run things, maybe she'll goof it all up. Maybe you should stay here with Babs, just in case."

"Nix to that," said De Vito, thinking, *No way in hell am I gonna miss out on a deluxe trip to L.A. that your old man is paying for.* "Where my girl goes, her man goes."

"I wanna speak to the boss," Chip said, swallowing hard and brushing his hair out of his eyes.

The sky was as gray as lead outside on this Monday morning. Chip stood at the reception desk of

The Whole Truth, an immensely popular tabloid whose offices were in a gigantic glass-and-chrome building.

The skanky blonde sitting behind the desk rolled her eyes and sighed. "For the third time, you need an appointment."

"But I have a big story for you!"

"So you've said."

"A guy with a big story don't need no appointment."

"*Everyone* needs an appointment."

"If I was Brad Pitt, you'd let me in."

"Brad Pitt wouldn't come in here. He has *people* who do those things for him." Then, "Do I have to call security to escort you off the premises?"

"What's your name?"

"Why do you ask?"

"Because," he told her, "after I sell this story for a few million bucks, I'm going to tell your rag how you treated me, and they're gonna fire you."

She snarled at him. "I'm having a hard time believing that *you* have a million-dollar story."

"That so?" Chip stepped backwards, as if she had just challenged him to fisticuffs. "I drove up her in a Rolls. I'm not some doofus off the street. I have juice; I know people."

She pursed her lips for a moment, then said, "Mr. Waller isn't available right now, but his assistant is. Go up to the eleventh floor and see him."

Chip smiled and nodded. That shit De Vito had told him was right: If the receptionist or other flunky says no, just start taking down names and threatening to have people fired. He'd watched De Vito start flexing on people like that a dozen times and it always worked.

Chip Tonucci, he said to himself, *you're unbelievable.*

Before departing their Park Avenue digs for their SoHo apartment, Frances took out her iPhone, called some of the girls in their stable and told them, 'Be chill. We're going to the Coast for a couple of days and Babs will be in charge *temporarily.*'

Then she called Babs. "When the girls come by, speak only if necessary. Don't drop any names and don't ask for selfies. Hear me?"

"I hear ya." Babs often did not hear and was far more interested in speaking than listening. Also, she considered Frances a gorgeous, pushy cunt. She much preferred dealing with handsome, charming De Vito.

"I'm glad you hear me. That's the main thing."

De Vito had suggested the night before that they give Babs the combination to their safe. Frances said no fuckin' way.

"Sweetie, what's she supposed to do with all the cash the girls deliver?" asked De Vito.

"She can stuff it all into condoms and hide them in her snatch."

De Vito from day one had said, 'Cash only. I mean it.' Everyone complied; usually the clients paid the girls, who dropped off De Vito and Frances' commissions. Always cash, none of it reported to the IRS. That way, De Vito reasoned, they would never get caught.

Until they did, of course.

Chapter 22

Kayce

I am not, nor have I ever been, a communist. Nor am I a slut, tramp or whore; I am simply someone who enjoys sex. And as I see it, God gave us sex so we could enjoy it and each other. What's so wrong with that?

Nothing. And if I enjoy men and sex, good on me!

As everyone who gives a damn about me knows, I've recently broken up with my boyfriend and have experienced some involuntary celibacy. Fortunately, I've just met two fine men— José with the killer bod and Richie with the killer mind and big heart.

O.K., so maybe Richie didn't have *GQ* looks like José, but he certainly did provide me with a memorable sexual experience. I can't remember exactly how it happened—that's a lie; I can remember it all. After I'd hauled out my iPhone and iPad and made all the arrangements De Vito insisted on—I resented doing that flunky shit because, after all, I'm a lawyer—Richie said it seemed like the right time to open a bottle of wine, so that's what he did. Scrambled eggs and wine? Well, why not?

We ate and drank; we got all nice and buzzed. When he kissed me, I kissed back and we kept it going for the longest time. Making out is an art, and Richie had had years of practice. Then we had sex. I don't know if I would call him a stud, but I would say he was a kind, gentle, patient lover, and to me that's pretty high praise.

Yea, Richie! Yea, me!

Now it's Monday morning and I get to go home. What's even better, I get to fly back first-class with Frances and her nasty boyfriend.

Richie came out of the shower with a white towel wrapped around his naughty bits. "Your turn," he said.

I'd thought about showering with him but decided against it. I'd had some of my finest sexual experiences in the shower and would have. But I didn't think we were ready for that, so I waited till he was through and then I went in. I felt all pumped up about seeing Frances again and escorting her and De Vito to Los Angeles. What would she and I say to each other? Would she remember me? Maybe she would but would pretend she didn't. I had a feeling that she was that kind of person.

After I showered and got dressed, I went into the kitchen and discovered Richie flipping pancakes.

"For a writer," I told him, "you sure seem handy doing domestic things." *You look pretty hot when doing domestic things, too,* I was tempted to add.

"That was fun yesterday," he said with a smile. "There I was, hanging out in my local coffee house, minding my own business, when this beautiful woman walks in and we sort of get this *rapport* happening."

My face went pink. I am not the kind of woman who is often called beautiful. But I certainly enjoyed

156

hearing it.

"When I got into New York and reached Manhattan and couldn't seem to locate the person I had come to see, I wasn't expecting to meet a man who would be so…helpful," I told him.

"Is that the best adjective you can come up with? I'm not really feeling too flattered."

"At this hour, on an empty stomach? Yeah, that's the best I can do."

"Then eat some hotcakes and drink some orange juice and get some nutrients into your body. Then you'll give me the sweet-talk I want."

I smiled and nodded as I sat down and stuffed my face with his hotcakes and washed them down with O.J. It seemed natural and right that I should have breakfast with this man with whom I had spent the night, if only because I would almost certainly never see him again. Also, I liked him and had no place else to go. I couldn't bear the thought of leaving Richie's warm apartment and stand outside Frances' door for an hour.

"Yummy hotcakes," I told him. "Yummy syrup. Not that no-sugar shit that diabetics use."

"No diabetics here."

"None indeed. Say, how did you become such a wizard in the kitchen, anyway?"

"Remember I told you that I had a real cunt for an ex?"

"Yeah."

"Well, she was—and still is—a chef."

"You mean like she cooks at HoJo's?"

"No, I mean like she cooks at Lutece."

My mouth fell open. "That place? Michelin gives it four stars!"

He nodded. "I said she was a selfish bitch. I didn't say she was stupid or unskilled." Then, "Now let me get philosophical for a moment. If we had stayed together, I wouldn't be here now, enjoying the morning with my new friend, a beautiful lawyer from Los Angeles."

Beautiful. That word. I've spent my whole life in a city where physical beauty is considered paramount, and I'm not considered physically beautiful. Maybe Richie's standards were so low that he really *did* consider me beautiful. Go figure people.

I swallowed a mouthful of hotcakes and O.J. "This is delicious but fattening. Out in L.A., they consider me a porker. A brainy porker, but a porker just the same."

"You have a beautiful body," he said. "Last night I made love to a beautiful woman."

I blushed some more. This guy was *such* a bullshit artist.

"Mind turning on the TV? I'd like to see if there's anything new on the Saul Rofstein case."

We watched *Good Morning, America.* They had a roundtable discussion about Rofstein and whether he killed Gina. If he did, was there a real chance he would buy himself a legal dream team who could get him an acquittal?

"Hand me your iPhone," Richie said.

"Excuse me?"

"Hand it to me so I can input all my contact information. That way you'll have the easiest time contacting me."

I shrugged and handed it over. Well, why not? I'd just spent half the night riding his dick. Anyway, what I lacked at that point in life was a friend in

Manhattan. Might as well be him.

He handed me his own smartphone. "You do me, I'll do you."

I punched my contact data into his phone and handed it back. "So, I guess I should be moving along."

"Got something for you." He handed me his scarf and cap. "You'll need these on the way to the airport."

"You're very kind."

"You need those items more than I do." He leaned over and gave me a nice firm hug.

I thought, what a pisser that he doesn't live in L.A. We could get together and have a very beautiful relationship.

Or maybe not.

Chapter 23
Hayley

Senator Strom Greggins woke up on a single bed in a bare, dusty room. He felt no pain, and in fact smiled at the relaxing warmth of painkillers in his body. Still, he had no idea of where he was or how he had gotten there. What the *fuck?*

He sat up and looked around. He heard footsteps and saw a pretty young woman hurrying up towards her. He noticed the gentle bounce of her firm breasts in her orange halter and started to feel like a man again.

"Ricardo! Whitey's wakin' up!"

A goateed Latino man half-ran into the room. "Dude, you went down pretty hard. We brought you here so's you wouldn't die."

"Where am I?" Strom asked. "I went down because someone shot at me."

"Shit happens, man." Ricardo danced around a little in his multicolored sneakers. "Bullet flew past and grazed you. Nothin' serious."

"Bullshit." Strom glowered at the man.

Ricardo arched an eyebrow. "Shouldn't swear when a lady's in the room." Then, "Look, nobody want trouble aroun' here, and you sure don't want bad publicity, seein' as who you are. That's why we're here an' you're here."

Strom shook his head. "You shot me. I know that much. I'm going to call the cops and have you busted."

"Hear that?" The beautiful young woman pointed at Strom as she spoke to Ricardo. "He wants you busted. How's *that* for gratitude?"

"Shut the fuck up. He's talkin' shit. Ain't no pigs comin' by."

"I've been shot. I'm bleeding," said Strom. Why don't you take me to the hospital?"

"Don't need no hospital," said Ricardo. "You're doin' jes' fine here. Anyway, we get the cops in here, they figure out I accidentally grazed you with a bullet? Shit, that means I'm goin' back inside, and I ain't about to let *that* happen. You hear me?"

"I have no idea what you're talking about," Strom said.

"Shit happened," Ricardo repeated, grabbing the modest bulge covered by his fly. "You got hurt, so we brought you back here to fix you up. Everythin' be cool, nobody goes to the hospital, nobody goes to jail. Work out jes' fine. I owe you one, an' when I pay you back, we be cool."

Strom nodded. He understood that Ricardo wanted to do him a huge favor to put things right between them. He was going to let Ricardo do him that favor.

Most people hated going back to work on Monday morning, especially after a fun weekend. Monday morning meant another full five days of work before they got to sleep in or play again. Hayley, though,

162

sprang out of bed beaming. Monday morning meant the beginning of five glorious days around Senator Strom Greggins.

She kept asking herself if he had told Joni yet. Had he gotten the chance to do so? If he hadn't told her yet, why not? He needed to stand straight, man up, show some balls and tell his old lady that he had met someone else and was ready to begin his new life with that special woman. He had told Hayley he intended to do exactly that.

She entered the office with a big, pretty blonde smile. She said hello to the new male intern and nodded at Maureen, the woman who arranged Strom's speaking engagements and whatnot.

"Well, isn't it a lovely day?" asked Hayley to no one in particular.

"The weather is awful," said Maureen. "Rain later on and maybe even snow."

"Weather isn't everything," retorted Hayley.

The two women disliked each other for a dozen reasons. Maureen had worked for Greggins for a decade, and when Hayley had been hired straight out of college, at a higher salary and with more responsibility, Maureen nearly burned with resentment. Worse, when Maureen—hardly the world's least observant person—began to suspect that Strom was playing slap-and-tickle with the pretty, tall young new hire from California, the older woman felt like punching the younger one in the nose.

"Senator Greggins," Maureen told Hayley, "will be out of the office this morning."

Hayley's face fell. "Why is that?"

"Because he won't be in."

"How do you know?"

"Because his wife called me and said so."

Maureen smiled because she received the call and not Hayley, and Hayley frowned because she considered herself Maureen's boss even though she really wasn't, and here was Maureen, acting like the top dog.

"Why didn't she call me instead of you?" Hayley asked, knowing that such a thing should be left unsaid.

"I've known her for years," Maureen said, lifting her chin. "We speak on the phone quite often."

"Oh." Hayley took a deep breath and admonished herself not to say anything nasty to Maureen. She marched into her small but cozy office and reminded herself of how much better off than Maureen she was—cuter, taller and smarter.

Had Strom confronted his wife already, and that was why he wasn't coming in? Joni might be throwing a huge temper tantrum and he needed to cool her out. Maybe was already cooled out and they were seeing a divorce lawyer that morning.

Hayley sighed and smiled. Her man had finally done what he had promised her he would do. She had done her thing, and now he had done his. Soon they would be together forever. She would give him a nice big kiss the next time they were alone.

Late on Sunday afternoon, Strom had returned home with a scratch but otherwise looked all right. When he opened the door and let himself in, Joni looked up at him with supreme indifference. "Everything all right?"

"Wonderful."

He tossed and turned all night, mentally replaying his meeting with Ricardo and telling him what to do. Strom didn't like any of it, and frankly believed that Ricardo lacked the intelligence to fulfill their plan. Well, they would try it anyway. Had Hayley really given him any options?

Nope.

Hayley was acting like such a boss, insisting that he dump Joni and marry her so they could have this kid, and if he didn't comply she would contact Joni personally and tell her about their affair and love child. Well, Senator Strom Greggins wasn't about to let Hayley Coleman push him around. No fuckin' way.

Ricardo. Who was he? An angry young Hispanic man with many crimes and misdemeanors. He had been incarcerated for the first time at age fourteen, and if charged with firing a gun at a United States Senator, he would go back inside for many years, something he had no particular desire to do. Plus, once the bullet grazed Strom, Ricardo had taken him to a private home rather than a hospital—therefore, the hard-luck Latino man would have faced a kidnapping charge, too.

The bullet that got Strom had been fired by a rival gang member who was after Ricardo. Had the bullet come an inch closer, it would have penetrated the senator's skull and killed him instantly.

But he was still alive, and the badass who felt responsible insisted on doing something nice for Strom to put things right between them, and Strom had every intention of getting that badass to do him a huge favor.

For the longest time Hayley sat at her desk and thought, *Shall I call or shall I not?* She told herself that since it was a workday, she had every right to call him at home and ask if there was anything she could do for him.

But maybe Joni knew about her relationship with Strom, and then calling his house would be a very stupid thing to do.

Still and all…she was at work, the place where she was normally so close to the one she loved, and he was at home, just a phone call away…why couldn't she call him?

She entered Maureen's office and blurted, "Did she say when he might come in today?"

Maureen stubbed out her cigarette—federal law prohibited smoking in their building—and looked up at Hayley with a smirk that suggested she knew why the young woman wanted so much to know about the man's comings and goings. "No, she didn't say anything about it. If she *had*, I would have *said* so."

Hayley nodded. "I understand. I guess he'll be in soon."

"Unless he isn't."

Hayley frowned. "Meaning…?"

Maureen smirked some more. "Maybe he has taken the day off to spend time with his wife while their children are at school."

Hayley blanched. *This old bitch knows about us.* "Take a day off to goof off with his wife? That doesn't sound like him."

"Their wedding anniversary is coming up," Maureen said. "Maybe they've gone out shopping for something special."

166

Hayley blanched some more and wandered out of Maureen's office, thinking, *Can't be. Absolutely, positively can't be. He loves me, not her.*

Chapter 24
Nelson & Frances

Nelson waited for Artie Jay to pick him up, and De Vito called to say that if they wanted to see Frances, they should come by the SoHo apartment.

"O.K., we'll do that," Nelson said.

Ria continued to obsess him. He told himself he was a fool to feel that way. It was just too weird—she was a famous singer but he couldn't think of one of her songs. He didn't know her phone number, and he wasn't sure he wanted it.

But if he wanted to contact her, how would he do such a thing?

The answer was: he wasn't meant to contact her. *She* would contact *him*.

A voice inside his head said, 'Stay away from her. She's bad news.'

A different voice said, 'She's the most exciting woman you will ever meet. Let her ride your dick as often as she wishes.'

Nelson had scarcely any idea of what to think or how to feel. Ria did her thing, which was to show up at his apartment whenever she felt the urge and she expected him to do as she pleased.

He realized she was every kind of weird and crazy. He knew he had to reject her before she kept messing with his head, but could he? Was he a good enough man to reject such a bad woman?

Frances squirmed as she sat in the back seat of the big shiny car. She had packed her suitcase and the driver stowed it in the trunk. He was now driving her to her SoHo apartment so she could meet with the legal eagle her father had sent. She rubbed her arms and took some deep breaths. She felt freaked out about the prospect of seeing Saul again. Frances had been estranged from her parents for over a year and still considered them asshole for refusing to provide her with handouts whenever she asked for them. She wondered, too, about her mother. Would the deceased be in an open casket? Probably not, since her killer had shot her in the face, thereby disfiguring her grotesquely and making it a bad idea to let her adoring public see her that way.

Frances remembered the last time she saw them. The two had attended the premiere of Saul's latest blockbuster and invited her along. Not wanting to sit through another Rofstein reeker, she had declined on the grounds that she had too many career-related things to do. But she'd dropped by their hotel and had breakfast with them in their ultra-deluxe suite. Frances always felt dazzled by them, the handsomest couple alive. Saul, slim and unsmiling, looked every bit the part of a zillionaire Hollywood mogul with his gray hair, generous mustache and paisley robe. Her mother, an incandescent beauty, sat there smoothing out her lovely black hair and smiling at her daughter.

Both of them had smiled at Frances, as if they were genuinely happy to see her.

"You look wonderful," Gina had said.

"You were smart to move to New York," Saul said.

She inferred that they wanted her to stay put, in this huge city so far from home, where in many ways she was no longer their problem.

He'd taken out a slip of paper and slid it across the table to her—a check for twenty thousand dollars. "A little something from me to you," he said with a grin. Chump change to him.

Thank you so much, Daddy, she thought as she pocketed the check. *It must have taken you all of fifteen seconds to make this amount of money.*

That was over a year ago. Now her mother was dead and very soon she would be flying back to Los Angeles to attend the funeral. She told herself to be an adult about it.

"Everything all right?" De Vito asked.

She shrugged. "Wonderful. Too wonderful."

De Vito nodded and said nothing more. Frances and her mood swings? Man, they freaked him out. First she was tripping out about Adel Nasrallah's son's bad behavior, then she was undecided on which outfits to take to California. Her mother's murder seemed irrelevant. He'd never seemed to understand his girlfriend and her ups and downs—but right now he was feeling pretty up about their trip to California and the good shit that might happen to him there. Her folks were filthy stinking rich and one of them was now dead. Maybe the survivor would part with some of his heavy money and his only child would be the recipient.

171

Nelson and Artie Jay agreed that they were doing the right thing by stopping by to offer their condolences to Frances. The three had attended high school together, and while the boys really had little use for her back then, they did have a few shared memories to laugh about, or keep quiet about—especially that prom night when, after way too many joints and beers, the boys had taken turns French-kissing and feeling up the girl. Her parents had wanted her to have a memorable evening, and she would have had just that except it was all floating around in bits and pieces due to the amount of alcohol and cannabis she'd consumed.

De Vito had asked them to come to the SoHo residence, and when they arrived, Artie Jay asked, "Why here? Why not your Park Avenue place?"

"Because Frances' dad thinks we live here," replied De Vito. "He's sending his lawyer out here to escort us back on the flight. Ain't he the sweetest thang? We're traveling first-class and the old dude is paying for it."

"He can afford it," said Artie Jay.

Frances walked into the room wearing a jumpsuit, boots and a leather jacket.

"What up, homies?"

"Haven't seen you in that outfit before," said Nelson.

"It's new."

With a touch of awkwardness, they took turns hugging her and murmuring "So sorry for your loss" into her ear.

"So sorry for having you here in this trashy

place," Frances said of the apartment that many in Manhattan would envy.

"We're gonna leave in fifteen minutes," De Vito said. "Quit actin' like you're a hard-luck case."

Frances sneered at him. She thought, *He can be such an asshole. Why didn't I hook up with someone like Nelson? He's handsome, rich and charming. If I was with him I could retire from this prostitution bullshit and we could live a life of sleeping late and goofing off.*

She figured that after her intoxicated tryst with Nelson way back when, he had lost all romantic and sexual interest in her and made no effort to pursue her. It was as if he were somehow ashamed of what they had done that evening. Also, Nelson and De Vito were friends; as long as De Vito and Frances were a couple, she and Nelson would never be more than friends.

"Thank you for stopping by and giving me your good wishes," she told them.

"Glad to do it," Nelson replied, thinking that if he and Artie Jay were sorry for her loss, *she* wasn't. Indeed, she seemed perfectly calm, even content. De Vito, however, seemed fidgety and twitchy, as if he'd just smoked a dozen rocks.

Nelson wondered for a moment how he would feel if anyone ever blew away *his* mother, the beautiful and feisty Lovey Skalbania. He felt sure that many people over the years would have shot her dead if they thought they could get away with it. He would then have her killer killed, for he was a Skalbania. He certainly wouldn't cope with his loss with an oh-well indifference like Frances.

Frances sighed. "Where's the lawyer guy, anyway? He should be here by now."

"Didn't I tell you?" De Vito asked. "The lawyer's a chick. She sounded young. She said you used to know each other or somethin'."

Frances shook her head. "I don't know any young women lawyers."

"Well, anyway, she's got this great reputation. Apparently she's one squared-away bitch."

"Probably a big fat dyke. Yuck," said Frances.

"We're gonna go now," said Nelson. He didn't like the way De Vito and Frances were speaking to each other. He predicted a bickering session was imminent and he didn't want to stand there and listen to them.

"You sure I can't talk you into flying out there with us?" Frances asked. "First class, you know."

"Can't do it. Got people to see and things to do."

She leaned in closer, as if wanting to hug and kiss Nelson, and he stepped back. Any physical intimacy between them would enrage De Vito. Nelson knew that, like most other women, Frances found him highly attractive. Most men considered him a formidable opponent when competing for women.

"Gotta split," said Artie Jay. "We want to open an *Attitude* in Moscow and have to meet with investors so they'll put up the cash we'll need to get it started."

"Break a leg," said Frances. "If you guys get it all shaped up, we'll fly out for opening night."

De Vito nodded. "A big party? Yeah, we'll be there. I've never been there. Would love to check it out."

"Bet your *asses* you'll be there," Nelson said with a laugh as he and Artie Jay wandered over to the front door. He flung open the door—and there stood

174

Kayce.

It seemed like a very long time before any of them said anything.

Chapter 25
Kayce

"Nelson!" I hadn't said his name in years. *"Nelson Skalbania!"* The cutest boy in school had grown up to be the handsomest man alive. I shouldn't have felt surprised.

Nelson was born with it all—looks, brains, charisma, a family with obscene wealth. He could have every girl he wanted—and certainly did. He and his best friend Artie Jay—also a major cutie—went through girlfriends faster than any other of the boys. Like everyone else, I heard stories about that prom night when he, Artie Jay and Francesca got high and had a *ménage a trois*; it was the only thing people at school talked about for weeks afterwards, so it probably happened. Frances walked around afterwards with a big, smug smile, even though I noticed that she was never one of the lucky chicks who got to *date* Nelson and be his *girlfriend*. I'm sure she was mad as hell about that for quite some time.

Now I was on my way to Frances' apartment, and here he was—Nelson Skalbania, my first love whom I had adored from afar. Who could walk right by me, look right through me and never know I was there.

"Have we met?" he asked, frowning. He wasn't just jerking me around; he really had no clue as to who I was.

I took a deep breath and said, "Probably not. I'm an attorney helping Saul Rofstein."

He nodded. "Frances' father."

I nodded, too. "I'm here to escort Frances to Los Angeles for her mother's funeral. Um, I went to school with Frances. I remember you from school, too, although I can't say that you and I *knew* each other."

He smiled, showing big, bright white teeth. What a cutie. What an absolute fucking cutie. "You've got some kind of memory. I forget everything but only the most important things, and sometimes I forget those things, too."

"Well, I'm a lawyer, so I kind of *need* to remember lots of stuff all the time," I told him.

"So you grew up and became a lawyer." He checked me out for a moment, up here and down there, as if to confirm that, yes, indeed, I *had* grown up.

"Yes, sir, I done." Then, "Anyway…"

The guy I'd spoken to on my iPhone, who called himself De Vito, stepped in. He was tall and skinny, with long hair and sharp features. He was handsome if you liked that crackhead look, which wasn't really my thing. I liked the *GQ* look. Nelson was more to my taste.

"You're the lawyer Saul sent over to take care of business, right?" De Vito asked, frowning, as if there had been some mistake.

"De Vito Silvera, right?" I extended my hand.

"I'm Kayce White." Lucky me, I thought. I got me a crackhead to escort back west. Lucky Frances. She got herself a crackhead for a live-in lover.

De Vito gave me a limp, clammy handshake. He and the others stood there, looking me over. While I have spent all my life in Los Angeles, I have never been anyone's idea of a California beauty, even though I have a moderately pretty face, a better-than-decent pair of tits and little if any body fat. They seemed to look at me with grudging approval, and my got-fucked-twice-in-as-many-nights glow probably lit up my face.

Artie Jay said, "Kayce! What up?"

I said, "It's all good." I thought, *How weird life is. These three people are all friends. Not sure if I have any friends except for the people I work with, and I think they're more* acquaintances *than friends.*

"Come on inside," said De Vito. "These guys were just leaving."

"Have a nice flight," said Nelson with another big smile.

"If you ever need a badass lawyer," I told him, "I'm Kayce White. I work for Bryan 'Frosty' Forst." Before I could think better of it, I plucked my business card out of my pocket and handed it to him.

You stupid bitch! I said to myself. *What are you doing? Hustling Nelson fucking Skalbania for business? Way unhip!*

Nelson and Artie Jay skedaddled, and I followed De Vito into a big, airy room that somehow seemed vacant.

Frances sat on a beige sofa, drinking a soda. Her TV was on and she sat staring at Barbara Walters or someone. She appeared ready to leave, dressed all in black—the kind of black where you walk into the most expensive stores on Park Avenue and say, 'Sell me the most expensive black outfit you have.' She completed the look with opaque black sunglasses, the designer type for which she probably paid three thousand dollars.

She looked away from the TV, gave me a glance, went back to her TV and gave me a long look. Her mouth dropped open and she got up.

"Kayce?" She actually took off her sunglasses, which was the highest—and perhaps only—compliment she had ever paid me. "For real?"

I nodded. I really had not expected her to have the slightest memory of me. We had parted years earlier and I was scarcely the plump, nerdy child I was then. When we were friends, I had thought her good-looking and dumb, a girl who knew little of books and facts but plenty about being cool and getting everyone to envy her.

"Yes it's me," I said with a big smile.

"Lookin' good, too. Slimmed right down."

"Wasn't easy, either." Frances had always been a pretty child, but not pretty enough for her gorgeous mother. I remembered when the swarthy teenaged cutie underwent a rhinoplasty because her nose was a tad too big, and breast implants because her pert young titties needed to be a bit bigger.

"You look good, too," I said, which was the understatement of the millennium. On our final Rodeo Drive shopping spree, she'd told me I was much too fat to wear the clothes most worth wearing, and I said I was O.K. with that because I was much too poor to buy the clothes most worth buying.

Back then I was a chubby size eight while

180

Frances was a cadaverous size zero.

"So you became a lawyer," she muttered.

"I certainly did."

"Nice for you," she said, sitting back down and sipping her soda. "I always figured you'd, uh, make something of yourself."

Yeah, right. We were chummy for a year and you often forgot I was at your side.

"Your father is very happy that you're flying in for a visit," I lied. "Also, I'm very sorry for your loss."

She swallowed a mouthful of soda and said, "Do you think he did it?"

"Excuse me?"

Just then De Vito came in. He took me by the arm and whispered, "Ignore her. She's full of grief."

And *you're* full of crack, I felt like retorting.

Frances got up. "Let's get out of here."

"Is the car here?" asked De Vito.

"It certainly is," I replied.

"Is the driver gonna come up here and get our luggage, or what?" he asked.

"I'll bring him up." I went from lawyer to gofer in five seconds. A shitty assignment.

Frances and De Vito. How long would these two last? They seemed alike, and different, in all the wrong ways.

I just hoped they wouldn't be too big a pain in my butt for the next six hours or more.

I figured out fast that Frances the adult was very similar to Frances the child. She hadn't learned a damn thing about how to treat people, or that it might be a good idea to treat others as she wanted

181

them to treat *her*. From the moment she got into the limousine, she ragged on the chauffeur about his driving, then started in on him about the inadequate heating and the limited channels on the TV.

Rag, rag, rag. She didn't shut the fuck up for one moment.

I kept waiting for her to ask about her mother's murder, her father's health, the number of people expected at the funeral. But no.

De Vito listened as she bitched. He nodded, shrugged, said nothing, forgot. To him it was probably just another day with Frances Rofstein.

He coped well. I envied him.

At the airport, a team from special services stood waiting for us. Frances got out, thrust her Louis Vuitton at the special-services woman and walked off.

They hustled us through check-in, but when the security guard insisted that Frances remove her boots, she said, "And stand on this filthy floor? I don't think so."

"It's the law," I told her. "Your belt and jacket, too."

"Fuck!" she yelled as a line of angry, inpatient people behind her waited their turn. Frances took forever and a day to remove her stuff.

De Vito had already cleared security and disappeared, leaving me to babysit his beautiful spoiled brat.

By and by I got them sitting side by side in the VIP lounge, so I left them in the care of their special-services escort and stepped aside to make a few calls on my iPhone.

First I dialed Frosty. He answered even though it was in the middle of the night in Los Angeles.

"That's my girl," he said.

I hated it when he called me that, and he knew I hated it, which is maybe why he said it. The thing is, I'm damned good at my job and everyone knows it; every law firm in southern California would love to hire me, so Frosty needs to mind his manners when speaking to me.

Next I called my father. He and my mother expect me to call daily; if I don't, they freak out. I had missed a day or so. I told him what I was up to.

"You're too important for that. That 'Frosty' guy should have sent a gofer."

"Well, he didn't."

I thought of Mark, the ex-boyfriend my parents wanted me to marry, then forgot about him and thought of Richie and José. Laid twice in as many nights! Yea, me!

I texted Hayley: *We're overdue for a long talk. Will call you when I get in.*

After I put away my iPhone I returned to Frances and De Vito. She sipped her third vodka over ice and maybe he was in the restroom sucking on the glass dick.

A crackhead and a lush, and they were my responsibility till they weren't.

Yea, me!

Chapter 26
Hayley

"Strom! Where have you been all day? I've been worried sick!" said Hayley. "It's *so* unlike you to take a day off."

"Everything is pretty terrific," he replied.

"Well, there's so much going on right now," she said, lowering her voice. "Between you and me, I mean."

"I'm a United States Senator. There's always plenty going on in my life that requires my immediate attention."

She chuckled. "Maureen thought you and Joni had gone out shopping for an anniversary present."

"Well, we didn't, and I hope you didn't think we did."

"Well, Maureen said—"

"Don't believe Maureen. She's an idiot."

"When you were a no-show today, I thought maybe something tragic had happened to you."

"Stop talking bullshit." Then, "Does anyone know you're on the phone with me?"

"No. Nobody knows. Hey, how come you called my iPhone number? Why didn't you dial my office line?"

"Because it's more confidential this way. It's

absolutely crucial that you and I are the only ones who know about our, uh, after-hours relationship."

"But I thought—"

"Don't think, just listen. I'm taking care of business and I know what I'm doing. Just trust me completely and be confident that I'm going to do what needs to be done."

"I trust you and love you and have every confidence that you'll do all the right things. But sometimes I just can't help getting anxious about everything."

"Well, there's this thing that has your name on it," he said.

She brightened up. "Really? A surprise? For me?"

"Just for you. You need to listen to me and do exactly as I say. Understand?"

"Yes, I understand."

"Good. Here's what I need you to do…"

Chapter 27
Nelson

"I think," Artie Jay told Nelson, "that Frances and De Vito are two of the weirdest motherfuckers on Planet Earth." The two hurried to their appointment with the Russians who had expressed an interest in helping to finance the friends' expansion into Moscow's nightlife scene.

Nelson nodded. "They're different, that's for damn sure."

"Frances has a heart as cold as the dark side of the moon. Her mother's been murdered and she's like, 'Well, shit happens, dude.'"

"She's a cool one. Remember high school?"

"I've done my best to forget."

"Forget what?"

"That prom night. We took turns bangin' her."

"It was consensual," Nelson pointed out. "Nobody raped anyone."

"I try real hard to forget about that night and what went down."

"Then maybe we shouldn't talk about it anymore. That was ten years ago."

Nelson's iPhone rang and at first he thought it might be Ria. He wondered if he wanted to hear from her, and he wondered, the next time she said, 'Come fuck me,' if he would drop everything and do as told. Nelson, who liked to consider himself his own boss and nobody's fool, often seemed to end up as her plaything.

"Hey, Ma," he said into the handset. No Ria this time, just Lovey Skalbania."What's doin'?"

"Keeping busy, Nelly, same as you."

"What can I do for you?"

"Return to Los Angeles forever."

"Excuse me?"

She laughed. "Just trying to get you all worked up. Seriously, I have a business proposition for you. Something I know you'll really like."

"That so?"

"It's something you've been on my ass about."

"Talk to me."

"Well, last night I fired the cretin who managed my nightclub out here. Turns out he was letting pushers deal dope on my premises. Plus, he was laundering money."

"Shame on him."

"Exactly. So I put his sorry ass on the slow boat to China."

"Yea, Ma!"

"Damn straight. So here's where you come in, Nelly. You and your boy are free to come in and make my nightclub the newest *Attitude*, if that's what you want, and I think it's *exactly* what you want."

"We haven't had this conversation in a couple of years, Ma. Artie Jay and I are going to open clubs in all the big cities, so my attention has been going in every direction. Right now we're going to meet with Russians who, if we're lucky, want an *Attitude* in Moscow as much as we do. So we'll have to get back to you about taking over your property."

"Bullshit, Nelly. I want an answer *now*."

"I gotta run this down for Artie Jay I can't say yea or nay without consulting him first."

"You have twenty-four hours."

"Really?"

"Yeah. If you can't get your shit together and fly out here to sign the deal, I'll find someone else who wants to operate a nightclub on my property."

Click.

"Want to tell me what's goin' on?" asked Artie Jay.

Nelson smirked. "My mother just offered me— us—her Oasis property as the site of the next *Attitude*."

"Sah-weet!" Artie Jay said, cackling. He slapped his thigh.

The Russians were four men with bald heads, fat stomachs and rumpled suits. Nelson disliked them immediately. He had inherited his parents' business acumen and instincts and knew at once that he and Artie Jay were wasting their time with these pushy, dirty foreigners.

The Russians wasted very little time in sitting down and telling the two young Americans what they wanted, which was tantamount to a ninety-ten split. They seemed to think that Nelson and Artie Jay were a couple of wide-eyed dummies eager to be exploited. The Americans heard them out, said, 'We'll get back to you on that,' and hurried out of the meeting room.

"Those guys thought we were idiots," Artie Jay said on the elevator ride down.

"Well, I'll have to call my ma tonight and tell her we'd be delighted to do a deal with her," said Nelson.

"The sooner the better. L.A. and Vegas seem like natural locations for our businesses."

"We better get to Vegas tomorrow. Maybe we should take the private jet."

"It's sort of *yours*, isn't it?" asked Artie Jay.

"Not mine personally."

"But you can use it whenever you like."

"Yes. I can, and so can Sass."

Artie Jay smiled. "How is Sass? Don't see much of her anymore."

Nelson shrugged. His mother had asked him to take a special interest in Sass and be a brother of sorts to her, and yet he hadn't contacted the girl in weeks. She'd mentioned something about having met someone new, so maybe her new boyfriend was the big brother Lovey thought she needed, so Nelson really didn't pay much mind to it, mostly because he had many other things going on. Also, Sass was a grown woman, capable of living her own life and dealing with her own shit. And if she couldn't, well, too fuckin' bad for her.

He admonished himself for thinking such things about her. But he was right—Sass was a beautiful, charming woman who attracted riff raff, losers and punks. One after the other. As long as her looks held out and her pussy stayed itchy, she would ride the dick of a bad boy till she grew bored with him, then find a new one.

"I'm going to call Sass," he said. "Offer to take her to Vegas. Ma would love to see her again."

"So we're taking your plane? So it'll be O.K. if I

bring my girlfren'?"

Nelson's eyes narrowed. "Didn't know you had one."

"Yeah, there's this chick I've been dating."

"Since when?"

"Since I started goin' out with her."

"This is the first I've heard of it."

Artie Jay grinned. "Well, you aren't exactly known for givin' a shit about anybody except Number One."

"Sounds serious."

"Well, I think I may have finally found the one for me."

"Bring her along. I'll check her out and tell you what I think."

Artie Jay laughed. "Love her or hate her—I don't give a *fuck* what you think."

"Yes," said Sass.

"Yes?" asked Nelson.

"Yes, I'll fly out there in the jet. Sounds like fun. Plus, I haven't been on that plane in a long time. Mind if I bring Al?"

"Who's Al?"

"My new friend."

"I hope this person isn't another one of your—"

"No sweat, Nelson. You'll like each other."

"Promise?"

So they agreed to meet at the airplane for an eight-in-the-morning flight. Artie Jay was bringing his girlfriend and Sass was bringing her squeeze. And Nelson? Well, he was, as the old song went, "Alone Again (Naturally)."

Chapter 28
Frances

Frances felt much ambivalence about returning to Los Angeles. As soon as she stepped off the aircraft, she got a big whiff of smog and instantly remembered why she'd left. She steeled herself for her homecoming. Looking around, she saw people hurrying this way and that and she smirked: Frances Rofstein had come home and nobody gave a rat's ass.

She felt glad that they would not be staying at Maison Rofstein. De Vito had been smart enough to make sure they had a suite at the Beverly.

Oh, she thought, that wonderful place. she'd cut class many times and hung out there, being very flirtatious with whichever horny male she encountered at the snack bar. She didn't look a day over her age—fifteen—and loved the look on his face once she told him her daddy was Saul Rofstein, the guy who sort of owned Hollywood.

Too much fun!

Now she was here with her boyfriend, a guy scarcely better than the ones she'd blown at the hotel, and she wondered what would happen over the weekend.

Kayce checked them in and walked them up to their suite.

"Your father wants to have an early dinner with

you," the lawyer told Frances.

"Will you be joining us?"

"No, I wasn't invited."

"Well, *I'm* inviting you." Frances grabbed her arm and looked at her with big, sad brown eyes.

"You must do this alone."

De Vito said, "She just invited you. It's rude to say no."

"I'm one of Mr. Rofstein's lawyers, not a friend or family member," Kayce said.

"Accept her invitation," said De Vito. "This is a rough thing for her an' she needs you. You're one of her oldest friends."

"Like hell I am!"

"Just make yourself useful, Kayce," De Vito said, pushing the woman out the door.

Frances got busy exploring their suite. She nodded and smiled as she sat on the bed, then inspected the bathroom and could find nothing wrong. She got on the phone and made an appointment to visit the spa.

De Vito went wandering through the hotel, his inner poor Chicago boy beaming at the beauty of it all. His home for the weekend, and he was staying here on *someone else dime!* Giggling, he gave himself the gentlest pinch to make sure it was all real. He smiled up at the sunny sky and let the gentle cool breeze kiss his face. He congratulated himself for becoming the live-in lover of Frances Rofstein and the most in-demand nightclub disc jockey in Manhattan. He wished he could reduce his crack consumption and remake Frances into a less bitchy girlfriend, but you couldn't have everything. He went by the pool and thought he saw Brad Pitt hanging out there.

Fuckin' A! This was his kind of place and these were his kind of people. Looks and money were the only things that mattered here, just as they were the only things that mattered to *him*, and he could definitely see himself doing some business in this place. De Vito Silvera—pimp to the stars, the man who set up beautiful young women with the horny men who just wanted to fuck them, not date or marry them. De Vito decided he wanted to get tight, real tight, with Hollywood stars; maybe Frances had the juice to introduce him to some of the heavies.

He nodded and smiled, thinking that this was where he and Frances belonged and he was going to make damn sure she knew it.

Wally Simons swiveled a bit in his leather chair as the lanky slacker sat across from him. "So, Chick," he asked, "what's going on?"

"I think maybe I have something you'll really like. Frances Rofstein. She's running a brothel."

"Serious stuff. Can you prove it?"

"Damn straight."

When Frances said she and De Vito were flying to her mother's funeral, that left Chick Tonucci's mother Babs in charge, and she took one nap after another while Chick went through Frances' and De Vito's belongings in search of proof of their illicit business dealings.

In their master bedroom he found a vast amount of designer clothing, shoes and handbags. Frances Rofstein must have gone into every store on Park Avenue and bought up everything she liked.

De Vito, too, reminded him of Richard Gere's

character in *American Gigolo*—dresser drawers filled to bursting with pricy articles of apparel.

Chick shook his head and let out a low, soft whistle. How many thousands of dollars had these two blown on all this shit? Did they really make that much money from procuring, or was she getting handouts from Daddy Rofstein?

He snarled. How come he busted his ass driving those chippies all over town to ride their tricks' dicks so that stuck-up cunt and her crackhead boyfriend could make all that money and buy all that designer shit?

Well, fuck you, Frances and De Vito. Your great gig is about to end, and I'll laugh my ass off as I watch you go to jail. I'm going to expose you to *The Whole Truth* and they're gonna pay me some heavy money for my trouble.

"Check this out." Chick thrust a manila envelope across Wally's cluttered desk.

"What is it?"

"Something that'll give you a boner."

"Better be something special. If you're wasting my time, I'll never do business with you again."

He looked through the many photos and held up a picture of Francesca when she was a teenager. "What a cutie. Of course, that's to be expected, considering who her mother is. Or was."

"Look at the other pictures."

Wally held up a picture of a moderately famous singer. "Is she who I think she is?"

"Yep."

"Didn't know she needed money badly enough to sell her body." Wally looked at a picture of an actress on a weekly series. "Her too?"

"Sad but true. I've driven them to their clients on many occasions."

"Have you?" Wally arched an eyebrow.

"They considered it easy money. Plus, it was all cash, period. The girls often got, like, ten large per date."

"Yes, but can you *prove* it?"

"Yeah, I can prove it. I have hotel receipts, dates, times, details. It's all there."

"Good deal," said Wally as he browsed through Chick's documents. "This will be of great interest to many people. If we hurry, we can include what you have in Wednesday's edition. It will be available for public consumption right after Gina Roff's funeral."

Chapter 29
Kayce

Wonderful! Frances has concluded that I am her best friend forever, and my boss Frosty is just about creaming in his pants over the news. To him, it meant that Mr. Moneybags Client—Saul Rofstein—was probably going to retain us as his personal counsel indefinitely, especially if he gets busted for his wife's murder.

Not that such an arrest will happen, though. While I was stressing out in New York, the Beverly Hills cops brought in two suspects.

Suspect number one is some lonely boy who was obsessed with the deceased. He did all of his communicating with her—love/hate letters, gifts, promises, threats—from his home in Atlanta, so nobody in California paid him much mind. But after the news media started reporting Gina Roff's murder, the stalker's brother revealed that his crazy sibling had boarded a Greyhound for Los Angeles with a pocketful of cash and the goal of meeting Miz Roff personally (one of the worst-kept secrets in southern California was Saul Rofstein's street address).

The other suspect was some guy who had been photographed having lunch with Gina Roff on the day before she died. They had dined at a restaurant in

West Hollywood and not even Saul Rofstein knew who her lunch companion was.

Was Gina riding the mystery man's dick? They went crazy on the Internet with speculation.

But more about me and my new best bud, Frances Rofstein.

"Frosty," I told my boss, "I would rather have dinner on my own. I don't like Saul Rofstein and he doesn't like me, so why should I have dinner with him and Frances? He treats me like a second-class citizen and he seems to think I'm your gofer. I'm a lawyer; a highly competent one. I insist on being treated with respect."

Bryan "Frosty" Forst, the coldest, most intelligent son of a bitch in town, told me, "It's all about how important lawyer/client relationships are. Clients depend on lawyers for legal counsel but also for friendship and camaraderie." Etc. & etc.

"O.K.," I said, "I'll do it."

I agreed, at least in part, because I wanted to sit at their dinner table and see how Frances and her father related to each other. As an A student of human behavior, I found that in a truly weird and twisted way I was eager to see these two fascinating, difficult people as they stared each other down and sized each other up. In court, I always watch the jury and study their expressions to try to discern what's going on inside their heads and hearts.

I looked at my iPhone. José had just texted me: *Dinner tonight?*

I thought of calling him but decided against it. I texted him: *Another night. Work to do.*

I didn't really give a crap if we had dinner or not. He was just there, this guy I knew.

Hayley had texted me again as I stared at the boring movie somewhere over America: *Please call! We need to rap! Got stuff to tell you!*

She said she would be getting into town for Christmas vacation in a couple of weeks. I wanted to hook up with her and do lots of girl stuff that I did only with her—spa, shopping, movies, whatever. I really ordered Hayley and wondered if anyone out there knew her but disliked her; I mean, really! How could anyone dislike such a big-hearted, caring person? She had big news and I felt eager to learn it. I truly hoped some good things were happening to her. She certainly deserved whatever good shit was going on.

As we stood waiting at the hotel's front entrance for the limousine to come by and drive us to Maison Rofstein, Frances squeezed my arm and gushed, "Thank you for helping me with this, Kayce! I know this isn't why you're here, but I really appreciate your doing me this personal favor."

Gratitude and humility from Francesca Rofstein! Wow!

"I remember you from school," she added. "Believe it or not, I was very envious of you. Maybe you didn't have megabucks like we did, but your parents went to those school events and actually gave a damn about you. I was way too envious of you."

Frances Rofstein envious of *me*? No freakin' way?

Frances opened her mouth to say something more, but just then De Vito hustled over after introducing himself to an NBA star who was a few feet away waiting for his car.

"You see the size of that dude?" he asked us. "Must be hard gettin' clothes and shoes that fit. Anyway, I gave him my card and demanded that he stop by and say hi next time he was in Manhattan."

Presently were arrived at Maison Rofstein and Saul personally greeted us at the door. After giving me the tiniest and most reluctant of nods, he shook De Vito's hand and sort of threw himself onto Frances for a brief, clumsy hug. Nobody said anything as we all entered the mansion.

I glanced at Frances and told myself for the hundredth time that she was one of the prettiest women I had ever seen.

We followed Saul into the gigantic living room that was dominated by a huge oil portrait above the fireplace of the Rofsteins. A waiter stood behind a remarkably long bar.

"Order whatever you like," said Saul. "My barkeep can fix every cocktail imaginable."

I observed that Saul's tan had faded and wondered why he hadn't made an effort to maintain it. Frances ordered a zombie and De Vito asked for a Jack over ice. De Vito wanted "Jack," as opposed to "Jack Daniels," because he thought that the hip, cool people in Hollywood called it by that name. He didn't order it because he liked its taste, either, because he grimaced each time he sipped it. Saul had a Jack over ice, too, which made De Vito smile.

I had a glass of white wine. Hardly the hip, cool drink, but at least it tasted good and I stayed mentally together while everyone else was getting fucked up. And getting fucked up was what they wanted to do, because Frances guzzled her zombie in three long slurps and asked for number two.

Oh, shit, I thought. People are drinking, getting drunk, and soon they're going to say shit that sober people would keep to themselves. Uh oh.

Have you ever been to a dinner where everyone snarls at each other but they all speak with politeness?

Someone who didn't know better would think he was attending the results of a Win Dinner with Saul Rofstein contest, in which several Saul fans broke bread with the King of Hollywood as their host sat among them, distant and bored.

Saul didn't have to say anything because De Vito seemed unable to shut the fuck up. He jabbered away on his usual crack high (I figured out fast enough that his frequent bathroom trips had nothing to do with elimination), he gave in to a case of verbal diarrhea and yakked away about the flight from New York, the weather, the state of the world in general and what a thrill it was to finally meet the splendid Saul Rofstein.

"I've seen every TV show you've ever made!" De Vito told him, then looked over to see Frances scowling at him. She had been his lover for this long and he hadn't said a word about admiring her father's work! What the fuck?

"I never got sick of your shows. They were like Big Macs—you always knew what you were gonna get."

I'd had a hunch that Saul was ready to dislike De Vito even before their first meeting—if only because De Vito was Frances' boyfriend—but the young man's compliments were so effusive and relentless that Saul, a man with the most monumental of egos, even by show business standards, just sat back and accepted them, helpless before the truth.

Frances and I looked at each other, exchanging the tiniest of shrugs, as De Vito went into endless detail about each of Saul's myriad hit shows.

At some point Frances stood up and said, "Excuse us for a moment." She nodded at me like, *That means* you, *bitch*.

I got up and followed her, leaving De Vito there to continue brownnosing Saul.

We entered a big powder room and locked the door. "First, I need a cigarette. Saul doesn't know I smoke." She lit a Camel.

"So…"

"Isn't this awful?" she asked, exhaling a long stream of smoke.

"De Vito seems to be enjoying himself. Your father, too."

"Saul will lose interest in the bootlicking soon enough. Anyway, thank you so much for being here."

"Didn't you know what a big fan De Vito is of your father?"

"Nope. He didn't say anything. What he *did* say was, 'Your old man is filthy rich and he should help you whenever you want a handout.' De Vito is just like, 'Gimme, gimme, gimme.' That's sort of his mantra. He's such a douche in some ways."

"You would have survived this without me," I said.

"I doubt it. Anyway, you're here, so I'm coping. Right after the funeral, I want to fly back to New York. Will you take care of that for me?"

Pleased to meet you. I'm Kayce White, Attorney-at-Law and Travel Agent/Gofer. Lucky me.

Back at the dinner table, Saul said, "Frances, during your stay I want you to go through your mother's things. Get the housekeepers to help you but make damn sure they don't steal anything. You know how hired help can be."

"Why do *I* have to do it?"

"Because there's no one else around here who's family."

"I just—"

"No backtalk, O.K.? She was your mother. She would have wanted you to do this for her."

"I seriously doubt that."

"Don't doubt it. I knew her far better than you did."

He stared at her. She faltered. It was hard to argue with King Shit of Hollywood.

We left Maison Rofstein at just before ten.

"Time to party down," said De Vito as we got into the car. "Where's the place to hang out these nights? Is the China Club still open? How about the Roxy? The Viper Room?"

De Vito Silvera was starting to get on my nerves. "I don't party much. Besides, I'm beat. I just want to go to bed."

"Like fuck! We're here, so we got to check shit out. Gotta hang out and see who and what's happening."

"You'll have to do it without me," I said.

"Count me out, too," said Frances. "I'm way too exhausted for drinking, dancing and whatever else De Vito has in mind."

"Shit, man!" De Vito shouted. "Do you know how *lame* you both sound?"

"Get the driver to take you to Sunset or

Hollywood Boulevard so you can party while Frances and I sleep," I said.

"You sound like a couple of old ladies," De Vito said, sneering.

"Maybe we are, and old ladies need lots of sleep. I'm sure you can meet some hip, cool people while you're out partying tonight," I said.

I heard Frances guffaw as she observed her boyfriend's temper tantrum because he wasn't getting his own way. O.K. enough-looking guy, but a spoiled-rotten crackhead just the same.

Frances and I climbed out of the car when we reached the hotel and the driver took off with De Vito in search of good times.

Frances waved at the departing limousine. "He'll be all right. Or at least the driver will feel obligated to look after him. For the rest of the night De Vito will not be my problem. See you tomorrow morning, Kayce."

"For what?"

"We need to go back to the mansion and go through my mother's shit."

I shook my head. "No can do, Frances. I work in this city, you know. I have an office and a bunch of things I need to do tomorrow. My boss expects me there in the morning."

Frances smiled. "No sweat—I'll just have Saul call him and tell him we need you here with us. Till I say otherwise, you belong to us."

"Oh."

Chapter 30
Hayley

Hayley slept a few hours before jumping out of bed and beginning her day. She was just too excited to sleep. Strom had promised her a surprise. What would it be? She was driving herself bonkers with anticipation. She knew it would be something wonderful, something especially for her.

She hummed a pretty tune as she decided to go jogging before work. She put on her sweatsuit and Reeboks, then went outside and ran her ass off.

Strom's words sounded in her head: *Take the highway till you cross the bridge and use exit 110. Keep going till you reach an abandoned Esso station and wait for me in the parking lot.*

She smiled, believing that she knew exactly what he had in mind. He would take her to view a house. Him and her. Just the two of them.

Of course! That was the surprise! Could it be anything else?

Strom and Hayley and their baby in their new house. How wonderful was *that*?

Chapter 31
Nelson

Artie Jay's new girlfriend, LaFonda, was a petite version of Whitney Houston before crack destroyed Whitney's looks. Totally gorgeous and eighteen years old, LaFonda was doing her best to break into the music business.

Nelson leaned over towards Artie Jay as they waited for Sass to arrive at the airport. "Jesus, Artie Jay, she's barely legal and so tiny! What was going on in your mind?"

"I was thinking that she may be just the one for me," he replied. "I'm thinking how wonderful life is when you've found someone you can really love. Of course, you wouldn't know anything about that."

Nelson ignored the insult. "We're taking her across state lines. Will we get busted?"

"Dude, she's eighteen, not eight. Knock off the retarded comments, O.K.? Shut your ass up and let's do what we gotta do."

Nelson shrugged. "Whatever, man."

The two men had been friends since high school. Artie Jay had always been popular with girls, and Nelson admired and respected him for his good looks, intelligence and suavity. But Artie Jay now had a serious, I'm-settling-down attitude that Nelson found completely unhip for someone so young. He had to admit that Artie Jay and LaFonda made the sexiest of couples, and she seemed sweet and warm—although sweet wasn't usually the way Artie Jay liked them. He liked his women to be good with backtalk and blow jobs.

Sass arrived only half an hour late. She was always late, like Romina, her late mother. Sass, ten years older than Nelson, was the younger man's niece, which made them both laugh hard and often.

"You're late," Nelson said, smiling.

She smiled back. "As always."

Nelson liked her smile. He wished she would smile more often. Her smile now was especially big and sincere. He figured it had something with Al, her new boyfriend.

A tall blonde emerged from Sass's car. The new "boyfriend" was actually a woman with short hair and a wide smile.

Sass grabbed the woman's hand and said, "Nelson, I want you to meet Al. She's the one I was telling you about. Isn't she just too beautiful?"

For every moment on their flight to Las Vegas, Nelson thought about Lovey and what she might think or even say about Sass's new relationship. Nelson had never pictured Sass as someone who might start playing for the Other Team, but then he told himself it sort of made sense. After all, hadn't she already gone through a series of criminals, druggies and mental defectives? Maybe she would have more happiness and success with a woman. She looked great and wore that big goofy smile he hadn't seen before. She and Al held hands and chuckled like kids out on a date.

Al was a tennis pro who lately was having some success. "We met at a tennis tournament," Sass said. "I was there with this divorced actor who thought he could get a career boost by dating someone who was a Skalbania. Anyway, Al had just broken up with her girlfriend and was there alone. We noticed each other, and here we are."

"Nelson," Al said, "I'm *so* thrilled to finally meet you. I was saying to Sass, 'It's time I got to meet your people! I'm sure they're *fascinating*!' And she said, 'The time is coming soon. I need to fly to Vegas with my Uncle Nelson. Come with me.'"

"Well," said Nelson, "I hope you like the rest of us as much as you like me." He looked over at Artie Jay and LaFonda, who were getting very friendly across the aisle.

He seemed to be the one without a partner. All by himself. *Alone Again (Naturally)*.

All he had was a giant boner for a music superstar who rode his dick and then left him as he slept. Yea for him.

Nelson felt grateful that the limousine's driver had turned on the air conditioning full blast. He had thick blood and didn't cope well in the Vegas or Phoenix heat. He grinned as the frigid air kissed his face. He closed his eyes for a few moments, and when he opened them, he looked out the window and saw a huge billboard on the Strip saying RIA! AT THE SERENDIPITY! ONE NIGHT ONLY!

Nelson nearly moaned. Was there no escaping that bitch?

The Serendipity, an elitist, exclusive boutique hotel, was operated by a couple of lesbians who were very chummy with Lovey and Sid.

Nelson closed his eyes again, concluding that he and his party would be at the Serendipity for the Ria concert, courtesy of one Lovey Skalbania, who would think she was doing her boy a favor by getting all of them tickets. When she had guests, especially from far away, Lovey liked to offer them the very best of absolutely everything.

So, what was Nelson gonna *do* about it?

He would go to the Gia show, of course. He was scarcely her biggest fan—her voice sounded to him like fingernails on a chalkboard—but supposed he could sit through her fifty-seven-minute act, unnoticed by the singer, just to placate Mama Skalbania.

"Unreal!" LaFonda pointed at the billboard. "Ria in Vegas! Oh, Artie Jay, let's check her out!"

Artie Jay shrugged, figuring that he was a guest of Nelson Skalbania, the son of Lovey Skalbania, who could move mountains in this town. "I'll see if I can get tickets."

"My ma's probably already got us all fixed up," Nelson said. "She knows people who know people."

"Or maybe just call Ria *yourself*," Artie Jay said. "After all, she's always checking you out like, 'Oh, baby, I could just eat you with a spoon.'"

Nelson swallowed hard. Had Artie Jay really observed that about Nelson and her without saying anything about it till now?

"For real?" Nelson asked.

"*Dude*," Artie Jay said, beaming, "you *know* that Ria be creamin' for y'all. She wanna ride the hobby horse with you. She wanna come on your cock."

"Aren't I the lucky one?"

Artie Jay smirked at LaFonda as she giggled into her hand. "Not sure if you lucky. Ria want you, not me, and I figure that make *me* the lucky one."

"Ria rocks!" squealed LaFonda. "If I liked chicks, I'd wet her down."

"Well, *Ria* likes chicks," said Al. "I do like a woman who's, uh, *flexible*."

Ria is one freaky bitch, Nelson thought.

He might have said something, or confided something, but at that moment their car turned into the parking lot of Oasis.

Chapter 32

Frances

As they sat in the dining room picking at their morning meals, De Vito, badly hung over, guzzled orange juice. Frances felt bored shitless.

"I wanna go back to New York," she muttered.

De Vito looked up at her. "Compared to New York, this place is heaven. L.A. is where it's at. You should have gone with me last night. I mean, there was some major *shit* happening on the Strip."

"Too bad for me." Frances, in her youth, had done major shit that would make De Vito's mouth fall open. She could imagine how impressed, even dazzled, her boyfriend had been last night as he got his first exposure to Los Angeles nightlife. She also knew it had its downside.

"This town is full of aging guys who depend on Viagra for boners, and the girls are often runaways or throwaways who come out here because they want to be models or pop stars. They often end up doing porn or working the streets. Let's hear it for my hometown! Yea!"

"We could do some great things here, sweetie." De Vito downed his second tall glass of orange juice and poured himself a third one. "Far as I can tell, nobody here is doing what we're doing in New York.

We could really take over in this city."

"Why do that when we're doing so great in New York?"

"Because, sweetie," he said, as if speaking to a very small, very stupid child, "the whole idea of doing business is to expand and prosper. Take over one market and move on to the next one."

She frowned. "But De Vito, you do understand that we've succeeded in New York because we're physically there to make sure things run right? We can't be in New York, do business in L.A. and expect to run things from three thousand miles away."

"Then maybe we should plan on spending much more time here." De Vito nodded. "We'll promote Babs to manager or something. She can run things back home while we're here or whatever."

"Putting Babs in charge of our Manhattan operation." Frances made a face. "Yeah. Great idea. I'll sleep well tonight."

"I'll find the right people to help with our expansion. You know me. I'm an outstanding judge of character."

Frances let out a big sigh. "I don't understand why you seem unable just to run the Manhattan operation and be content with that. Expansion is totally unnecessary."

"Wrong attitude, sweetie. Expansion is the very best thing there is. Expansion has made America great."

Frances lost her appetite and pushed away her plate. Why was De Vito such an asshole so much of the time? She was so sick of L.A. and he didn't seem to care about her feelings.

She checked her watch and thought, *Where is*

Kayce? Frances felt grateful that Kayce was there to help her through this *mishigaas.*

Frances tried to think of her good times with Kayce but came up with very little. They had hung out together for a while, sure, but Kayce had always put books and school first and had scarcely any fashion sense. Plus, the poor thing never had much cash or many credit cards in her wallet, and Frances was damned if she'd lend or give her friend money. Come to think of it, Kayce pretty much had been a party pooper.

Well, that was then and this was now. Kayce, now a lawyer, was here to help, and that pleased Frances because De Vito had no desire to help his girlfriend.

"Hey! Isn't that Jake Gyllenhaal?" De Vito said in a quiet but urgent voice as the famous actor walked by. "He's bigger than I thought. His sister Maggie is tall, too. Must run in their family."

"Nice for Jake and Maggie. De Vito, do you have any idea how *lame* you sounded last night, kissing my father's ass? You embarrassed everyone, including him and me."

De Vito straightened up. "I resent being called 'lame.' I am not lame. Anyway, what's your problem this morning, sweetums? On the rag? Is that it?"

"You and me both."

He scowled. "Excuse me?"

"You heard me. I'm wondering if we're really right for each other.'

De Vito frowned. "I'm trying to figure out what's going on at this moment. You seem really bitchy right now, and I'm not sure I like that. I know you're upset about your mother, even if you don't know it—but that's no reason to take things out on me. We're in L.A. now, and we should be enjoying every moment of it instead of bitching and moaning at each other.

"Well, you want to know something? It's been an awful few days, a really tense time…but we still have each other, right? Let me take you out to dinner tonight."

"De Vito—"

"Don't try to fight it. There ain't nothing that you can do. Just hang back and let me make all the arrangements. I know just what we want."

"Are you seeing anyone?" Frances asked as the car took them to Maison Rofstein.

"No one really special." Kayce was damned if she would tell Frances about her sex life.

"Good for you. Always keep your relationships casual."

Kayce sighed, hoping that Frances would soon stop asking such personal questions. She remembered, years earlier, the smug, patronizing look on Frances' face when Kayce revealed that she did *not* have a pocketful of cash to blow on designer clothes and accessories.

"Do you live in a house?" Frances asked.

"No, an apartment."

"I'm glad. Apartments are better. I have an apartment in Manhattan."

"I know. I was there."

Frances wanted to point out that Kayce saw her SoHo shithole, not her Park Avenue palace. But she said nothing, mainly because Kayce, if shown the

SoHo place and then the Park Avenue suite, would probably say, "I don't think either of these is better than the other one."

They kept quiet till they reached Maison Rofstein. As they waited for the huge wrought-iron gate to swing open, a couple of photographers leapt from the shrubbery and began taking pictures.

Frances looked away. "No! They can't take my picture! The people in New York must never know who I am!"

Kayce smirked a bit, remembering all the TV cameras and reporters who'd provided such generous coverage of Gina Roff's funeral, as if the woman had been some head of state.

As soon as they reached the house, the housekeeper took them upstairs to Gina's vast dressing room, which was even bigger than Kayce's entire apartment. Once again, Kayce thought of how some people had so much while others had so little, and those with so much seemed so quick to cry poor-mouth.

Frances collapsed into a pink love seat as if she'd just walked a thousand miles. "I can't deal with this shit. I'm too exhausted. You'll have to do it for me."

Kayce instantly remembered all those times during high school that Frances said, *"I didn't do my homework; you'll have to do it for me,"* or, *"I'm not in the mood to get my own lunch; you'll have to get it for me,"* or, *"I'm not interested in Hayley's party; you'll have to give her my regrets."* Kayce, whose young life had been so full of doing things she did not wish to do but did anyway simply because she had nobody else to do them for her, did those things for Frances because Frances was cool and Kayce was not and Kayce wished to remain friends with her.

But this morning, Kayce, now an adult and a lawyer, had had enough of Frances' bullshit. "Too bad for you," she said. "I have important work to do. Looks like you'll have to do this yourself."

"No! You're bought and paid for! I need you here!"

"Don't worry, I'll send my assistant, Chloe. She's a tireless worker and you'll adore her." Kayce White hurried out of the room.

"Bitch!" Frances screamed.

From his private cabana at the Beverly, De Vito checked things out to see what was going on. Alas, very little was happening due to the early hour. He wanted, and expected, a dozen or two movie or TV stars to arrive and hang out so that he could introduce himself. He had fantasies of handing his business card to some female L.A. stars and talk them into becoming his first West Coast chippies.

De Vito exited the cabana and lay down on a *chaise longue* by the poolside. He ordered a screwdriver because he'd heard that was the favorite drink of cool people in Beverly Hills. He wanted to say to everyone, 'Hey! I'm De Vito Silver from New York and I'm cool!'

He smiled to himself. So far, so good. The night before, he'd gotten into quite a party scene. Tits and ass? Shit, man, L.A. was the place. Black girls, white girls, blonde girls, redheaded girls, brunette girls, girls with fake titties, girls with fake lips…and all of them looking for a man with bucks, a dude with juice who could make a phone call or two and get the girls' acting careers started. Too bad virtually all of them would fail abysmally.

De Vito visited a couple of especially fashionable nightclubs. As a prominent nightclub disc jockey and prosperous pimp in Manhattan, he'd decided to take on L.A. and knew that the three things he needed, but sadly lacked, were contacts, contacts, contacts. So he'd gone into a Sunset Strip nightclub, headed straight for the bar, checked out the crowd and slipped the bartender his card.

"Are the owners around?"

"Your card says you're a D.J. Sorry, but we're not hiring right now."

Presently, the club's manager and a part-owner, came by. De Vito introduced himself and they shook hands.

"I'm from New York," De Vito explained. "I'm here because my girlfriend's mother, Gina Roff, died and they had her funeral this week."

Doug's eyes bulged. "Gina Roff' daughter is your girlfriend? Really?"

No, you fuckin' douche, I just made it up. "She sure is. We live together in Manhattan."

"Lady was murdered," Doug said, shaking his head. "What a tragedy. How about if I buy you another drink?"

"Cool."

As their conversation progressed, Doug said, "I really admired Gina Roff. She was beautiful and popular to the end. The world never lost interest in her. I used to be in the business myself."

De Vito nodded. "You look familiar."

"I was in *Ma's Family*. She was a good-lookin' single mom and I was one of her obnoxious kids. We lasted for a few years." Doug smiled. "Fame is the most addictive drug of all. They treat you like you're something special, and when it ends, you're nothing again."

De Vito took a long look at Doug, who appeared to be a pushing-forty, beaten-down-by-life child star who, all these years later, still didn't know what to do with himself.

What a loser, he thought. *This town is just begging to be scored, and I figure I'm the man to do it. But I'll need some help, and this poor doofus could do me some big favors.*

"So, Doug," he said, "let's get together and talk some more."

Doug nodded. "Yeah, let's do that."

"Tomorrow would be ideal. Lunch at the Beverly? I have a business deal about to happen that you might find lucrative."

"Tomorrow it is. I'm always looking for new opportunities."

They shook hands. De Vito smiled. *Am I slick or what? Just got in and I'm a player. Getting connections and making shit happen.*

Yea for me!

Chapter 33
Kayce

I got a text from Richie and read it on my way to the office. *Miss my Angeleno girl. Who am I gonna make love to now?*

I smiled. I liked it that he missed me. I texted him back: *Your pancakes were way too yummy. Eager for more. We'll get together...soon.*

I kept smiling all the way into the office. My smile disappeared as soon as I saw Frosty. He ragged on me about my failure to be Frances Rofstein's slave and babysitter.

"I am a lawyer," I retorted, "not a slave or babysitter."

He nodded, which was his way of acknowledging my point. "You and I are going to attend the funeral. Out of respect to the Rofsteins."

"That means I'll have to miss dinner with my family."

"You have dinner with them every week. I'm sure they'll survive."

I reached my office and buzzed for my assistant, Chloe. She was my own personal intern, and while I had promised her services to Frances and assured my old friend that Chloe would serve her well, I knew that Chloe was as obtuse and incompetent as anyone

I had ever met. Chloe, the daughter of one of Frosty's colleagues, seemed unable to learn anything, period. She forgot shit ten seconds after I tried to teach it to her.

Naomi, a Valley echohead, lived only for shopping, dancing and handsome men. She replayed *Lifestyles of the Rich and Famous* over and over.

Then it occurred to me that Naomi and Frances might truly enjoy each other. They had much in common and genuinely seemed to believe they were vastly superior to the rest of the human race.

"Here's the address," I told her. "Try not to be too impressed when you get there. Mind your manners and try to maintain a professional attitude."

"Cool!" Naomi shouted. "Now I don't have to do this boring office shit!"

After she'd taken off, I sat at my desk and took a look at my other work. Frosty always got the cases involving celebs or washed-up show-business people, and often assigned them to me. A shoplifting beef involving a struggling veteran actor and a pawnshop. The other one, aggravated assault, concerned a black rapper and a photographer who got up in the rapper's face. The rapper told the photog to back the fuck off, and when the shutterbug didn't, the rapper kneed him in the nuts. Mostly mundane, but I would do my best with them because both cases involved fairly well-known offenders.

At times I regretted the fact that Saul Rofstein had not been charged with Gina Roff's murder. What a case! Frosty would have tried it himself and I would have sat right beside him, assisting him in whichever way possible.

At some point I dialed my veterinarian to check

on the status of my dog, Kurt Cobain. Kurt freaked out whenever I tried to put him up in a kennel during my business trips, so I bribed my vet to take him in.

"I'll come get Kurt today," I told the receptionist.

"Not possible. He's already gone."

"What? Gone? How?"

"Your friend came in to get his cat, and when he saw Kurt Cobain, he said, 'I'll take him, too.' He insisted that you knew about it and would be O.K. with his taking custody of the dog."

"What's the guy's name?" I asked.

"Mark something."

"He's my ex-boyfriend and he had no right to ask you for custody of Kurt."

"Well, Kurt sure seemed delighted to see him. The two were very happy together."

"I guess Kurt belongs to Mark now."

"I'm terribly sorry if we did the wrong thing," she said with a catch in her voice.

I called Mark on his iPhone. I wasn't sure why I still had his number, but I did have it so I dialed it. I got his voicemail.

"This is Kayce," I said, doing my best to sound as cold as fuckin' ice. "You kidnapped Kurt Cobain, and I want you to call me so I'll know when you're going to return him." Click.

I snarled at my phone as I hung up. How dare that son of a bitch pull a stunt like that!

By dinnertime Mark had yet to call back. I knew that the only way to get Kurt back was by going to his house personally. *Mark bought a house*, I said to myself. During our years together, he had never mentioned wanting to buy a house. Which probably meant that he had never expressed a desire to make a house-buying commitment with *me*.

I had never actually been inside of his house, but after learning that he had taken possession of it, I drove by it a couple of times with grudging admiration at its spacious lawn and the big house, with its Old Colonial style architecture, made me think for a moment that I had been a fool to call it quits with Mark. He had more brains and bucks than I had given credit for having.

I parked across the street, marched up to his front door and rang the bell.

A cadaverously thin woman, tall and artificially blonde with a salon tan, opened the door and snarled at me.

"Yes?"

"Yeah, hey, I'm looking for Mark." I tried to look past her.

"And who might you be?"

"My name is Kayce White. I used to live with him."

She frowned for a few minutes, as if totally unable to comprehend that someone named Kayce White had once lived with Mark. Then it registered.

"He has our dog. The dog's name is Kurt Cobain. I want him back."

"You can have him. I don't like that mutt."

"So where is Kurt Cobain?"

She looked puzzled. "I thought he killed himself in 'Ninety-four."

"No, I mean the *dog* we named Kurt Cobain."

"I'm pretty sure I locked it in the backyard."

"Why would you *do* such a thing?"

"Because it never shuts up."

"Kurt is barking," I told her, "because you're mistreating him. Where is Mark?"

"Not home yet."

"Then give me Kurt and I'll go away."

"Does he know you're here? If I let you take the mutt, will Mark will O.K. with that?"

"Yes, I'm sure he will."

I stepped inside and observed right away that the place was a mess, filled with all her stuff. His only obvious possession was a huge, flat-screen TV and his funky old leather reclining chair. He'd kept that awful old chair but let me go. Some people just had their priorities all out of whack.

I stood still and listened as Kurt barked somewhere in the distance. Then Mark entered the room.

Mark Kron. My ex. The man who I had lived with, planned on marrying and whose babies I assumed I would have.

For a moment we stood there looking at each other and I could remember exactly why I had gotten involved with him. Nobody had ever accused him of being ugly.

"What the hell is happening here? Why are *you* here, Kayce?"

"You stole Kurt," I said, putting my hands on my hips.

"He is *our* dog."

"No, *my* dog."

"You left Kurt at the vet. He seemed very distressed, so I took him home with me."

"You were completely out of line."

"Bullshit. We found him together."

"And when you moved out, we agreed that he would keep living with me."

He scowled. "No, *you* decided that. when did *I* ever have any fuckin' say-so in anything?"

"Your blonde bimbo, the chick I just met, doesn't even like Kurt, so why do you insist on keeping him?"

"You are such a control freak," he said. "Always got to have everything your own way. Kurt was our dog. I'm entitled to have him."

"No. Absolutely not."

"Looks to me like I already have him."

Just then the girlfriend got into it. "Kayce, if you want the mutt, take him with you. The two of you are giving me a hellacious headache!"

"She's right," I said. "Give me my dog back and I'll fuck off."

Mark's mouth curved into a humorless little smile, the way it always did when someone challenged him to a fight, physical or verbal.

Had I ever loved this man?

Maybe once, but certainly not now.

"Fine," he said with his mirthless little smile.

"Hand him over and I'll fuck off," I repeated.

A few minutes later I was out the door with Kurt Cobain, both of us happy to be together again.

I had to stop by the office first before we went home; plus, I had agreed to have a late dinner with José. He wanted to take me to some chic restaurant in L.A., and I wanted to look my sexiest for him when he showed me off at this hip eatery. He would probably try to seduce me, and would succeed.

I told myself that after dealing with that prick named Mark I would need the comfort of the prick that belonged to José.

I drove to the highrise where I worked and Kurt just curled up and went to sleep on the backseat, knowing Mama would be back presently.

In the elevator I rode up to the forty-ninth floor. Naomi looked up at me and beamed. "Frances was too much fun! We had the best time!"

I shrugged. "Going through a murdered movie star's clothes with her daughter doesn't sound like a good time to *me*, but whatever turns you on."

"Mr. Forst wants you to look at these." She handed me a bunch of pictures. "O.K. if I go home now?"

"Shoo."

She smiled. "Thanks. See ya."

Frosty had enclosed a note with the pictures: *Kayce, look very closely at these pictures of Gina Rofstein. Tell me if you can tell who the man is. Saul is very eager to know.*

Yeah, boss, I'll bet he is. His wife is out with another man and the next week she's murdered, so of course he wants to know who this other dude is.

I took a long look at the pictures. Damn, Gina was gorgeous! Right to the end; never lost her looks. In the pictures she sat with a man, clinking glasses and smiling, siting in a restaurant in the Malibu hills.

It took me a few moments, but I figured out who her lunch companion was.

Hayley's father.

Chapter 34
Hayley

All Hayley could remember was pulling into a deserted Esso station and sat there, entertaining herself with her own pleasant thoughts. When a young Latina rapped on her window, Haley, being a kind young white woman, rolled it down to ask how she could be of assistance.

Then she blacked out. When she awoke, she observed that she had been bound and gagged, blindfolded and stowed in the trunk of a car. Panic seized her right away, but as it faded, she felt relieved that she was still clothed and her cooch had been left alone. For now.

Help me, help me, she said to herself in the darkness. *Strom, come rescue me.* She thought that if she repeated that mantra often enough, her man would come get her.

"You sure that chick gonna survive?" asked Lupe, Ricardo's adolescent girlfriend. Lupe, otherwise pretty enough to be a model, had a nasty white scar that ran along the hairline of the left side of her face, the result of a knife fight with some other girls. Her *madre* had given her a bunch of shit over that one. "Don't you know that your looks are all you've got? You're grounded for two months!"

"Fuck," Ricardo muttered with an exasperated shake of his head. "Ain' I tol' you a dozen times now? We just wanna scare her into a *miscarriage*, not kill her."

"She just had to put a condom on, or take it out before he shot his load," said Lupe. "That's been known to work."

"Sometimes it don't work. You got a baby livin' wit' yo' mama to prove condoms an' shit sometimes don' work," Ricardo said, sneering. "Anyway, it's not her that wanna lose this baby—it's what Senator fuckface wants. Far as Senator fuckface is concerned, what he wants is the only thing in the world that matters. He keeps forgettin' that he works for the people."

"Senator fuckface," she said with a mean laugh as she guzzled from a can of Rockstar and let out a huge belch. "Why you doin' him this favor, dude?"

"Let's jes' say I owe him."

"How long you gonna keep her?"

"Till she ain' wit' baby no mo'."

"Then take her to an abortion clinic," said Lupe.

"No can do. Gotta make it look like she lost the baby. No mo' fuckin' questions."

Ricardo had been dating her, if one could call it that, since she was fifteen. Lupe didn't rag on him that much, was there when he needed her most of the time and made herself scarce when he wanted to be alone (or with someone else). Plus, she could blow him like a porn star, and to him that was one of her

232

finest attributes.

Only problem was, Lupe's baby had been fathered by a rival gang member who felt that the infant meant that Lupe belonged to him rather than Ricardo, so the baby's father had tried many times to kill Ricardo. Consequently, Ricardo had thought about terminating his relationship with Lupe.

But not now. He had the white politicians secret squeeze locked up in the trunk of the car and needed to do what must be done. Dumping Lupe right now would be dumb, and Ricardo tried, always, not to be dumb.

"It's formal tonight," said Joni Greggins to her husband.

Strom disliked such events but knew he had to attend this one because while Hayley was missing, Strom needed to be out, around and highly visible.

Nobody had yet noticed Hayley's absence. Since she resided alone, it could take days before anyone reported her as a missing person. Once Ricardo, after vacating Hayley's womb, returned her, Strom would express outrage to the media about what had happened to the dear girl. Then he would discreetly cut her loose.

If Strom got lucky, Hayley's terror over her abduction would provoke a spontaneous miscarriage. Then she would be set free, and Strom would be emancipated as well.

He had told Ricardo only to scare her, not rough her up. He didn't think Ricardo was smart enough to figure that out on his own, but Strom felt he had run out of options and needed to rely on Ricardo for help in this matter. Besides, Ricardo had said, 'I owe you. I'll do whatever you want.'

Joni appeared in the doorway of his dressing room. She was dressed in a white gown and wore tasteful, conservative diamonds. "You aren't ready yet."

He nodded. "Give me a few minutes." Adding, "I've got things on my mind."

Hayley feared she would puke and choke to death on her own vomit. The car bounced again and again, throwing her about.

She promised herself that Strom knew of her disappearance and would soon come looking for her or at least tell the cops she was missing.

Or maybe not. His middle name was Looking Out for Number One, and he was very much the kind who wouldn't necessarily consider Hayley's missing-in-action status *his* problem. Strom was notorious for his reluctance to take on others' problems as his own, which was an odd way to be when you worked as a United States Senator.

She reminded herself that her car was still parked in the lot of that crumbling Esso station, and that Strom at some point would travel there, see that her car was vacant and make *some* effort at ascertaining her whereabouts. Unless he didn't give a shit, and Hayley had to admit that such a possibility did exist.

But what if a worst-case scenario were to come true? What if one of those bad guys had made off with her car after abducting her, so that Strom wouldn't know how or where to begin searching for her?

And, again, what if he just didn't care enough to begin the search.

Chapter 35
Nelson

As he stood there checking it all out with Lovey and Artie Jay, Nelson just couldn't get the smile off his face. Soon the nightclub inside the Oasis would be his, and he could just picture how good it would look as soon as he got done with it. He would change its name to *Attitude* and it would be the finest, freakiest, funkiest nightspot in Las Vegas, just as the *Attitude* in Manhattan was the best hangout in the Apple. He had been after Lovey to let him take over, but she had said, "I'm not sure if you can do it. What if you fuck it up?" Well, he'd shown her what a fuckup he wasn't: *Attitude* was making colossal profits in New York, and he had plans for such clubs in Miami and Atlanta. But for now he had Las Vegas to conquer, and what a boner he got from *that* prospect!

"You know that I'm going to make some big changes to this property," he said to Lovey.

"Surprise, surprise," she retorted.

"You want us to make it our own, don't you?" He noticed for the hundredth time that his mother, with her svelte figure, long dark hair and hazel eyes, was still the prettiest woman around. She was also the shrewdest businesswoman he had ever met.

"Yes, I want you to make it work. That's why I

offered it to you," she said.

"No, you offered it to me because you knew you could trust me not to sell crack and meth to the customers."

"Not at all. There are many nightclub operators I could have brought in—"

"But you didn't. And do you know why?"

Lovey shook her head. "Tell me."

"Because you need me."

"That so?"

Nelson smirked. "You know it is."

Lovey nodded. "I need you, Nelly. You too, Artie Jay."

Artie Jay smiled. "Thanks, Missus—"

"Lovey."

"Lovey." Nelson's mom always gave Artie Jay a king-size boner.

"Artie Jay," Lovey said, "I've known you and your family since you were twelve years old. Your father operated on my father, and your mother is just *much* too charming."

"And did you know," Nelson said, "that Artie Jay still has the world's biggest crush on you. But now that he's met the love of his life, you're probably safe."

"Too bad for me," Lovey retorted.

Artie Jay's face went crimson. "Why don't you tell her who's trying to get into *your* pants?"

"Do tell," said Lovey.

"Ria," blurted Artie Jay. "She's always making eyes at him and licking her lips."

Nelson sneered at him. "Like hell she does."

Lovey chuckled. For years she had known the most famous people in the world, and many of them

238

impressed her as being, well, not altogether deserving of their fame. Ria, however, deserved every bit of it. "She's one of the best singer ladies in the business, and I've heard them all," she said to Nelson and Artie Jay. "If she's attracted to you, Nelly, you should feel very flattered." She added, "I've got tickets for all of us to tomorrow's show. I can't wait."

"Forget about Ria's show," said Nelson. "Don't you want to hear about the great things I'm going to do with *Attitude* in Las Vegas?"

"Oh, I think I can figure that out for myself," said Lovey. "But you're dying to run it down for me, so ahead."

"That illuminated staircase? Indoor fountains? Paintings on the walls? All of that shit needs to go. Way too ostentatious. Our Vegas *Attitude* needs to be identical to the one in Manhattan—laid back, real cool."

"Ostentatious isn't necessarily a bad thing," Lovey told him. "Business was always good. We turned people away."

"It's not about the money the people pay to get in. It's about the people themselves."

"And what kind of people are you after?" asked Lovey.

"No tourists unless they're great-looking people. No fat people. No people who obviously lack fashion sense. It's like I told you from opening night—you need to make this a hip, cool hangout for people who know how to dress and conduct themselves. It's no coincidence that our New York club is called *Attitude*. That's what it's all about. We want sexy chicks who dress to show off what they've got. We want rich guys who drive Ferraris. We want visiting celebrities. But everyone has to have this *attitude* thing down."

"Nobody has ever accused you of being indecisive," said Lovey. "I just hope that your 'whatever works in Manhattan will work in Las Vegas' business strategy is the right one."

"Not gonna haggle with us?" asked Nelson.

"Nope. Now let's write a deal so we can go have some fun."

"Let's do that!"

Later on, Dee, Nelson's half-sister, got his attention by pounding on his door at the Oasis, then jumping into his arms as soon as he opened the door.

Nelson hadn't seen Dee in a few months but whenever they met he was amazed at what a beauty she'd become. Of course, she was still as wild as a tameless horse. Tall and dark and lean like their mother, she had a big blonde smile and sparkling green eyes. Unlike Lovey, she had no head for business or much of anything else except having fun.

"Hey!" he said with a big, embarrassed laugh as he pried her off. "You're getting a little too old for that sort of thing."

Dee threw back her head and let out a huge, delighted laugh. "Never too old for lovin' my big bro! Anyway, Mom said you were here, so I flew out just to spend some quality time with you. Ain't I jus' the sweetest thang?"

"You have your moments."

"Do you love me?"

"Most of the time."

"Say it, then. Say, 'I love you, Dee.'"

He shrugged. "I love you, brat."

240

She cackled. "Close enough." Then, "So where's your homey?"

"Huh?"

"Artie Jay. Where is he?"

"Who wants to know?"

"My best girl Peaches wants to know. She said, 'Go get his gorgeous black ass and bring it back to L.A. so I can do evil things to it.'"

"Peaches is way too young for him. He'd get busted."

Dee went over to the minibar, took out a can of Dr. Pepper and popped it open. She took a long drink and said, "Here's the deal, Nelson. I think you and I should become roomies. I'd love Manhattan."

He shook his head. "Not gonna happen."

She made a face. "Come *on*. I'd do my thing and you could do yours."

"For real? Would you let me?"

"Be serious, Nelson."

"I am. I'll stay in Manhattan and you'll stay in L.A. and go to college. Sound like a plan?"

"Don't wanna go to college. It's a waste of time."

"That so?"

"Yeah. Mom didn't go, and she's done all right. You went for something like fifteen minutes before you dropped out. This chick is too cool for school, baby."

"A college degree will help you a lot, Dee."

"Ha!" She laughed, then plopped down onto the sofa and stretched out.

"I mean it, Dee. Get that sheepskin. You'll be glad you have it."

"You're starting to sound like Mom. Well, I

don't want to hear it. Guess I'll just have to take off and make it on my own."

"Really? Where would you go?"

"Wherever, baby. Like I said, I'm too cool for school. I need adventure and experience, and no classroom is going to provide that." She added, "Nobody is gonna tell me I can't do that."

Nelson sighed. Lovey and Sid had a big problem with this kid.

"You mentioned adventure and experience. What did you have in mind?"

Dee shrugged. "Oh, the usual. Bang lots of men, live on the edge, tempt the Reaper…"

"Oh, please."

"Look, Nelson, let's understand something. I'm me. I'm my own boss. I'm not your kid sister or Lovey and Sid's daughter. I'm me, me, me."

"You have been since day one."

"And I'm going to live my own life and do my own thing."

"And when is that going to happen?"

"When I feel the time is right."

"And then you're just gonna bust out and live dangerously?"

"Fuckin' A."

"Well, wild child," he said, grabbing her hands and pulling her off the sofa, "you can be a badass some other day. Tonight we have dinner with some important folks, so you better mind your manners."

"I'm serious, Nelson. I'm gonna be my own person, and that's just how it is."

Chapter 36

Frances

"Just box it all up and have it put into storage," Frances told Rosario. "I'm much too upset to deal with this matter right now."

"Yes, Miz Fran," said Rosario. "Miz Gina's jewels? What we do with them?"

Frances assumed that all of her mother's jewels—the ones worth stealing, anyway—were in a safe-deposit box at the bank or stashed in a safe somewhere in the house. "Leave it for now. I'll figure out what to do with them later."

What Frances wanted to do most of all was to get out of there as fast as possible. Being back in Maison Rofstein was such a bummer—she was starting to feel physically ill. She had grown up in this house and all the bad memories of her childhood started filling her head. She decided that what she really needed was to get out of her childhood home and do something to take her mind off her mother's imminent funeral.

Downstairs, Frances discovered Chloe, Kayce White's assistant. "I'm Chloe. I work for Kayce. Your housekeeper let me in. I'm here to help you."

Frances looked this way and that, saw no sign of Saul, and smiled. "Come with me. We're going shopping."

De Vito made damn sure that he had a great table, just by the pool, where he could see everyone just fine. He knew he could have ordered lunch in his cabana, but sitting at that table just by the pool was even better. Who wanted to be locked away when he could be out in the open? See and be seen, man. That was the cool thing to do. De Vito wanted to be a player, and players were out there, in full view of everyone.

He had already spotted one chick who he thought would be ideal for their L.A. operation, if such an operation actually materialized, which he believed was a definite possibility. She was tall and blonde, with nice big titties and a heart-shaped ass.

The girl was also with some white-haired old fucker with a deep tan. De Vito knew that, in Hollywood, the most powerful people often were pretty ordinary looking, so maybe the white-haired dude was a heavy right up there with Saul Rofstein. The pretty girl wore a bikini so skimpy that it left very little to the imagination, and De Vito noticed that she shot a glance in his direction every few minutes. He guessed that she really wanted to get laid and that her white-haired dude just couldn't rise to the occasion. De Vito had his business card ready in case she came by.

Doug Haslett arrived nearly half an hour late, wearing a white-on-white outfit. He frowned. "You said to meet you in the Polo Lounge."

"Not me. I'm a New Yorker. Gotta be poolside."

"How about this southern California weather? Getting a tan in December."

"That's why I'm thinking of moving out here," said De Vito.

"That so?"

"Yeah. I like the weather and scenery." He nodded in the direction of the girl in the bikini.

"Her? She's nothing special. You've been to my club. You've seen the fine pussy hanging out there."

"And they all want to be actresses, right?"

Doug chuckled. "Or they don't know what they want to be. All they know is that they want to stay young and pretty and have fun."

The server came by and took their drink orders. De Vito asked for a Corona and Doug wanted a Jack over ice.

This guy likes his booze, De Vito thought. *That will make it easier for me to exploit him. He'll help me take over this town even if he doesn't know he's doing it. He's gonna make sure every Angeleno around knows who De Vito Silvera is.*

Frances had fun spending the day with Chloe. They went up and down Rodeo Drive, then Melrose Avenue and a few other spots. Frances spent close to ten large on a couple of outfits and felt happy with what she got.

She even gave Chloe a limp little hug as they parted and Frances returned to her hotel, loaded down with boxes and bags and showing off her big, smug smile. Shopping always reminded her of how much fun it was to be Frances Rofstein and that it was just too bad the rest of the world couldn't be her.

De Vito had crack. Frances had plastic. Everyone had his own drug.

She thought for a moment of picking up her iPhone and calling Babs in Manhattan to make sure their business there was running right. But then the hotel called to remind her of her spa appointment in an hour.

Babs would have to wait for that call. Frances got ready for her spa visit. She had her priorities straight.

As De Vito and Doug sat having lunch, De Vito's phone rang.

"Never guess where we are," said Nelson.

"Tell me."

"We're in Vegas!"

"No shit? I thought you were in Manhattan, stayin' put for a while."

"Nope. Here in Sin City with Artie Jay and his chick."

"Didn't know he had one."

"Well, he does now. Barely legal, petite. He's saying she's the one."

De Vito wasn't especially in Artie Jay's barely legal girlfriend. He had big things he needed to figure out. "You still haven't told me why you're out west. Got somethin' big goin' on?"

"Oh, just a li'l ol' thang. My ma called and said, 'You want to take over my club concession out here?'"

De Vito hooted. "You've hit the fuckin' jackpot!!"

"Kind of. Anyway, I'm calling to see if you and Frances want to fly out here for a day or so. You can use my private plane."

"*Private plane?* You never use that thing!"

"Well, lately I've been using it to get to places faster. So, how about it?"

"Vegas might be fun."

Nelson laughed. "*Might* be?"

"The only pisser is that we need to be back in L.A. for Gina's funeral."

"No sweat. We can all fly back together. Sid is out of town on a movie shoot or something, so I've agreed to be Lovey's escort to the funeral."

"So Lovey is going to the funeral?"

"Yeah. She thinks it would be a good idea to remind the world, 'Gina Rofstein and Lovey Skalbania were friends.' Which I guess they were. Sort of."

"I'll run it down for Frances," said De Vito. "But count me in, even if Frances says, 'No fucking way.'"

"So I'll go ahead and make some phone calls. Later."

Click.

Doug looked at De Vito. "Maybe it's none of my business, but I think that was an important phone call."

"That was my best friend, Nelson Skalbania." De Vito watched as Doug straightened up and arched an eyebrow. "He's flying me out to Vegas on his private jet."

"*Nelson Skalbania*, Lovey Skalbania's zillionaire son who owns *Attitude* in Manhattan?"

"Same guy. We're like this." He crossed his fingers. "We want do some deals together."

"Nice work if you can get it."

"Tell me about it." Then, "Say, Doug, maybe

you and I should do a few deals together."

"So," De Vito asked when he finally caught up Frances that day. "How goes it?"

"Had better days." She said nothing about her shopping spree or visit to the spa.

"It's always difficult, losing a parent and then having to go through their stuff and funerals and all."

"No fun."

"Well, tonight I have a wonderful dinner planned for us," De Vito told her. "And tomorrow I'm flyin' you out to Vegas for the day."

Frances raised an eyebrow. "Vegas? Why?"

"Just because." Then, "Nelson's there already. He's sending his plane to get us."

"Vegas? Nelson? Something's going on." Frances liked the sound of that.

"Nelson's mom is sellin' him that nightclub she owns. He and Artie Jay are turnin' it into the newest *Attitude*. He's goin' to your mom's funeral with his mom, and then we're all flyin' back here together. You O.K. with that?"

She nodded, although she really wanted to scream with delight.

"Then it's settled. Nelson is making all the arrangements." De Vito didn't know if he was happy or disappointed that Frances would be joining them.

Just before they left for dinner, with Frances still in the ladies' room and De Vito combing his hair, Saul called. De Vito answered the phone.

"I'm expecting the two of you for dinner," Saul said.

"Uh, we've already made plans. We're going to

Spago."

"Then I'll meet you there."

Click.

De Vito, who had the most colossal respect and admiration for Saul Rofstein, was O.K. with having him as a dinner guest, but he knew that Frances would be outraged as soon as she learned her father would be breaking bread with them.

He decided not to say anything about Saul when Frances came out. He would just look very surprised once they were in the restaurant and Saul joined them.

Frances came out wearing one of her new outfits. De Vito looked over and smiled at her, thinking that his girlfriend may be a brainless spoiled brat but she sure as hell was a beauty.

"Got this today," she said, striking a few poses for him.

"You're too gorgeous. Way too gorgeous."

She beamed. He always knew just the right thing to say.

Chapter 37
Kayce

The first thing I tried to do was contact Hayley about what I had just discovered. I wasn't sure what I would say to her, but job one was just getting in touch with her.

I called her but she did not answer her phone. Then I texted her: *Contact me ASAP. That means now!*

Then I began thinking about Dr. and Mrs. Freddy Coleman, Hayley's parents. I didn't know them especially well, but Hayley as an adult had always spoken of them with the deepest affection, and when she and I were much younger and she had me over to her house, Freddy and Val seemed to get along as well as any other married couple I knew.

Freddy Coleman was a renowned plastic surgeon; perhaps that was how he had met Gina Roff.

Valerie Coleman had worked for Freddy as his assistant; she married her boss. I remember her as a public-relations specialist, pretty enough woman but no breathtaking beauty.

Freddy, however, was a handsome man, tall and lithe, with an earthy charisma.

I hadn't seen either of them in a few years but always made a point of asking about them and Hayley assured me that they were as well as ever. Her father had a very exclusive medical practice; he had done rhinoplasties, facelifts and boob jobs for some of Hollywood's elite. Generous with his time and expertise, he had done more than his share of *pro bono* work with children and Third World folks. His daughter spoke of him with much pride.

Freddy Coleman struck me as being a very unlikely adulterer, but those pictures were what they were—two people who were totally horny for each other.

Wow! I thought. Freddy Coleman. *Shall I call and tell Frosty that I've identified the man with Gina Roff? Or maybe I should call Hayley and check things out with her first.*

I decided to keep it to myself for the time being.

The only thing I decided to act on immediately was my dinner date with José. I was in the mood for a large, filling meal and then bumping uglies with my man.

What the fuck? Am I becoming a wanton woman?

No. Just a human being with an itch to scratch.

I dashed home, fed and hydrated Kurt Cobain, took a shower and got dressed. Then I hurried off to dinner with José. When I entered the restaurant, I saw him sitting at the bar with a Hollywood Clone. I call them that because they all look so much alike that even their mothers probably couldn't tell them apart. They have blonde hair, fake tans and artificial breasts. The minimum height requirement for a Hollywood Clone seems to be five-seven and all have zero-percent body fat.

José spotted me right away and stood up. The Hollywood Clone did not. She had no intention of getting off her heart-shaped butt.

"Hey!" I called out with a big smile.

The Hollywood Clone shot me the briefest glance. José gave me a big hug.

"Glad you're back," he said in a voice loud enough to be heard by the blonde chick.

"Did you now?" He smiled, and I couldn't believe how white his teeth were.

"Damn straight."

Hollywood Clone sneered at me. Then she stood up. "I've got a party of six over there waiting for me," she said, and I guessed she wanted José to insist that she sit with us for a few more minutes.

But he didn't.

"Lovely seeing you again, Heather," he said.

"Be sure to call me," she told him. I thought it odd that she would depart without our being introduced.

She took off and I sat in her seat, which was still warm from her heart-shaped ass.

José sat, and offered me an embarrassed smile, as if he'd been getting a hummer from her and I'd caught him with his woody in her mouth.

I didn't ask him any questions, mainly because playing the role of jealous girlfriend wasn't my kind of move. Besides, I wasn't sure José was even mine in the first place.

"Heather is just an old friend," he said.

"Great tits," I retorted. "Wonder where she got 'em."

He laughed. "I'm glad you've got a sense of humor." Then, "Are you jealous?"

I just screwed some guy in Manhattan, so maybe you're the one who should be jealous. "No, you're free to talk to people."

"Heather and I called it quits a long time ago."

I didn't want to hear about the other chicks he'd banged. Especially when I had every intention of letting him bang *me* that evening.

"I'm glad you two called it quits. Echoheads don't seem your type."

He smiled. "That's what I like most about you."

"What?"

"You're a feisty broad. You don't give a shit. You just say what you think and if the other person doesn't like it, too fuckin' bad."

"And you *like* that about me?"

José nodded. "Many beautiful women are afraid to speak their minds."

I blushed. Was he calling *me* beautiful?

Apparently he was.

Well, this dude was going to get his dick rode in major ways tonight.

There is something way too much fun about sex. Once you've been without it for a while, you sort of forget how yummy it is. But once you start getting it on again, you wonder how you ever survived that period of celibacy.

After a big, delicious dinner, José paid the check in a hurry and we practically ran to our cars. He sped home and I tailgated him. I would have invited him back to my place, but thought that Kurt Cobain had been freaked out enough for one day; he didn't need to stand outside my bedroom door and wonder why I was making all kinds of weird noises with this strange man.

As soon as we reached his place, I jumped into his arms and we tore off each other's clothes.

Presently we were in our birthday suits, my titties squashed against his chest and his boner poking me in the tummy.

Then his doorbell rang.

"Hide in my bedroom," he said.

I did as told. I hid underneath the covers.

Soon José entered the bedroom, still naked and stiff as a flagpole. I thought of John C. Holmes. I thought of T.T. Boy.

"I hope you didn't answer the door like that," I said.

"I covered my junk with my hand. Good thing I have big hands."

I giggled. "People have always told me that size doesn't matter."

"Those people lied." Then, "So, you're ready for an adventure, right? Ready to try something new?"

"Bring it on, baby." I was so aroused that I could barely breathe.

"I love trying new things."

I kept my eyes closed as he yanked the sheet off my body and began moving his long sweet tongue down my sweating, heaving body. He spread my thighs and kissed me lower, lower, lower…

With a deep moan I arched my back and thrashed from side to side. Any man who knows how to eat pussy is a special fellow indeed. José really seemed to know how to pleasure a woman.

He stopped for a moment. I wondered why.

He kept pleasuring me and I gave myself over to the longest, loudest orgasm I'd had in some time.

"She talks too much," José said as he kissed my neck.

I thought, *What the fuck? How could he be kissing*

my neck when his lips are still glued to my cooch?

Then I figured it out: the lips at my cooch belonged to a third party.

Chapter 38
Hayley

"Do not contact me," Strom had told Ricardo. "If contact becomes necessary, I will contact you."

Ricardo didn't give a shit. He had a job to do, and once it was done, he and Senator Greggins had nothing more to say to each other. If Ricardo had trouble in doing this job, then he would feel free to contact Senator Greggins. The only thing in Ricardo's mind was making sure he never went back to prison. He would rather die than be locked up again.

This job of abducting Greggins' squeeze and making her suffer a spontaneous miscarriage was becoming a pain in Ricardo's ass. He thought it would be simple: Grab the chick, drive her around a bumpy road and the baby would be gone, period.

But after much driving over many bumpy roads, they'd stopped when Lupe said she was tired and hungry. Ricardo decided to pull over and open the trunk so they could check on the status of Hayley's crotch.

He decided he would love a cheeseburger and beer as he opened up the trunk. "You take a look at her coochie."

"What the fuck, Ricardo?" Lupe said, sneering.

"You check her out. I ain't no gynie."

"Oh, and I *am?*"

"Well, you got the same snatch as she does."

"But it's your deal. You made a deal with that white big shot."

They drove back to their rickety, aging house and pulled Hayley out of the truck. They'd knocked her out with Chloroform and she was still out cold or just faking it. Ricardo tied the woman's wrist to the bedpost and then traipsed into the living room and collapsed into a reclining easy chair. He grabbed the clocker, turned on the TV to ESPN and stared at the screen for the longest time.

His favor for Greggins, he decided, had become one fucked-up pain in his ass.

Ricardo knew he had to get rid of that broad. He also knew that he had to do it soon, *real* soon. He cursed himself for taking on someone else's problems, as he had done so many times in his life.

Soon Ricardo started to doze in front of the TV set. Lupe hurried outside and went through the car's interior, looking for the white woman's purse. When the abduction first happened, Lupe had tossed the purse into the back seat of the car, and now it occurred to her that the purse might contain things that Lupe would like to have, such as cash.

Much of the time, Ricardo was the king of the idiots. When he explained what the white guy wanted—an abortion for the white woman—Lupe thought Ricardo a fool to go about it this way, but she always went along with whatever he wanted, because he was her boyfriend and it could be hard for a chick to get a boyfriend when she already had a kid. Also, having an older boyfriend, especially one with gang connections, was a good thing whenever she had a beef with someone at school, which happened rarely because she seldom bothered to attend school. Everybody watched his step around her at school because nobody wanted Ricardo to get up in his face.

Lupe concluded that she was entitled to the contents of the purse because she was due some kind of reward for helping Ricardo in this little misadventure.

After finding the purse, she hurried back inside and hid it under the kitchen sink. As soon as she heard snoring coming from the living room, she would go through the purse and look for goodies. Ideally she would find cash, which she always needed because Ricardo always gave her squat. She had to loot his pockets to get whatever she needed.

"Hey!" he shouted from the living room. "Get me a brew an' don't take your time about it!"

She knew what he wanted: a beer and a blow job. It was always best to give him what he wanted as soon as he wanted it.

Hayley woke up and discovered that she had been removed from the trunk and now lay in bed. She could smell stale smoke and old onions; she had no idea that Strom had been in same room just a couple of days earlier.

She tried to sit up but vertigo made the room spin. She needed to urinate and feared she would vomit. Someone was watching a sports event on TV in the next room. Hayley could swear she could hear the choppity-choppity of a helicopter in the distance.

Where had they taken her?

What were they going to do with her?

She was hardly famous, and her family had no money, so what was the point in kidnapping her?

Hayley told herself that she didn't have to worry. Strom would arrive soon to rescue her. Then he would leave his wife and begin his new life with his new wife.

Chapter 39
Nelson

The dinner with Sass and Al, Artie Jay and LaFonda, Lovey, Dee and Nelson went well. They were joined by Raven, and Cassie, the lesbian couple who owned the Serendipity Hotel. Nelson, as usual, felt impressed by his mother's ability to make everyone feel relaxed and wanted, even though Dee spent much of the evening bugging her.

Lovey adored Sass's girlfriend, while Al kept blushing every time she looked at her hostess. Raven and Cassie beamed as they sat together holding hands; LaFonda and Dee were into some serious chick-chat.

LaFonda and Dee, Nelson thought. *There they are, rapping away big-time. Well, why the fuck not? They're about the same age. Artie Jay needs to find someone a little bit older. He and she won't last too long.*

At last he had a few moments alone with Lovey. "What's up with my little sis? Why is Dee bugging you so much?"

"Isn't she awful?" Lovey asked, rolling her eyes. "But what can we do?"

"You can start by backing off and letting her make her own decisions. She's nearly eighteen. She's smart enough to decide what she wants to do."

"She's not as smart as you were when you were

her age. Anyway, she's still only seventeen. I would hate to see her go through the same shit Sass went through at that age."

"Why are you under the impression that such a thing might happen?"

"Oh, *please*. Dee is young and beautiful and she comes from a stinking-rich family. You and I know that every jerk-off out there who's too lazy to work wants to hook up with someone like her so he'll have an easy, fun life. Therefore, I want her in college until she matures and smartens up a little bit."

Nelson shook his head. "N.G.H., Ma."

"What's that mean?"

"Not Gonna Happen."

"Why do you say that?"

"Because she's ready to go out there and do her own thing. Don't mean shit how *you* feel about it."

"That so?"

"Damn straight. No college for her, period. She said so herself."

"Too fuckin' bad for her, because I'm not about to let her run wild at her age."

"Not sure you have any choice in the matter, Ma. She comes of age, she can do her own thing. The law says so."

Lovey let out a huge sigh. "She's too damn much like me when I was her age. I never listened to anyone but Number One."

"Well, then maybe you should be able to see things from her perspective."

"Oh, I try that all the time."

"You were married at sixteen."

"Yes, and my father was responsible for it. Of course, it didn't work out."

Nelson smiled. "Ma, you've turned out to be quite a winner. You're a self-made woman, a millionaire."

She shook her head. "The world is a different place now. I fear for Dee. I wonder how she'll get along."

"Things were difficult and dangerous then, too, Ma."

"Yeah, but I fear for Dee, not myself. I was always street-smart. I could read people and situations. I knew what to say and do."

"Dee's not so dumb herself. She wants to move to New York, you know."

"She wants to be your roomie."

"To hell with that. I love her but I'm not about to become her keeper."

"Then tell her no. You and Sid will get her to do the right thing."

"We're working on it."

"Good luck with that," Nelson said, smirking.

"But enough about her. What's going on with her big brother?"

"I'm keeping busy with *Attitudes* Las Vegas."

"I meant your love life. Anyone special right now?"

"Nope. When I meet her and say, 'She's the one,' you'll be among the first to know."

The next morning, Dee flew back to Los Angeles. Nelson took her to the airport; on the way, he again urged her to go to college, then said nothing more about it. If Dee wanted her freedom, she was going to get it. He only hoped she would use her freedom wisely.

He spent most of the day at the new club with

Artie Jay. Both men fairly slathered with longing at its possibilities as they consulted with an architect and interior designer.

Nelson kept looking at his watch; he wanted to get back to the hotel to say hello to De Vito and Frances as soon as they arrived. He wasn't altogether sure why he had invited them to Las Vegas; he had made an impulsive decision and now partly regretted it. Perhaps he wanted a barrier of people protecting him from Ria, that sexy bitch who chewed him up and spat him out for sport.

Where, he wondered, were all the nice, sweet, intelligent women, the ones Nelson was supposed to choose from and marry? They sure as hell weren't spending their evenings at *Attitude*. He was sick to death of the models, wannabe actresses, party chicks and bored heiresses.

He spent a few moments thinking of Kayce, the lawyer he'd met at Frances' place in Manhattan. She had mentioned attending the same school as he and Frances in Los Angeles. He couldn't remember her— she had probably been a homely kid, which meant he had paid her no attention at all—but now, as an adult, she had given him her business card and seemed like a personable, down-to-earth kind of woman, which was certainly the type he wanted right now. He had her phone number, so why didn't he call her? She handsome a good attitude and wasn't anorexic, which meant she probably might enjoy some gourmet dining and not feel guilty about tucking away a steak dinner plus dessert and a cocktail or two. He concluded that he should have asked De Vito to bring her along.

But he'd missed that opportunity. Anyway, what did he want from Kayce? Probably just someone to sit with and talk to so he wouldn't have to think about Ria.

He decided he could deal with Ria and her bullshit. *Bring it on!*

Like most other superstars known worldwide by one name, Ria expected everything—and that was just for starters. Her demands were outrageous, and nobody, it seemed, would dare to say no. She paraded through life knowing that people feared her, or worshipped her, or both, and that she would get away with every kind of misbehavior.

Ria's thing was to use and abuse people. She loved to see how much of her mistreatment people would accept. To her, life was little more than a great big game, and if her way of playing that game resulted in the deaths of some of the other players—well, life was a bitch.

Men turned her on…but once in a while, she wanted a woman's touch, too.

Nelson Skalbania turned her on. He seemed much different from the other young men she had become attracted to. Nelson had money, style, charisma. Also, even though she had criticized his performance in bed, the man did have much sexual prowess; she could tell he had already made love to many beautiful women despite his young age.

Therefore, when Nelson made arrangements to see Ria perform in Las Vegas, she learned within minutes that he would be in the audience. The news pleased her enormously.

Raven, commitment-owner of the venue hosting Ria, personally gave her the news. "Lovey Skalbania and her party will be there, including Nelson, Lovey's very handsome son."

Ria shrugged. "Would these people interest me?"

"Haven't you ever met Lovey? She's too fascinating! I need to introduce you two."

"I'm very selective about my friends and acquaintances," said Ria. "But if you think they are my kind of people, please invite them to have a private dinner with me after my show."

"Absolutely! You'll love them!"

"I certainly hope so, because I hate to be around people I cannot love."

By the time he had concluded his meeting about *Attitude*, Nelson looked around and observed that he was alone. Artie Jay and LaFonda had skedaddled, as had everyone else, including Lovey, who had escaped to her office to deal with some business matters that couldn't wait till morning.

He decided that what he really wanted was to make some excuse and not attend Ria's concert that evening, but then he realized that all the arrangements had been made and he was committed to going to her show.

Ria would be on stage singing her ass off as the audience sat there and adored her. It wasn't as if he would have to touch her or have any sort of intimate contact with her.

With nothing better to do, he decided to get into the limousine and ordered the driver to take him out to the airport. He thought it might be fun to meet Frances and De Vito himself and the three of them could ride back to the Oasis together. On their way, they might even stop in at one or two of the Strip's swankiest casinos and play some blackjack.

As he strode through the lobby, he saw a copy of *The Whole Truth*, and its headline freaked him out.

Oh fuck!

Chapter 40

Frances

On the Skalbania flight were two flight attendants—Claudia, a pretty German blonde and Laddawan, an attractive woman from Thailand. Both women, polite and efficient, knew how to cope with whatever crap happened five miles in the air. Both ladies had been working for the Skalbania family for several years and knew that they had a problem. They had a two-person girl-huddle in a section of the aircraft and discussed ways to handle it.

De Vito Silvera was a passenger, sitting alongside his lover, Frances Rofstein. They were the problem, sort of. They were en route to Las Vegas, and the flight attendants wondered about what the lovebirds might find once the touched ground.

"Should we tell them now, or let them enjoy their flight and then panic when they get into the airport and walk by the newsstands?" asked Claudia.

Laddawan said, "We should tell them now."

Claudia said, "No, we'll let them find out for themselves later on."

They agreed to disagree. Then they took the matter to the pilot, a fortysomething man deeply in lust with Laddawan.

"You should figure it out for yourselves," he

said, staring at Laddawn's perfect young breasts and hoping these two young woman did not notice his throbbing boner. His favorite crazy fantasy was to leave his wife and three young children so he could run away with Laddawan and spend the rest of his life making love to her.

"O.K.," said Laddawan, "then it's settled—we tell them."

"We tell *him* and he tells *her*," said Claudia. "It's better that way."

"Let me see this rag that contains the scandalous story," said the captain.

"Don't have one on board," said Laddawan. "Claudia thought it was best to leave it back at the airport."

"If it's one of those real sleazy tabloids," said the captain, "then the story you're so concerned about is probably based on lies." When Laddawan snarled at him, he added, "Of course, you could always take this Silvera guy to an isolated part of the aircraft and run it down for him."

"I can do that," said Claudia.

"So can *I*," retorted Laddawan.

"I have experience in dealing with things."

"Oh? And I *don't*?"

Claudia sighed. "So maybe we'll take him aside and tell him together?"

"Sounds like a plan," said the captain. "You two do what you have to do. Tell me how it works out."

"I have a feeling," said Frances Rofstein as she chewed on some nuts, "that I may have been abused sexually as a child." She swallowed and frowned as

Nelson's Learjet hustled them out to Las Vegas.

"First time you've said anythin' to *me* about it," replied De Vito.

"Well, I'm starting to remember shit. I guess coming back to L.A. has something to do with it."

"I didn't force you to make this trip. You said yes to it." De Vito shook his head. His old lady was on the rag. Again.

"You *suggested* that we make this trip. You've had one eye on my father's money from the moment you figured out who I was and who my parents were. Furthermore, as we speak we've left our *business* in the care of your fat cousin Babs and her semiretarded son Chick."

"I'm sure they're doin' O.K. with it," retorted De Vito, although he had to admit to himself that her appraisal of his cousin and her son was very accurate.

"Have you called Babs yet? Have you?"

"Frances—"

"I didn't think so. My father. Your hero."

"Well, what of it?"

"Maybe years ago he had his finger in my cooch."

"Maybe he didn't. Anyway, when did you start thinking such bullshit?"

"So you think it's bullshit, huh? Well, *you're* an idiot for saying that to me, and *I'm* thinking it's time for me to go to a shrink who'll help me dig up my childhood traumas so I can overcome them."

"I take that back—it isn't bullshit," said De Vito, deciding to humor her because the alternative was to let her work herself into a rage and knee him in the gonads. Frances, a tall, strong girl, could probably take him in two minutes if it came down to a fight. He added, "I think you're havin' some feelings about your mom's murder."

Frances nodded; her eyes moistened up. Yes, her mother's death was affecting her—and she was reacting to Adel Nasrallah's son's mistreatment of her. Why hadn't De Vito confronted either of the Nasrallahs about that bad date? What kind of boyfriend/protector did she have if he did nothing to defend her honor?

She shifted in her seat and thought, *I must dump this chump. He's bad news. All he cares about is smoking rock, making money and looking out for Number One. Plus, the way he'd brownnosed my father as if Saul Rofstein were King Shit of the Universe!*

Later, dude

Frances wondered if she should just tell him so now, leaving her free to hook up with Nelson once they arrived in Las Vegas.

She smiled. Hooking up with Nelson. Yeah, she'd love to cuddle that handsome man for a good long while. But that could wait till they got back to New York and life settled down into a nice, quiet routine.

Nelson was a definite possibility as her next boyfriend. She was sure he was attracted to her—everyone found Frances Rofstein attractive—but he and De Vito were friends, and that might complicate matters. She had to be sure that the timing was right. If she gave De Vito the heave-ho, Nelson would almost certainly offer her some sort of comfort.

And from that some sort of comfort…who knew?

"Mr. Silvera?" Claudia tapped De Vito on the shoulder. "Mind if we have a word with you?"

"What?" De Vito feared these two lovelies were not flight attendants but air marshals who wanted to take him aside and bust his crack-smoking ass.

"Please come with us," said Laddawan.

"Why? There a problem?" De Vito asked, swallowing hard and wiping sweat from his forehead.

"We need to speak in private," said Claudia.

All three glanced over at Frances, who had curled up and drifted off to sleep.

De Vito took a deep breath. These flight attendants had singled him out as the person they needed to deal with. Just him, nobody else. Couldn't be good news. Fuck.

As he followed them into the galley, De Vito concluded that there must be mechanical trouble with the aircraft and they wanted him to try to land it or something. But did he really look like the kind of guy who had a mechanical aptitude? Where were the fucking pilots right now, anyway?

De Vito stared for a moment at the flight attendants. Both looked way too cool, calm and collected for there to be any kind of midair mechanical crisis.

"So….?" he simply said. He thought, *This Hawaiian chick, or whatever she is, is way too fuckin' cute.*

"Mr. Silvera," said Claudia, "there is a situation we thought you should know about. It involves you personally."

"There a problem with the plane?"

"Oh, no, nothing like that," said Claudia. "It's a *personal* matter."

"Then tell me what it is."

273

"One of the tabloids has just run a headline story about you and Miz Rofstein. Clearly you know nothing about it yet."

De Vito smirked. "There's no such thing as bad publicity."

Claudia shook her head. "In this case there is. The story asserts that she is a madam and you are a drug addict who gets girls to participate in your prostitution ring."

"Naturally," said Laddawan, "we assume that this is all quite untrue, but we felt you should know about it because many people will probably believe it and want to ask you questions about it." She looked him up and down, thinking he was handsome in his own decadent, strung-out sort of way. Was the story true? Probably, she concluded. He looked the type to engage in very decadent behavior.

De Vito licked his lips. His brow grew shiny with sweat. His armpits were flooded. How could this have happened to him? To *them*?

He knew he didn't have the option of withholding the information from her and whisking her through the airport and into the car, pretending the tabloid story simply did not exist. Frances, when she learned about it, would go ballistic and blame him for everything. Whenever shit went down, she pointed her finger at De Vito and said, "It's all *his* fault!"

"Where is this freakin' tabloid?" he asked, snarling.

"We don't have one. We read it while we were on the ground," said Claudia.

"What the *fuck*!" De Vito kept his voice low but his lips quivered with anger. "You tell me that some sleazy tabloid has raped us in print, then you say you don't even have a copy to show me! Jesus H.!"

"You're out of line, Mr. Silvera," said Claudia.

"Yeah? Well, too fuckin' bad. Now, what you gotta do is shut the fuck up about this shit to Frances. Not one fuckin' word. Think you can do that?"

Claudia nodded many times.

De Vito shook his head again and stormed off.

"How dare he speak to us that way1" Laddawan said in a hoarse, sneering whisper. "That story is probably true. How could such a gentleman as Nelson Skalbania be friends with an asshole like De Vito Silvera?"

"We shouldn't have said anything. We should have just let him find out about it after we landed."

Frances slept even as they landed. De Vito just let her be. Damn, would she shit a fuckin' brick once she found out about that tabloid story!

De Vito decided he wasn't going to stand for that kind of bullshit. First thing he needed to do was get a copy of that tabloid and read every word of that story. Then he'd sic every badass lawyer in Manhattan on that scandal sheet and sue them through the balls. Saul Rofstein would pay for it, of course, because he would be as outraged as De Vito and Frances were by that assassination of her character.

If that rag reported on De Vito and Frances' Manhattan business, who the fuck blabbed about it to that rag?

Sonofabitch! He needed to know exactly what was in that story. This was the worst possible time for such a scandal, considering the murder and the

275

funeral. Saul would trip out once he found out about the tabloid story.

It couldn't be as bad as all that.

Or maybe it was worse.

Chapter 41
Kayce

Did I feel humiliated and degraded by José's threesome? Damn straight I did. How could I have allowed myself to get involved in their little freak scene?

Am I a prude? Hardly. But a *ménage a trois,* without my consent? What kind of bullshit was that?

He sneaked in a third party so she could go down on me! What kind of a despicable sack of shit would do such a thing? And to think I actually *liked* him!

Well, guess who Number Three was? Yes— California Girl, the blonde bimbo from the restaurant. Plenty of fake blonde hair on top, but bald as a baby's butt between the legs. Out here in L.A., men seem to like that bald-coochie look.

Once I got hip to this freak scene, I jumped out of bed, sort of scooped up my clothes on my way through the living room and beat cheeks out of there. José ran after me, yelling, "Come back, sweetie! I thought you were down for threesomes!"

I jumped into my car and sped off. José ran alongside my car, covering his package with one hand while thumping on my car. At home I got into my shower and did my best to scrub away all of

Hollywood Girl's spit from my clit.

I pulled on a tracksuit and fashioned my hair into a ponytail. I put the leash on a restless, yapping Kurt Cobain and we jogged around the block a couple of times.

Kurt got loud as we neared my apartment. I could see why: Mark was there, right outside my front door. He held two extra-large cups of Starbucks rocket fuel plus a bag of chocolate-chip cookies.

"Hey," he said.

"What you want?"

He handed me a cup of rocket fuel. "Just wanted to say sorry for being such a jerk. I know I was out of line when I took Kurt." Then, "Mind if I come in for a few minutes?"

"Bad idea. I'm running late."

"Just five minutes."

I sighed. I really didn't want him to come in, but I have this neurotic unwillingness to hurt people's feelings, especially after they've given me a cup of rocket fuel. Plus, those cookies looked way too yummy.

"All right." I nodded. "Five minutes."

"Your roomie is a tough chick," he said to Kurt as we went inside.

"Cookies?" I asked, pointing at his bag.

"Your favorite."

We sat at my coffee table and sipped rocket fuel as we nibbled on cookies. I felt tired and bored. I had no clue as to why Mark had come for this visit and wanted to make our conversation as brief as possible.

"You bought a house," I said.

"Yeah. Did you like it?" He smiled as he swallowed a mouthful of cookie, acting like we were

278

still a couple.

"Big and fancy. How nice for you." What I really wanted to say was, *Hey, asshole, that was one of the things we were going to do together. Remember?*

He nodded. "Great investment, too. There is always a demand for a quality house."

"You going to marry her?" I asked.

"Katrina? No. It's just a temporary thing."

"I wonder if *she* knows that."

He ignored my remark. He looked me up and down. "You're lookin' good. Nice and svelte. Have you lose weight?"

"Are you saying I was fat?"

"No. You've always been beautiful."

Beautiful. I've never really used that word to describe myself, but I liked to hear it from others.

I munched on a cookie, took a big drink of rocket fuel and wiped my mouth. "Well, Mark, thanks for stopping by. But like I said, I really need to get busy now."

"I hear ya, Well, we'll do this again soon. O.K.?"

I shrugged.

At the office a few hours later, I got mad at myself for not telling Mark to buzz off. Some nerve he had, showing up uninvited. Did he even say what he wanted?

Naomi knocked on my door and came in with a dozen red roses. "Someone out there likes you," she said. "Also, Mr. Forst wants you in his office right away."

I snatched up the note attached to the roses.
Can you ever forgive me?
José

I seriously fucking doubt it.

Then I checked my iPhone to see if Hayley had gotten back to me. No...and when I called her office, they couldn't tell me much. I wondered if she knew about her father and Gina Roff. Hayley and her dad had always been close; maybe he had told her what he was up to.

I sighed and shook my head. I had to tell Frosty the name of the man in the photo with Gina. No more procrastinating; I had to tell my boss what I knew.

Frosty sat at his huge desk, a pinched look on his unhandsome face. He was holding a copy of a tabloid and, as I sat down, flung the item at me. I caught it.

"Read," he said.

I did as told. I swallowed hard.

SLAIN MOVIE BEAUTY'S GIRL RUNNING HOOKER RING WITH CRACKHEAD BOYFRIEND

Next to the headline was a big photograph of Frances wearing a big blonde smile. Damn, she's gorgeous, I thought.

"I'm going to guess that you were as ignorant of this as I was," said Frosty.

"I had no idea." The words came out in little more than a whisper.

"I sent you out there. To New York. You spent time with them."

"A brief time. They didn't tell me about this."

"A good lawyer learns a lot about people in a

brief time."

A good lawyer shouldn't dress like a pimp the way you do.

"I apologize if I let you down. But I do know the name of the man with Gina Roff in that photo."

His eyes widened. "*Do* you?"

"His name," I told him, "is Freddy Coleman."

"How do you know?"

"Because I used to go to school with her and Frances. We all knew each other and each other's family."

"You know many people."

"I've lived out here for quite a while."

"Saul wants to see us. He wants to minimize the damage this tabloid story has caused. Also, I want to find out how well he knows Freddy Coleman."

"I guess you want me to attend your meeting."

"Absolutely."

So I had to go back to Maison Rofstein. I wondered if José would be waiting for me outside the mansion. That would be just my luck.

Chapter 42
Hayley

After a night on that hard bed, Hayley wondered if she had actually slept or not. She had a bad stomach ache and felt concerned for the health of her unborn child.

Who were these people and what did they want of her? And why hadn't Strom utilized all of his resources to find and rescue her?

Then it occurred to her that, whatever this nonsense was, maybe, just maybe, Strom himself was one of the participants.

Chapter 43
Frances and Nelson

Nelson wondered if De Vito had seen a copy of *The Whole Truth*, and, if so, how bad a temper tantrum had he thrown?

Nelson tucked a copy of the tabloid inside of his jacket as he paced up and down in the airport.

As he watched De Vito and Frances exit the Skalbania Learjet, Nelson could tell that Frances knew less than nothing about the scandalous story. Her smile was big and bright, her walk bouncy.

"I am so eager to see Ria's show!" Frances said as she pulled Nelson in for a big hug that was just a bit friendlier than he would have liked. "Ria has the most *amazing* voice. I could listen to her all day and half the night."

De Vito frowned, his eyes darting this way and that. He definitely had some major shit on his mind. "Gotta take a whiz," he said as they walked towards the limousine.

"You could have gone while we were on the plane," said Frances.

"Pisser was empty then."

"I'll show you where to go," said Nelson. To Frances he said, "Get yourself something to drink in the car."

The two men walked away and presently entered the airport terminal.

"I guess you know about it," said Nelson.

"Fuckin' A. That rag is *everywhere*." Then, "I haven't actually seen it, but your two stews ran it down for me. Is it bad?"

Nelson nodded. "Yeah, it's bad. Real bad."

He reached into his jacket and pulled out a copy of the magazine. "Read it and shit a brick."

De Vito stood there and did as told, his lips curling around the words. *The Whole Truth*'s informer had provided names, dates, places, prices, even pictures of girls with masks and even Frances yukking it up with some of her beautiful whores.

"I need to make a call," he said at last.

"To your lawyer?"

"No, to my fat-assed cousin in New York who's supposed to be makin' sure that this kind of shit doesn't happen to us."

"There's nothing you can do about any of it now. It's all a matter of public record. Next week there'll be another scandal and yours will be mostly forgotten about."

"Fuck that bullshit." De Vito, breathing hard and sweating, ran a hand through his hair. "Let those assholes get away with this shit? Not fuckin' likely. I'm gonna get some badass lawyers and sue the balls of some motherfuckers."

"Gonna cost some heavy money. Lawyers don't work for free."

"I've got money." De Vito for a moment flashed on his and Frances' stacks of greenbacks in their Manhattan safe. "I'm gonna teach some tabloid scumbags that they can't fuck over De Vito Silvera and get away with it."

"Well, if you just leave it alone, it'll be like a pile of dog shit—it'll just dry up and blow away."

"You don't get it, Nelson. They've dragged my name through the dog shit, an' I can't just stand here an' do nothing. I gotta fight back—that's just the way De Vito Silvera is."

"Bad deal."

"Too bad for me. What I need from *you* right now is this—take Frances back to the hotel while I try to figure out what I'm gonna do."

"O.K."

"See, she don't even know a thing about this shit storm that's hangin' right over us. This is one of the few times when I wished my name was Frances Rofstein."

"Well, she's going to be hip soon enough. The funeral's in a couple of days. Reporters will be shouting questions about your scandal."

De Vito groaned.

"We need to deal with things as they are, De Vito, not pretend that things are the way we wished they would be."

"You're turnin' into a real philosopher."

"I'll take Frances back to the hotel. You need to remember that this scandal will wither up and blow away—if you let it."

Frances sat in the limousine sipping champagne, thinking that nothing tasted quite as good as ice-cold bubbly. She licked her lips and pondered her options.

She made it clear to Nelson how much she liked him by giving him that extra-long how-ya-doin'? hug at the airport. She grinned. That man just got handsomer every time she saw him. Well, she was pretty freakin' gorgeous herself. Once she cut De Vito loose, she would help herself to Nelson. Without De Vito skulking around, she was the finest catch around. She would say, "Here, De Vito, our hooker service is all yours," because after that bad scene with Adel Nasrallah's son, her gig as madam wasn't fun anymore. She'd walk off into the sunset, so to speak, with Nelson.

Her new man would be able to keep her very comfy, of course, so she wouldn't have send chippies all over town. Nelson was, if he wasn't already, an honest-to-God *billionaire*.

Yeah, just as soon as they got back to Manhattan, she would say, "We're over, dude. Out you go." They would split the money in the safe and go their separate ways.

On Thursday they would attend the funeral. On Friday they would fly back to New York. On Saturday she would give her crackhead the bad news.

We're a done deal, De Vito. Better find yourself a new madam if you want to keep on pimping.

"What up?" Nelson said, easing himself into the limousine and greeting Frances in the black slang that seemed so popular everywhere.

"It's all good," said Frances, supplying the appropriate reply. She looked at him, told herself for the hundredth time that Nelson was the handsomest man around. She wondered what they would name their children. "Where's De Vito?"

"In the crapper. Got an upset stomach. He'll

288

meet us back at the hotel."

Frances beamed. Time to get busy getting acquainted with her new man. She looked straight ahead, confirming that the partition prevented the driver from hearing her, and said, "De Vito crack habit just keep getting worse. I'm not sure how much longer I can put up with him."

Nelson shrugged. "Seems to have his shit together most of the time." Right now was the worst time for her to start fretting about De Vito; presently she would have much bigger problems.

"Like hell he has 'his shit together.' *You* don't have to live with him. *You* don't have to catch him sucking on that glass dick, then listen to lie about how often he gets high."

"Hard luck."

"He's the biggest pain in my ass. Know something, Nelson. I'm going to dump his worthless ass."

"No snap decisions, O.K.? You need to talk to him first. Maybe you can work things out."

"He's not intelligent and reasonable like you, Nelson."

Nelson didn't like the sound of that.

"Maybe you underestimate him. Maybe he's more intelligent and reasonable than you think." Nelson wished she would change the subject.

"I'll tell you something." Frances pursed her lips, then open her mouth to say more. "De Vito has never been part of our crowd. You, Artie Jay and I? We've always been tight. In high school, everyone wanted to join our little clique."

Nelson frowned, totally clueless about what she was talking about. He and Artie Jay had rarely spent time with Frances—except for when they were seniors and got trashed that night and fucked their brains out. After that, the two boys had made a point of avoiding her and the bevy of rich girls who flocked about her.

He reached over, grabbed a bottle of ice-cold Evian water and took the longest drink of his life.

"Don't want any champagne?" Frances asked.

"Never during the day. Gives me a headache."

"More for me, then. I'm looking forward to the Ria show tonight. You'll have to sit next to me so you can catch me when I faint."

Nelson rolled his eyes. Why was Frances acting so weird? Suddenly he liked the notion of spending the evening watch Ria perform. The singer was currently the biggest star in the world and probably would know if Nelson Skalbania was in the audience. If so, she might invite him backstage to say hello, and then invite him to fuck her all night in her suite. If so, he might even let her seduction happen.

Chapter 44
Kayce

Didn't Ernest Hemingway once say, "The rich are different from the rest of us"? If so, he was absolutely right. Well, Saul Rofstein was about as rich as they get, and he stood before me, madder than anyone I had ever seen. Face bright red, eyes blazing with rage, voice loud enough to be heard from three miles away.

He paced around, changing direction every few seconds, as if the cretin who'd published the tabloid were in the room, too, dancing about. His publicist, Bim, was here, wearing a suit and sitting in an armchair, looking as wimpy as his name.

Saul, as always, ignored me. Then he swung around and faced Frosty, as if my boss were the one to blame.

"This is disgusting and despicable! What are you going to do about it?"

"We're getting an injunction to stop next week's issue," replied my boss, utterly unflappable. That was why they called him Frosty.

"You mean they're going to publish *more* of this nonsense?" Saul shook his head in disbelief. What if the story *wasn't* nonsense? That surely was the part that really freaked him out.

Frosty shrugged. "Whenever these tabloids get

something this scandalous and substantial, they spread it out over as many issues as possible. Apparently their informant had an armload of material to sell them."

I had already read the story. If my name had been De Vito Silvera, Frances Rofstein or Saul Rofstein, yeah, I would be feeling humiliated. I got mad at Frosty for saying that there was more to come. He hadn't told *me* that. Why the fuck not?

"What's *in* next week's story?" I asked Frosty.

Saul turned to me and pointed his finger in my face. "*You* were in New York with them! Why didn't you know about any of this?"

I threw out my arms. "Wasn't my fault."

"Her idiot crackhead boyfriend! He's to blame for this. I should have had him wiped out or thrown in prison by now."

Bim cleared his throat. Frosty and I looked at each other, shocked.

"Saul," said Bim, "you need to be very careful of what you say, even in your own home. If anything tragic were to happen to Mr. De Vito…"

Saul nodded. "Where the hell are they? I called the hotel and they were gone for the day. What gives?"

Frances had texted me that she was flying out to Las Vegas to see Ria's show but would be back in time for the funeral. I laughed at how effortlessly she and her people zoomed off to Sin City to see a performer whose tickets were, as the showbiz trade magazines said, "absolutely, positively impossible to get." Well, if your name was Rofstein or Skalbania, the word *impossible* simply didn't exist.

I ran it all down for Saul.

"They went to Vegas? Why? To see if they could find some more sluts to turn out onto the streets of New York? How do you think all of this makes *me* look? I'm the King of Hollywood! People look up to me! I did not raise my daughter to do what she's doing in Manhattan! I did not raise her to do that!"

I had to fight not to roll my eyes.

"They'll be back first thing tomorrow," I said.

"So what?" He turned to Bim. "Get me a plane. We're going out there."

Bim did as told; we headed out to LAX and boarded a Learjet. No time to go home, take a shower, put on some fresh panties and brush my teeth. I called my neighbor and asked her to walk Kurt Cobain.

Frosty didn't like this spontaneous flight to Vegas any more than I did. He especially disliked being ordered around. People didn't tell Bryan "Frosty" Forst where to go or what to do; *he* told *them*.

Bim had gotten us a private jet owned by the movie studio, but once we boarded it, Saul acted as if he owned the damn thing. He lit up a cigar that looked and smelled like a long, skinny turd. He neither offered any of us a cigar nor asked us if we minded his smoking.

"That picture we have," said Frosty, "is of Gina and Freddy Coleman."

"I knew she was seeing him," Saul said, his lips taut with anger.

"Are you saying," Frosty asked him with much annoyance, "that you knew it was Coleman in those tabloid photos? Why didn't you tell the cops? Or *me*, for that matter. Last time I checked, I was your lawyer."

"Gina wanted it kept nice and quiet. She was going to get a facelift."

I almost chuckled. So Gina went home and laid that line of bullshit on Saul and he bought it.

"You need to tell the detectives exactly how much you know, what you know and how you came to know it." That was Frosty's thing. Cooperate with the authorities and be aboveboard in everything so that nothing can ever come back and bite you in the ass.

"I am under no obligation to do any of that. They get paid, don't they? Let them find out for themselves."

Saul's cigar stank like the oldest, funkiest outhouse. Its smell filled the cabin. I feared I might retch. Then he slurped down two double Scotches over ice.

Frosty and Saul decided to put me in charge of finding out where in Vegas De Vito and Frances were staying.

Lucky me.

Once we landed I called Frances' iPhone but got no answer. Then I tried De Vito's number.

"De Vito Silvera?"

"Who wants to know?"

"Kayce White."

"What you want?"

"Just calling about tomorrow. Frances told me you two will be staying in Vegas tonight. When will you be returning to California?"

"Don't know. We flew in with Nelson and we're flyin' back with him. It's his plane."

I didn't know Nelson had a plane. Lucky son

of a bitch.

"So where's Nelson?"

"At the Oasis."

"Is your whole party staying there?"

"Too many questions."

Click.

I had all the information I needed.

On our way from the airport in the biggest white stretch limousine I had ever ridden inside, I checked my iPhone for voicemails and texts while Bim called the Oasis and told them to prepare a room suitable for Saul Rofstein.

I had heard zero from Hayley and her silence started bothering me. She wasn't the type just to fuck off without a word to anyone.

I sat up as soon as I saw a voicemail from Freddy Coleman. I listened.

"Kayce? This is Freddy Coleman. My wife and I just received an awful call from the D.C. police. They say they have discovered Hayley's car; my name is on the pink slip. I can't reach her, and I know that you two are very friendly. Do you have any idea where she is? If so, please call me as soon as possible."

I put my iPhone back into my pocket and leaned forward. I asked the driver, "How long before we reach our hotel?"

"Maybe a few minutes, maybe an hour," he replied. "Depends on the traffic."

"See if you can do the 'few minutes' thing. Mr. Rofstein has things to do, people to see."

"O.K., ma'am."

I cringed at the *ma'am* as I sat back and tapped

my fingers on my thigh, wanting to call Hayley's father but needing to do so in private.

Since I would be sitting in that big, awful car till it reached the Oasis, I thought about other things. De Vito said that Nelson Skalbania had his own Learjet. Hmm. How did he acquire such an item?

Then I recalled that Nelson was the son of that ballsy/beautiful woman Lovey Skalbania, who was married to Greek shipping zillionaire Dimitri Skalbania, who had died when Nelson was a little kid. Nelson and his cousin or niece or someone would inherit the whole works at some point.

Well, I supposed that the Learjet was part of "the whole works."

"We almost there?" Saul scowled, looking more like an angry pit bull than a zillionaire media mogul.

"Few minutes yet," I said, thinking again that his cigar smelled like feces. "Vegas traffic is a bitch."

"Fuck this shit!" Saul turned to Bim. "Get on the phone and have the cops give me an escort. I want to get where I'm going *now!*"

Chapter 45
Hayley

Senator Strom Greggins knew the main thing about being an elected leader: whenever there's trouble, pretend that everything is copacetic. But he fretted all the time, hoping that Ricardo had done his job and that Hayley, recipient of an abortion, would reappear and say, "I have no idea what happened to me." If he was, she would say that her ordeal had ruined her feelings for him.

Getting a dope-dealing gangster to make the abortion happen? Not a good idea, looking back on it...but at the time, it seemed irresistibly convenient.

So where the hell were Ricardo and Hayley? Had the job been done yet? If not, why not?

Strom sat at his desk, staring at the cell phone number Ricardo had given him. As much as he wanted to call that number and demand an update, he knew it would be foolish to do so. He smirked, acknowledging to himself that, throughout his life, his main concern was to look after his own ass. He was absolutely indifferent to Hayley; couldn't she see that? Why did she care for him when she knew he didn't give a crap for her?

He'd told Ricardo exactly what to do, and to notify him when the job was a done deal. So why hadn't that notification happened?

Just then his secretary entered his office.

"Senator," she said, "a police detective is here. He wants to speak to you. Are you available?"

Lupe got out of the house because she told Ricardo she needed to go out to buy food. Ricardo devoured junk food; incarceration had taught him zero about healthful eating.

Lupe was O.K. with that. She too loved junk food because she cared only about the taste of food, and junk food was full of salt and sugar, so it *always* tasted good.

During one of Ricardo's naps she'd emptied Hayley's purse and stuffed it all into her Louis Vuitton knockoff bag. Hayley had some shit worth taking, most notably an iPhone. A fuckin' new iPhone with every kind of fancy app. Lupe giggled with glee. She had a cell phone of her own, of course, but it was a dimestore piece of shit that crapped out all the time. But now she had this honest-to-God iPhone that did just about everything! Yea for her!

The only hassle was that this new gadget was too good. Too fancy and complicated for a cyber-retard like Lupe.

She stuck in her earbuds, managed to get some music happening on her new iPhone and half-danced her way to the grocery store, completely unmindful of the three teenaged girls who surrounded her, kicked her in the booty and stomach, stole her purse, snatched away her iPhone and continued with the beat-down till she faded to black.

Chapter 46
Nelson and Frances

"So, Nelly," said Lovey Skalbania, "I have some good news for you. Those Ria tickets I bought? They're all yours. Please remember that Raven and Cassie will be there. They also expect you to attend their dinner after the show."

"Those ladies are *your* friends, and you're taking a powder for the whole evening. Please explain that to me."

"Sid's been on the road for most of this year and he's going to be in Los Angeles for something like three hours on his way overseas. I want to spend every minute of that time with him. You got a problem with that?"

"You two sure do have your priorities straight. I guess that's why your marriage has lasted so long. You actually give a shit about each other."

Lucky smiled. "Yes, Nelson, that's how it is. My husband comes first."

"So I'm gonna see Ria, then there's that dinner…"

"Stop sounding so glum. Ria is the biggest star in the world right now. Her voice makes me cry sometimes, when I'm in the mood to cry."

Shit, thought Nelson. *Looks like I'm going to be the host. Sass and Altogether, Artie Jay and LaFonda. Frances and De Vito. Double shit!*

Why couldn't he just fly back to L.A. with Lovey and let the others enjoy the concert and dinner without him?

Because he had promised his mother he would do this favor for her, and they both took favors very seriously.

Also, because running out on his group in Vegas was just the kind of thing De Vito would do, and as always Nelson needed to prove he was De Vito's superior in every possible way.

Triple shit!

Speaking of De Vito…Nelson smiled and shook his head at the big mess his friend had gotten himself into. How, he wondered, was De Vito coping with this crisis? Had he told Frances about it? If so, how was *she* coping with it? When they last spoke, Frances started bitching about De Vito's crack habit and told Nelson she wanted to call it quits with her man. Well, this scandal certainly wouldn't help matters.

Nelson took out his iPhone and called Sassy. He asked, "What up?"

"Oh, Al and I are just about to go into the casino and do some gambling. This is her first time, so I'm going to teach her blackjack."

"Well, don't let her gamble with *your* money. That could get expensive."

Then he called Artie Jay. "How they hangin', big man?"

"Everything be cool. We just be chillin' up in our suite till showtime."

300

"Meet you in the lobby at seven."

"I hear ya. LaFonda's all pumped up about tonight. First she's gonna see Ria, then she's havin' a fancy dinner. She's like, 'This can't be real!'"

Nelson laughed. Artie Jay was the best catch around and LaFonda knew it.

When his mother first opened the Oasis, she had invited Nelson to buy a suite in the luxury-apartment development attached to the hotel. He declined, and now realized he had done the smart thing. Las Vegas was for bachelors or guys getting married who were desperately in love or falling-down drunk. It was also for guys willing to be shaken down in the casino. Nelson was none of the above. Lovey adored Las Vegas but Nelson wasn't Lovey. He did, however, look forward to the prospect of making *Attitude* the most popular new nightspot for miles around. He had already promised himself that he would commute from New York to get the club open and operating, then hire a manager who would follow Nelson's instructions precisely.

Sick of listening to himself think, he decided to head on down to the casino and hang out with Sassy and Al. He also decided to spend less time alone and more time with others.

De Vito finally reached Babs in New York, and by the time he did so he had figured out a few things. *"That shit in the tabloid! It was your dumbass son who fucked us over!"* he shouted, hyperventilating with rage.

"I had zero to do with it. I have had no contact with anyone from that tabloid."

"I'm not sayin' it was you. I'm sayin' it was

fuckin' Chick. I *know* it was!"

"If Chick done it," said Babs, her voice quivering, "he done it without sayin' a word to me. I would never do you like that, De Vito."

"Don't bullshit a bullshiter," De Vito said, still struggling to breathe. "How'd he get those photos if you didn't help him? You're in charge of the business right now. You musta helped him."

"He stole 'em." Babs burst into tears.

"Where is that dickhead?"

"Don't hurt him, De Vito. He's a good boy at heart. He means well."

"Oh, you're breakin' my fuckin' heart."

"I'm serious. Someone musta confronted him an' said, 'Tell us what you know. It could be worth lots of money to you.' He's naïve. He doesn't know about things."

"Too bad for him. When I catch up with him, I'm gonna waste him. Simple as that."

"Please don't do it." Babs whined.

"Say, Babs, I have a great idea. Why don't you get off your fat ass and find him? Chick owes me for this. He's trashed my business and made a joke of my reputation."

"I apologize for this, De Vito." More tears.

"You should fuckin' apologize."

Click.

As he stood in the men's room, several men were relieving themselves. One of them said, "Bad day, huh?"

"You got no fuckin' idea." He threw open the door, stalked outside and immediately saw piles of *The Whole Truth* at the newsstand. He kicked the tabloids every which way and, cursing to himself,

302

headed out of the airport to find a taxi.

Nelson had gotten De Vito and Frances a suite at the Oasis that was even better than their digs at the Beverly. As she walked through their room, Frances daydreamed of the day De Vito was no longer in her life and she was married to, or at least shacking up with, Nelson Skalbania.

But that would happen sooner or later, preferably sooner. Frances knew it would happen because she was the sort of person who could make such things happen.

Where was De Vito, anyway? He was certainly in no hurry to get to the hotel from the airport, and he knew how much she resented it when people were late and kept her waiting.

She thought of expediting the termination of their relationship by picking a fight with him as soon as he got to their suite. Or maybe she could just cut him loose after the funeral.

But Frances had read a few pop-psychology books. She knew the different between "instant gratification:" and "delaying gratification," and her response was, *I want what I want when I want it, and I want it now.*

That meant she would wait till he entered their suite and tell him to get the fuck out of her life.

Unfortunately, she couldn't do that. She had to wait till it was time to leave town, then fly back to New York with him. Otherwise, he could go back to Manhattan alone and loot their safe. She *knew* he was more than mean and angry enough to do such a thing, and their safe contained a few hundred thousand dollars in cash.

Then she thought, *Fuck that nonsense? Why am I even willing to split the money with him? It's all mine; I did all the work. Fuck you, De Vito!*

She smiled. Yeah, she could easily pretend everything was cool with him, then transfer the greenbacks into a safety deposit box. De Vito would go ballistic, of course, but tough titties for him.

Frances admonished herself to think things through before actually *doing* anything.

Feeling lucky, De Vito sauntered into the vast, opulent Oasis casino and stopped at a roulette table. He placed a two-thousand-dollar bet on black, and black came up. Within a few moments his two large became four. He grinned at his good fortune and for a moment half-convinced himself that maybe his luck was changing. Maybe that tabloid scandal would dry up and blow away like dog shit.

Good luck with that.

He headed over to the cashier's cage and converted his checks into cash. Then he spotted Sassy at the blackjack table, sitting next to a tall, pretty blonde.

He headed on over. "Hey," he said, tapping Sassy on the shoulder. "You're Sassy, right? We met at *Attitude* in Manhattan once or twice. I'm De Vito Silvera. Nelson and I are tight. We'll all be hangin' together tonight."

"De Vito," Sassy said with a big fake smile. "Nelson told me about you. You play the music at the club."

Damn, she was a cutie. A tad older than he

would have liked—wrong side of thirty—but filthy rich like Nelson. He'd heard plenty about Sassy Skalbania and her thing for bad boys who presumably just needed a good woman to straighten them out. If he ever called it quits with Frances, he might just consider hooking up with someone like Sassy, who was good-lookin', probably a real heller in the sack and had more money than De Vito Silvera could amass in ten lifetimes. Yeah, Sassy was definitely worth his time.

"By the way," said Sassy, "this is my lover, Al."

De Vito shook hands with the tall blonde, thinking, *Too bad the heiress is a dyke.* Then he thought that a *ménage a trois* was a kick he hadn't tried in a while, and both women were giving him a very serious boner.

Then Nelson came up from behind and clapped him on the back. "Long time, no see."

"Yeah, I took a nice long piss at the airport."

"Looks like you've met Sassy."

"Gentlemen," Sassy said with a little shrug, "I'm trying to teach Al, so could we do our little pow-wow later?"

"We hear ya," said Nelson. "De Vito, let's leave them be."

The two men walked across Lovey's casino.

"I won a pile of money at roulette. Got this huge wad of cash in my jacket pocket. Hope your mom won't be too upset at how I cleaned her out."

"Don't worry about it. For every winner there are a thousand losers. Have you told Frances about the tabloid story?"

"I'm thinkin' she might go the rest of her life without knowin' about it."

305

"Then you're not thinkin'," said Nelson.

"Right now, I'm thinkin' that De Vito Silvera is very lucky, an' when that luck happens, the whole fuckin' world better watch out."

Chapter 47
Kayce

I couldn't believe it when Saul Rofstein actually got his police escort. Two motorcycle cops appeared. They put on their lights and wailers and traffic parted like the Red Sea. People probably wondered if the president or someone else of major importance was in that car. What would they have thought if they had known that V.I.P. was just an asshole Hollywood mogul who wanted to get to his hotel faster?

The Oasis was *such* a gem! Unlike most of the other, it practically smelled of class and sophistication.

My last time in Sin City was when Mark took me to New York, New York for his college reunion. Not much fun but we had terrific sex. I guess something about that town gave him a boner.

Flunkies of all kinds surrounded our car as we stopped and the doors opened. As soon as Saul climbed out, everyone seemed to be in a big hurry to kiss the big man's ass. I practically guffawed at the spectacle of it all, but Saul, King Shit of Hollywood, clearly had received such treatment myriad times, for he just ignored those brownnosers and headed into the lobby, then to a private elevator and up to his room. Bim had gotten him a glorious four-bedroom suite that was a vision of turquoise and silver.

How long would we be staying? A couple of hours? But when you were Saul Rofstein, only the best would do, and when you thought you were getting less than the best, you sure as hell got an upgrade.

I knew that Freddy Coleman was anxious and needed to hear from me, and I would feel awkward about calling him from Saul's suite, so I told the guys I needed to go to the lobby drugstore for Tampax. They waved me off, but Frosty admonished me to come back soon.

Downstairs, I sought out a quiet corner to call my own. As I took out my iPhone, I looked up, and who did I see? De Vito and Nelson.

I had, as the old song went, nowhere to run. Those two guys had already spotted me and were half-running straight at me.

"What the *fuck*?" De Vito threw out his arms, scowling. "I thought you said you were in L.A.!"

I shook my head. "I didn't say I was in L.A."

"What the *fuck*?" he repeated, moving closer.

"Leave her alone," Nelson said, smiling.

"Somethin's bad. I can tell," said De Vito.

"Here's the deal," I said. "I flew out here with Saul Rofstein. He's mad as hell about this tabloid story and he wants to take Frances back to L.A."

De Vito swallowed hard. His face turned white.

"Saul is here?" he asked.

"Certainly is," I said.

"Shitfuck! He didn't believe that tabloid, did he?"

"Yes, De Vito," I said, "he kinda did. That's why we're here."

"Maybe," Nelson said, "De Vito should go see

Saul and explain that it's all a big mistake."

"I think," I told them, "that maybe De Vito should have no contact whatsoever with Saul, whose attitude right now is, 'I want someone to pay for this, and if it's De Vito, I'm fine with that.'"

De Vito stood there sweating profusely, as if John Gotti had just ordered a hit on him. "I need to speak to Frances before her old man does."

"Kayce," said Nelson, "do us a favor and don't tell Saul you've seen us."

"Done," I said.

"I gotta split." De Vito took off.

"I'm thirsty," Nelson said. "Want to get a drink over at the Serendipity?"

"Let's do that," I replied, thinking that I had promised Frosty I would be right back, but that was before Nelson Skalbania offered me a drink. If Frosty didn't like it, he could go screw.

An hour had passed and I had scarcely thought of Freddy Coleman or Frosty Forst as I sat drinking with Nelson. We yakked away at each other, and he came across as one of the most interesting people I had met in a long time—good-natured, down-to-earth, comfortable in his skin. Over the years I had convinced myself that he was probably someone not worth knowing, just another guy too impressed with his own good looks and a lifetime of having things go exactly his way.

But he was not that way at all. Not at all.

He told me about his success with the nightclub in Manhattan; he'd taken over retail space that other proprietors had failed with a dozen times, and he'd turned it into *Attitude*, New York's chicest hangout. He aimed to do the same with his mother's Oasis space. He had countless ideas for his latest project and endless confidence that it could become Las Vegas' newest jewel. Then he started asking *me* about what *I* wanted and needed in this crazy thing called life.

Yowza! He and I were having an actual conversation. Most men, when on first dates, usually went on and on about themselves. Of course, this was hardly a date; it was just two people having a drink as they talked about De Vito 's predicament. Personally, I didn't give a crap about De Vito, but I admired Nelson's loyalty to his friend.

A date with Nelson would be fun. I was sure of that. Alas, the Nelsons of the world didn't date the Kayces. I wasn't in his league. Very few women were. Maybe that was his problem—he was too rich, too handsome, too good for just about every woman on Earth.

"Do you mind if I check my messages and make a quick call?" I asked him. "I'm still at the office, sort of."

He shrugged. "Do what you gotta do. Step aside if you need privacy."

I shook my head. "It's just that there's someone in D.C. who seems to have gone missing and I need to call her father to see if he's located her."

Nelson nodded. Handsomest man alive. Probably the fuck of the century, too.

"Oh," he said. "I have some news for you. I've got a couple of extra tickets to Ria's show tonight. Want them? Bring a date if you want."

"I'm here alone. I'm not seeing anyone right

now."

"Me neither," he muttered.

We stared at each other for a few minutes, then heard the loudest commotion as Ria, the biggest star in the world at that moment, entered the casino with her five-man entourage.

Nelson tried to look away but then looked back at her. I took a nice peek. Over the past decade I had seen Linda Ronstadt, Stevie Nicks, Bette Midler and Barbra Streisand in person and was shocked to see how puny and unremarkable they were in person, all scarcely over five feet tall and with their share of wrinkles. Ria was different—tall and strapping, a woman who could fill any room simply with her presence.

Nelson checked the time on his iPhone and signaled for the tab. "I'll walk you back to your hotel. Remember, you know nothing about Frances and De Vito or where they may happen to be."

"I hear ya."

The check arrived, Nelson threw down some bills and we took off. As we reached the exit, we heard a *very* familiar voice.

"Nelson."

He turned around. "Ria." Then, "What a nice surprise."

She smirked. She knew when she was being bullshitted. "A surprise? No. You're coming to my show tonight."

"Yes. Looking forward to it, too." Then he grabbed my arm and hustled me out of there.

Frosty was pissed in major ways. Surprise! "Where

311

have you been?" he asked, his lips taut with anger.

"I'll be very honest with you," I lied. "I ran into my auntie and cousins. Hadn't seen them in years. We had a coffee and chatted for a bit."

"Get caught up with them on your own time. we have business to do here."

"I hear you." I nodded, sticking out my chest. The best way to deal with Frosty was to show him you weren't some wimp he could push around. "I promised my people I would have breakfast with them tomorrow, so I'll have to stay here overnight. I can fly out tomorrow and be at the funeral."

I wasn't asking him, I was telling him. Frosty wasn't used to being told; if you wanted to do something, you asked his permission—and he often said no. "Saul can't find Frances. He's tried their suite but got no answer. So it's your job to find her and bring her to him—minus De Vito Silvera. Silvera will get his later."

"If Saul can't find her, how can *I*?"

"You'll find a way."

Chapter 48
Hayley

The young Latina lay there for some time before someone bothered to call 911 and get her some help. The doctors observed that she had significant head injuries and the damage to her right eye was so severe that they had to wait till the ophthalmologist arrived to see if they could save her eye.

The big problem was that she was brought in without identification. To the hospital she was just another Jane Doe.

"You can't be serious." Strom Greggins shook his head as he looked at his wife. "Another charity event? Don't you know how much I hate those things? Don't you?"

"You're missing the point." Joni Greggins rolled her eyes. "The people who go to these things are the same people who keep you in office. They vote for you and they enjoy seeing you at these functions. You seem to forget that."

He craved a blow job at that moment. He yearned for the sight of Hayley's sweet face as, eyes closed, she took his big stiff cock into her mouth and together they eased his phallus all the way down her throat. She sucked and she sucked and she sucked. She never refused and always let him ejaculate into her mouth. She even swallowed his load. What a lovely girl!

"Hello?" Joni waved her hands in the air to get his attention. "You have an hour to get ready for this event. It's not black tie, so a suit will do."

I didn't know I was married to my mother, Strom thought.

Strom grinned, wondering what would happen if he bent her over his desk and fucked her from behind. Joni was a good-looking woman, always had been—she was far too vain ever to let herself get fat and matronly. What would happen if he went to town with her at that moment? She would scream, of course, and that would make him even hornier.

Hayley, Hayley, Haley! I hope that idiot didn't kill you.

A detective had told him that they had discovered Hayley's car abandoned in the parking lot of an abandoned Esso station. Did Senator Greggins have an idea where she might have gone?

He had made a face of grave concern. Then Maureen said that Hayley mentioned a dental appointment.

"I hope it's nothing serious," he said. "I don't know what we would do without her."

"Please contact us if you hear anything," said the detective.

"Absolutely." Strom thought, *Why didn't that imbecile stash the car somewhere?*

"By the way," Joni said, "Eduardo from the community center called. He wants you to call him back. There's a matter he wants to discuss with you."

Strom nodded. He couldn't imagine what

314

Eduardo wanted.

Ricardo was beside himself that Lupe had gone out for food and not come back. He believed she had run off to be with her baby—a kid fathered by another man, one of Ricardo's rivals.

He muttered some nasty words and promised himself that he would punish her as soon as she returned. No bitch disrespected *him* that way. What a motherfuckin' insult!

Now he had to get that pregnant white bitch out of the house by himself. It was a hassle; he was a busy man who had people to see and things to do. He had a prosperous drug-trafficking business that demanded his constant attention.

Sweating and shivering, Hayley began loosening the knots on the electrical cord that bound her wrists together. She could tell she was making progress.

Whoever was in the living room sure liked to have the TV turned up loud. Then it occurred to her that maybe nobody was in the house. Where was that Latina? Where had she gone? Also, where was Strom? Why hadn't he burst through the door and rescued her?

The more she thought about it, the more she convinced herself that Strom probably had personally ordered her abduction. If so, he surely wanted to have her unborn child aborted; perhaps that was his way of making an inconvenient situation go away.

She cursed him and tried for the next while to free herself.

Chapter 49
Nelson and Kayce

Seeing Ria at the Serendipity reminded Nelson of how much better-looking most stars were on billboards or other media where their flaws were removed by artists. One of the reasons for Ria's remarkable popularity was her beauty—big eyes, small straight nose, full lips. But when one saw her in person, close up, her crow's feet and mouth lines were unmistakable.

So there he was, sitting with a normal, young, perfectly attractive woman with ample curves, soft pink lips and big, surgically unenlarged eyes. Ah, Kayce White. An honest, good-hearted, pretty young woman lawyer. If he wasn't careful, he might fall seriously in like with her.

After they parted, he went back to his suite feeling better and more optimistic than he had in a long time. She was single and so was he. Maybe they were meant to be together. A part of him really hoped so. Being single was getting way too boring.

Ria. Biggest music star in the world. Biggest pain in the ass in *his* world. Yuck.

He took a deep breath and smiled. At that

moment he realized that there could, and would, be life without Ria for him.

He decided to take a shower. After stripping naked, he entered the oversized bathroom, turned on the water and stared for a few moments at the overhead TV, which he'd tuned to ESPN.

Nelson wondered how much Lovey would like Kayce. His mother would like her because Kayce was smart and had balls, so to speak. Lovey liked ballsy women. Dee would hate Kayce because Dee hated every female who paid attention to her brother, because the attention Nelson paid to Kayce meant less attention Dee would get.

He closed his eyes and let himself enjoy the water. The TV was on so loud that he failed to hear the shower door as it opened.

"Hey, Nelson," he heard in Ria's unique voice as she grabbed his cock. "Your friend down here happy to see me?"

"Who let you in?" he yelled.

"I let myself in. I'm Ria. I can move mountains. I can open locked doors."

He tried to back away, but she had his cock in a tight grip, so he had nowhere to go.

"Right now, I want to give you a nice big blow job," Ria said. "Since nobody ever refuses me anything, I suggest you just stand there and enjoy what I am about to give you."

He tried to think of something to say or do, but she got on her knees and took his member into her mouth. His cock immediately got as stiff as a flagpole, and he cursed his phallus for its cooperation in this matter.

Whether in the recording studio or elsewhere,

318

Ria did everything to the very best of her ability. She blew him with such expertise and relentlessness that he threw back his head to scream but was drowned out by the noise of the TV.

After he ejaculated into her mouth for the third time, she shouted, "I must leave." She left as abruptly as she'd entered, and Nelson felt grateful he didn't have a girlfriend to apologize to. What would he say? 'I was in the shower, minding my own business, when in came Ria and she blew me three times'?

Feeling exploited and manipulated, he got out of the shower, toweled himself off and dressed.

She raped me, he told himself, *and my cock said O.K.* He snarled at his flaccid long prick.

'I can move mountains. I can open locked doors,' she'd said. Yeah, lady, you sure as fuckin' shit can.

He let out an exasperated sigh and headed downstairs.

So I was out there in Las Vegas, all by myself. I had to kill some time before my date with Nelson. Saul and the others had left town, so they had checked out and their huge suite was no longer mine to use, so I had nowhere to stay, but that wasn't necessarily a problem. I decided to buy myself a new dress and maybe get freshened up at a hair salon. Also, this was downtime for Sin City, so I needed to whip out my American Express card and book myself a room for the night, unless Nelson made me a better offer…but no, I shouldn't think that way. Not yet, anyway.

I went through the Oasis' prodigious shopping arcade and found the most irresistible Versace dress plus the perfect pair of shoes to go along with it.

After buying the dress and shoes, I kept my Amex card out and got a haircut at the beauty salon. I even let their beautician talk me into letting her do my makeup. This was *so* not like me!

I looked in the mirror and got a little freaked out at the glammed-up Kayce. Did I like who I saw? I didn't know, but felt eager to know how Nelson felt. After all, I had done all of this for him.

Artie Jay and LaFonda looked as goofy as little kids when they met up with Nelson in the bar at the Oasis.

"What's up with those big smiles?" Nelson asked as he ordered a screwdriver.

"You'll never guess," said Artie Jay.

"You're right, so tell me."

"We just got married!" LaFonda said, her voice mostly a squeal.

Nelson's jaw dropped. "What?"

Artie Jay nodded. "Just like she said. Would've been nice to have you there, but it was this *spontaneous* thing. Didn't have time to for much of anything except 'I do.'"

Nelson shook his head. "Don't know what to say. Your mom's going to shit a brick when she finds out."

Artie Jay laughed. "No, she's just gonna love my wife and be proud of me for having such good taste in women."

"Hope you're right about that."

"Hey, Nelson, I just got married. Wanna pretend you're happy for us or somethin'?"

LaFonda said, "I'm so excited about seeing Ria

320

tonight! Can we go backstage and say hi after the show?"

"Absolutely," Nelson said. He felt heartbroken at the sudden demise of his closest friendship. He and Artie Jay would never again have the closeness and camaraderie they'd enjoyed as single guys.

"Where did Frances and De Vito go?" Artie Jay asked, looking around. "Got to share the good news. Break out the bubbly and do all that fun shit."

"Something came up. They had to fly back to L.A."

"Too bad," said Artie Jay. "Hope it's nothing serious."

Nelson shrugged. At that moment he considered Artie Jay the biggest fool on two legs. Impulsively marrying in Las Vegas! How lame was that? No prenuptial agreement or traditional wedding. Artie Jay's parents were going to trip out in major ways.

Presently Sassy and Al appeared, both beaming.

Nelson frowned. Everyone seemed to be having fun except him. He knew that Ria was the one who'd fucked up his mood. He would be all smiles now if she hadn't let herself into the shower with him. He should have tossed the bitch out of the shower immediately.

But that didn't happen. His big *schlong* had gotten stiff right away and told his brain not to turf the nasty cunt.

Why was he always letting the little head do all the thinking.

As I made my way through the casino in my new outfit and face, I started getting attention from men that I was unused to and wasn't sure I liked. Also, my beautiful new dress wasn't made for a brassiere, so my zoomers were jiggling as never before.

What was the deal here, anyway? Why had I gone to all this trouble?

The answer was, because I was trying to compete against the myriad other women who presumably were chasing Nelson as much as I was.

I started feeling angry at myself. Frances Rofstein had always made looking her best to be her top priority in life, and I had always striven to be better than the Frances Rofsteins of this world. So why was I standing there, all dolled up, waiting for this cute, rich dude? I was Kayce White, hotshot, badass lawyer from L.A., dammit!

I arrived at our destination, thinking I would just tell him I couldn't stay, so sorry, can you ever forgive me…

But then he stood up, tall and muscular in his open-necked blue shirt and black jeans, all smiles and dimples and white teeth. Just too damned handsome.

"Hey!" he said, pulling me in for a fine little hug. "Is this the new you?"

"Hey!" I said. "The old you is lookin' pretty good."

He threw back his head and laughed. Then he introduced me to his party, and I kept getting lost in his handsome face.

I had a feeling I would remember this evening for a very long time.

Chapter 50
Frances

Frances nearly shook with rage as she and De Vito boarded a commercial flight back to Los Angeles.

She seethed as she looked at him. That son of a bitch was trying to destroy her! She had firmed up her plans for a blissful future with Nelson.

The whole problem, as she saw it, was that her crackhead boyfriend had ruined their business by going out and hiring his fat cousin and her retarded son. What a couple of losers! How many times had she warned De Vito about those two? But did he listen? Of course not. So now those two assholes had gotten hold of sensitive documents and sold those items to that tabloid, and now the whole world thought she, Frances Rofstein, was a madam!

De Vito, full of dread, had confronted her with the issue of *The Whole Truth*. She'd gone ballistic, throwing roundhouse punches that he had effortlessly blocked or dodged. 'Your father wants to take you back to California and keep you locked up for the rest of your life,' he'd told her.

'Let's get out of town. Let's go somewhere,' he'd added.

'But what about the Ria concert?'

'Who gives a shit? Saul is after us. That's more

important than anythin' else. He sort of blames me for the mess we're in.'

With the deepest reluctance, she nodded and packed her suitcase, bitching all the way to the airport. Presently they boarded a commercial jet that didn't even have first-class.

"We're at the back of the plane," she said to the flight attendant. "It's near the restroom. It's smelly. This won't do."

The flight attendant rolled her eyes. "This flight is full. You're lucky to have what you've got."

The flight attendant walked away. Frances whimpered for a few minutes. "This smelly plane. These ugly people. I hate this."

"It's a short flight," De Vito said, wishing she would shut the fuck up. "Not sure if we should go back to New York to stay in L.A. for the funeral."

Just then the woman across the aisle leaned over and said to Frances, "I don't mean to be rude, but are you the TV producer's daughter who turns tricks?"

"No, she's not," said De Vito.

"Yes, she is," the woman said. "I read that magazine this morning." She shook her head. "Must be hard up for money to do that for a living."

"Get me a glass of champagne," Frances told De Vito.

"Gotta wait till we get to the hotel."

De Vito had an idea. Go back to California and attend Gina Roff's funeral. Let the media go crazy as they observed Frances Rofstein, daughter of the slain movie star and omnipotent Hollywood producer, subject of the latest scandal, making a public appearance. They could follow that with appearances on TV. Yummy!

Now the only thing was getting Frances to go along with it.

Chapter 51
Hayley

After getting buzzed on Cisco wine, Ricardo looked outside and concluded that soon it would be dark enough to remove Greggins' chick from the house and dump her in the first place that seemed convenient.

He had been sitting in his recliner drinking all day, getting angry at Lupe for taking off, leaving him with nothing much to eat.

He couldn't believe she would have the balls to fuck him over that way. All females were little whores, including the *gringa* in the next room. That bitch was starting to smell in major ways. Time to get rid of her.

Ricardo sighed with frustration. It really sucked when he was stuck in the house, unable to take care of business or do much of anything else. The TV was full of retarded shit—all those channels and nothin' on. He decided that what he really needed was some porn to make his cock nice and stiff.

He went to his cousin's collection of DVDs and checked them out. He settled on *Sherrie and Her Blonde Pussy*. He wasn't that interested in blonde pussies but he inserted the disc into the player, drank some more Cisco and unzipped his fly. Pleasuring himself was one of Ricardo's favorite pastimes.

"Does she have any identification at all?" asked Detective Harrison.

He and the female physician, Dr. Byrne, stood at Lupe's bedside. Tall and rangy, with a deep voice and graying hair, he reminded her of a Hollywood cop— he had that no-bullshit way about him that she found comforting.

"No identification. No nothing, in fact. She had on her top and skirt and not much else."

"That neighborhood? The crime is out of control. Every kind of riff raff is out there. It's a shame, considering it's our nation's capital and all. I guess it will get worse before it gets better."

Dr. Byrne, who hadn't had a date for the longest time and was quickly getting fed up with masturbation, wondered if this cop was married.

"There are neighborhoods here in D.C. that even I wouldn't wander around in. The gangs and whatnot, you know."

"I'll call you if she wakes up and starts talking," said Dr. Byrne.

The detective nodded. "You do that."

Hayley nearly had the cord loosened to the point where she could remove them and get herself free. The worst was over, sort of.

But once she could move about freely, where would she go, and what would she do? Were her captors in the next room? Was anyone standing guard outside?

She had no money or identification; her clothing

was filthy. Also, she was famished and practically dying of thirst.

But she wanted, more than anything, to get out of there, to confront Strom and demand to know what part he had played in her abduction.

Strom Greggins, she said to herself, *if this was your idea, God help you.*

Chapter 52
Nelson and Kayce

Nelson supposed he liked it that everyone seemed to like Kayce. After all, Kayce was smart and good-looking and looked way too yummy in her Versace dress. Artie Jay was ogling her boobs and Al kept checking them out, too. Sass and LaFonda weren't paying much attention to Kayce because both were just too amped up about getting to see Ria perform. Ria! The biggest star in the world, the woman with the most beautiful voice in the world.

Nelson sighed. He didn't want to sit there and watch Ria sing her songs for two hours, but he didn't know any way out of it.

"Ria is really thrilled that she's going to see you people after the show," said Raven. "Too bad Lovey won't be there."

Nelson nodded. "She sends her regrets."

"Oh, wow!" LaFonda fairly screamed. "I can't believe I'm going to see *Ria* tonight! She's just, like, the best singer lady ever!"

"And she doesn't go on tour every year," said Raven. "You may not get this chance again for a very long time."

"Amen to that," muttered Nelson.

Nelson's friends seemed like decent enough people. I remembered Artie Jay from high school—he was the good-looking black kid with the fancy car, designer clothes and rich parents who probably expected him to be that much better than everyone else. His girlfriend was tiny, young and sweet and seemed quite thrilled to be seeing Ria in concert, as if that was the best thing that had ever happened to her.

I must admit that I am not Ria's biggest fan, although I'm aware that something like half of all worldwide music sales are Ria's CDs and downloads, and I certainly admire success. Musically, I'm kind of stuck in the 1960s and '70s.

I wondered about Nelson's taste in music. What did he like? Or did he just not give a shit about music at all? I knew so little about him. I was so eager to learn more.

As we headed for our seats—front-row center, the kind you expect when you're Lovey Skalbania's son—he said to me, "If you don't like this show we can always bail and catch up with the others later."

"Negative," I replied. "If we did that, Ria would see us."

"No way."

"Way."

"So," he said, "where did you get that dress?"

"I bought it just for tonight."

"You fill it out very well."

I blushed in major ways, and I am *not* a blusher.

I thought for a moment that maybe I should have flown back to L.A. with Frosty and Saul.

This evening could be the start of a life-changing relationship. Was that something I wanted?

Yes, yes, oh, absolutely.

Before Ria appeared, a hidden voice admonished everyone not to take pictures or use our cell phones during the show.

"Shit," Kayce muttered to Nelson. "I have a very important call due soon."

The house lights dimmed and emcee reminded everyone of how famous and accomplished Ria was. Then a huge curtain opened and the star entered to waves of applause. She wore a gown and had her hair up; she had a zillion-piece orchestra and all the players were dressed in black.

Ria sang and waved. The crowd went bananas. Nobody, but nobody, could sing half as well as she— her voice was almost freakishly powerful and soulful.

Her act was to sing some, talk some, then sing some more. Part of the attraction was that the audience never knew just what she would say to them, what outrageous shit might come flying out of her mouth.

Nelson squirmed in his seat. He'd been in the shower, minding his own business, when she'd helped herself to him and his cock. He promised himself he would never let her eat his junk again.

He looked over at Kayce and saw her sending a text message. Obviously she felt as bored with Ria as he did.

"If my voice sounds good tonight," said Ria, "it's because of my sexy lover Nelson Skalbania. He knows just how to bring out the best, and worst, in me."

The audience applauded and cheered. Nelson

blanched.

Artie Jay leaned over and beamed at Nelson. He made a fucking gesture with his hands.

Kayce put down her iPhone and looked up at woman who had just claimed to be Nelson Skalbania's lover.

"Let me explain," continued Ria. "Before I perform, I need to *perform*. I need to do exercises that will make my body stronger. So I got Nelson to help me with that. Thank you, Nelson, for stretching the parts of me that need stretching."

The crowd screamed some more.

The thought of Ria and Nelson in the shower together made me gag.

"Ignore her," he said to me, as if I had the option of doing just that. Some things cannot be unsaid.

"I have a situation in D.C.," I told him. "I need to leave for the airport right now." I stood up and squeezed past everyone else. He stood up and followed me. I gave him an excuse to walk out on the incredible Ria.

No big loss for either of us.

Chapter 53
Frances

De Vito was happiest when at his busiest, and right now he was busier than he had ever been. That shitty tabloid had gone after him, but he had a plan for retaliation that was just too delicious to resist.

"Here's the gig," he said to Frances as their flight eased on down into LAX. "We're not gonna go back to stay at the Beverly, because Saul wants us to do that."

He booked them into the Sunset Babylon under a false name.

"But what about all my stuff? My clothes and shit and everything?" Frances practically wailed.

"I'll send for it as soon as I can."

She plopped down onto a sofa and buried her head in her hands. "De Vito, we are just *way* too fucked."

"I've got it all covered. We just have to stay cool and be very optimistic."

She sighed. "If you say so."

De Vito found something she liked on the TV set, then poured her a glass of Cristal and went into the next room. He took out his iPhone and made his first call.

He knew that his first call was probably the only

one he would need to make.

Fawn Leibowitz could make shit happen. She was the last person in the world you wanted to have as an enemy. She was big and bold and loud, with short, frizzy red hair and loads of flab.

Everyone respected or at least feared Fawn Leibowitz, especially Doug Haslett, who remained friendly with his former manager even though she hadn't done a damn thing for him since the cancellation of his sitcom in the 1990s.

De Vito called Doug and said, "I guess you've heard about my scandal in that tabloid."

"Everyone in town knows about it."

"I need some help. Spin doctor, damage control, whatever you wanna call it."

"You need my former manager, Fawn Leibowitz. She knows everyone worth knowing."

"Then I'll need to see her today. Can you make that happen?"

"Affirmative. But I'll need a fee for making it happen."

"Done."

Precisely one hour later, De Vito and Doug sat in Fawn's office, waiting for her to arrive. Her walls were covered with Hollywood memorabilia and the room reeked of stale cigarette smoke.

De Vito checked the time and glanced over at Doug. They were right on time, so where the fuck was this woman who, according to Doug, would fix De Vito's problem?

"She'll be here any moment," Doug said. "She's different, but she has all the connections and juice to

336

handle your predicament."

Fawn came in a few minutes later, wearing a multicolored muumuu. "So, fellas, what's this problem that's so urgent I had to cancel some appointments because of you?"

"Fawn," said Doug, "this here's De Vito Silvera. You probably saw him in *The Whole Truth*."

Fawn nodded. "The crackhead boyfriend who's pimping in Manhattan."

De Vito grunted and stood up.

"Siddown, kiddo. Learn to take a joke and you and I will get along just fine." Then, "So, De Vito, what do you want from your current notoriety? Fame, money, people's envy? Because I can get it all for you."

"For real?"

"Fuckin' A."

De Vito sat back down.

The movie ended, and Frances yawned. She zapped through the channels, watching everything for a few seconds and going to the next one.

Then she came upon CNN and realized they were doing a story on Gina Roff. Frances called for De Vito, then realized he wasn't in. Damn! He was never in when she needed him.

"Wally you heartless bastard! How they hangin'?" Fawn said into her pink telephone, her voice a blend of sassy cheerfulness and don't-fuck-with-me nastiness.

"Fawn Leibowitz," retorted the editor-in-chief of

The Whole Truth, "you're the only one I know who's got bigger balls than I do."

"And don't you ever fuckin' forget it."

Fawn's conversation was being blared out on speaker-phone. De Vito and Doug sat there listening. De Vito admired Fawn for being able to speak that way to the honcho of that tabloid and get away with it. He was also impressed that she had his home number and that he would take her call on his day off.

"I'm going to guess," Wally was saying, "that I've offended one of your clients, and that's why you're calling me at home while I'm entertaining a young ladyfriend."

"Got another hooker, huh?" Fawn winked at her audience. "I wonder if she's one of De Vito's chippies."

Wally groaned. "Don't tell me that *De Vito Silvera* has put you up to this."

"Yes, sweetie. So you better tell me who gave you the story, or I'll bust a lawsuit up your worthless ass."

Wally groaned. "Fawn, every fuckin' word we printed is the truth."

"Yeah, and I'm still wearing a training bra. Better email me part two of this story."

Click.

Fawn reached into her desk and pulled out faxes. She tossed them across the desk to De Vito and said, "That's part two of the tabloid story."

"Didn't you just tell him to send you part two?" De Vito asked. "Why would you do that if you already had part two?"

"Where is Frances, anyway?" Fawn asked.

"Back at the hotel. We're hidin' out from Saul. He says that when he gets me he'll rip me a new

338

asshole."

Fawn laughed. "Oh, Saulie. He broke my cherry when I was fifteen. He had a nice big cock, but I've seen bigger."

Chapter 54
Hayley

Ricardo got sick of porn, so he cursed out Lupe some more and regretted that she wasn't around to blow him. He thought of beating off just to alleviate his boredom but then decided against it. No food, no coochie. What the fuck was he supposed to do?

Then he thought of the white bitch tied up in the bedroom. She was starting to stink up the joint in major ways, but she still had a perfectly decent snatch. Also, if he shoved his big stiff cock inside her long enough, he could abort her fetus, couldn't he? Get that Senator Greggins off his ass and everyone would be happy.

He could do that white chick right now. Blindfold her, shove his cock into her, knock her out with chloroform, put her in the car and dump her out at some corner far from home and never think of her again.

To hell with Lupe. He no longer needed her assistance. He could do this thing all by himself.

He crept towards the bedroom door and opened it a crack. The room was dark enough for him but he could see the woman moving on the bed.

As he got ready to pull out his big boner and introduced it to her, the telephone rang.

Dammit! What the fuck! He decided he had better answer it in case someone was calling on business. He closed the bedroom door and picked up the receiver.

Eduardo was on the line.

For the longest moment Hayley's heart beat so loudly that she feared whoever was at the door would hear it. She could scarcely move. The cord was nearly off when she saw the door open the tiniest inch. Then the phone rang and the person closed the door before going to answer it.

Now her limbs felt heavy as iron and she couldn't will herself to take off.

Get your shit together! A voice screamed inside her head. *Run! Run! Do it now!*

Drenched with sweat, she undid the cord and made herself put her feet on the floor. She couldn't find her shoes and guessed that they had fallen off at the time of her abduction. Well, she could make do without them for the next while.

She hugged herself as she stood up and lurched towards the window, hoping that soon she would be free.

"No fuckin' way!" shouted Ricardo. "I ain't never listenin' to a word you got to say!"

"No need to get loud," said Eduardo in a calm, even voice. "All I want is for you to come down to the center tomorrow to listen some and speak some."

"What the fuck *for*?"

"The people who know what's going on are saying that your life is in danger."

"Ain't nobody after me. And if they are, my boys'll get them before they get me."

"They'll get you if they want you bad enough."

"Kiss my ass! You don't know shit!"

Click.

Eduardo always broke Ricardo's balls, trying to get him to go to the community center and become a solid citizen. What happened last time he went there? He nearly got capped, that's what. Also, his main rival was the father of his girlfriend's child. What kind of fucked-up shit was that?

Time to kill his rival—the bastard would deserve it. Plus, why did Eduardo want him to go out to the community center? What was there to talk about, how the Redskins were gonna play that season? Shit, for all Ricardo knew, Eduardo wanted to kill him and take over Ricardo's lucrative drug trade. Well, too fuckin' bad.

Hayley pulled open the window and half-threw herself out of it, unable to see anything in the nighttime darkness. Her heart continued to thunder and her limbs burned as her feet touched the grass and she ran...just ran.

Chapter 55
Nelson and Kayce

Nelson and I headed out to the airport. I told him I had an emergency and even ran it down for him. He agreed that it was important, and added that he could fly me out there in his private jet. When I said no, he said yes. So there we were, on our way to the airport.

Freddy Coleman had practically implored me to help him with this matter. He and his wife were already in D.C., so what could I do but give them my full assistance? And when Nelson insisted that I go there on his plane, with him, how could I refuse?

Hayley was missing and nobody seemed to have any idea of her whereabouts, so that meant she had been kidnapped. Or maybe even raped and murdered.

I had scarcely a clue as to what I could do to help, but Hayley had been my best friend for so many years and I felt a deep obligation to provide moral support to her parents.

I telephoned Frosty to give him an update.

"You're flying off to D.C. and neglecting your duties here? What the hell is your problem?"

"No problem here. In all the time I've worked for you, my job has been my first priority. Just ask my last few boyfriends."

As much as I valued my job—working for Frosty Forst was something to brag about—I knew I would jump ship at some point to work for someone who would pay me much more money and not rag on me quite so much.

Then I called my neighbor. "I'm going to be gone for a few days. Please be kind to Kurt Cobain for me."

"I'll treat him like my own," he said.

"Everything going O.K.?" Nelson asked.

"Fine," I said, thinking of what Ria had said about having sex with Nelson. We can never unsay what we have said, and Ria's remark stood between us like Mount Everest as we sat inches apart, and yet miles away, in that limousine.

He was not the man for me, so why was I pretending otherwise?

Nelson, because of his good looks, noble parentage and obscene wealth, had gone through life having everything pretty much his way. He had learned plenty from his parents, and even though he had been a small child when Theo died, Nelson had acquired a great deal of knowledge about his late father, such as how Theo had managed people with endless charm, compassion and control.

Lovey wasn't Theo. She had her own way of dealing with people and resolving conflicts. She seemed to have an instinct for doing business and making things happen.

Both of Nelson's parents had been tough yet honorable and conscientious. They knew what they wanted and how to get it. Winners with a capital W.

Nelson wanted to succeed, too. He knew he had been born into ludicrous privilege, but he had always treated others as he wished to be treated and he had never tried just to get by on his cover-boy looks. He'd always said to himself, 'What am I good at? What do I like doing?' He had found his niche as a nightclub proprietor and, so far, succeeded.

He had always prided himself on being the gentlest of gentlemen, being sure to let his girlfriends down easy whenever it came time to say goodbye. He tried to be a *mensch*, a good man.

But now Ria had made him look ridiculous in front of everyone in attendance at her sold-out Las Vegas show. He was mad as hell. At Ria, certainly, but mostly at himself.

As soon as Ria ran her mouth about their liaison in the shower, Kayce had begun treating him like some rich *schmuck* whose company she had to endure because he was doing her a favor she badly needed.

He wasn't sure what he might say to her. Should he explain things? 'You see, Kayce, I was alone in the shower, minding my own business, when Ria got in with me and *blew* me against my will..."

Kayce was the first woman he had liked in the longest time, and that fuckin' Ria had ruined it for him. Fuck!

Their car pulled up to the airport, and a couple of special-services people hurried over to escort them to their Learjet.

Once they boarded the aircraft, Kayce intentionally sat across the aisle from Nelson. When the flight attendant came by and asked her if she wanted or needed anything, Kayce shook her head with a smile.

Nelson leaned over and half-whispered, "Kayce, there's a bedroom at the back if you want…" Then he grimaced, thinking that he'd just said something like, 'Wanna fuck?' He meant absolutely no disrespect to her.

But he sure had a boner for her. Yessie. A great big boner with her name all over it.

The problem was that Ria had stopped any chance of that happening.

Life is a weird thing. Whenever something big happens, all the rest of it seems trivial. A couple of hours ago, I had been practically creaming in my undies for Nelson, but now I felt totally indifferent to him. Had I really spent my afternoon dolling myself up just for him?

Now all I had on my mind was Hayley. Where had she gone to? Had someone really kidnapped her? If so, why? She was hardly someone I would have characterized as a V.I.P.; her family was comfortable but far from rich, so I was unsure as to what her abductor thought he could get from her people.

I had few if any answers, and that felt weird, because much of my job involved saying to Frosty, "Give me fifteen minutes and I'll get you a hundred answers."

I checked my iPhone to retrieve her Hayley's messages and looked for clues. *We must talk soon! So much to tell you!*

Now, what the hell did *that* mean? Had she gotten back with her old squeeze, or had she met someone new?

Her big news was definitely about a man. No

question about it.

I looked over at Nelson. He sat back, eyes closed, probably worn out by being blown by Ria a few hours ago. That woman freaked me out. If she wanted Nelson, she could have him, so far as I was concerned. Only thing was, the already sort of *had* him but didn't altogether *want* him, and that was the story of her life—she could have everything she wanted and therefore didn't want any of it, at least not for very long.

I looked down and observed that my sexy new dress showed far too much of my better-than-average tits, and my shoes were way too uncomfortable, so I picked up the shopping bag that contained my change of clothes and said to the flight attendant, "Where can I go where it's private?"

"I'll show you," she said.

She escorted me to a fully appointed bedroom. A *bedroom*? On an airplane? With a plasma TV, a king-sized bed and walk-in shower. Yowza!

I wondered if Ria had flown in this aircraft. Or if Nelson had fucked her in this bedroom. She probably had a jet of her own. Filthy rich people owned such things because they could. They couldn't relate to the rest of us and our workaday hassles.

As I changed, I thought of Hayley and where she might be.

Kayce came back out in her khaki slacks, white blouse and loose-fitting jacket. She had scrubbed off most of her makeup and put her brassiere back on. Nelson decided she was the prettiest woman he had seen in a very long time. She had a world-class pair of titties and he would be honored to marry her and have her as his wife for the rest of his life.

Dammit! Why did Ria have to run her mouth on stage like that in front of everyone?

"I need to make a call," Kayce said to no one in particular, heading for an isolated part of the plane.

Nelson nodded, thinking that at least she had accepted a ride on his private jet and therefore he wasn't a total douche. He also realized that, for all he had, he lacked the thing he wanted most—a steady girlfriend, and he was eager to find out if Kayce White might be that person.

Probably not, he concluded. *That bitch Ria did us in.*

Chapter 56
Hayley

As she ran to nowhere in particular, Hayley felt her legs burn and heart pound. The raindrops hurt as they landed on her head and visions tormented her of Strom Greggins, smug and grinning, the bastard behind her abduction. She ran and ran and ran, with no idea of where she was going.

Muttering, snarling and swearing, Ricardo tried to forget about that nasty phone call. He forced himself to concentrate on the blow job happening on the TV screen in front of him.

That fuckin' Eduardo! The two men had known each other all their lives and Ricardo could never figure out why they were friends, since Eduardo had always been such a bully and manipulator. Ricardo, ashamed of his alcoholic mother, went looking for a family and stability and ended up hanging out with Eduardo, who lured him into gang life.

Over time, Eduardo concluded that being a badass had gotten boring, so he became a holier-than-thou community leader. Ricardo now had no use for that asshole.

He sat and stared at the TV screen until finally he

got a better than average boner. He knew his erection had to do with his hatred of Eduardo as much as the skin on the idiot box. Well, a stiff dick was a stiff dick. He decided to try it out on that cute white chick who'd been riding Greggins' stiff dick.

Ricardo got up and headed for the bedroom door.

Chapter 57
Frances

De Vito frowned and scratched his head. "Did you just say they've made an arrest?"

"Yes," said Frances. "It's on TV."

"Who got busted? That weird guy from New Orleans or somewhere?"

"What bad guy?"

"Some drifter who came out here to meet Gina Roff. The cops said he was a person of interest."

Frances smirked. "Maybe they've busted my papa."

"You should take this more seriously."

"You should take your crack habit more seriously." Frances sighed, thinking once again that the time had come to cut this guy loose.

"There's this woman you should meet. Her name is Fawn Leibowitz."

"That so? What's she gonna do for us?"

"Well, we have a problem, and she's gonna fix it for us."

Frances rolled her eyes. "Just like that?"

De Vito nodded. "Damn straight. We're gonna have dinner with her tonight at the Chateau. Ten o'clock."

"Too late. It's been a long day. I want to turn in

early."

"But you need to be there with me so's you'll understand what she's gonna do for us." Then, "She's very eccentric an' loud so don't get too freaked out. She's just the person we need right now."

Frances met Fawn and immediately thought, *I'm tall and slim, dark and beautiful. I'm better than you are.*

Fawn thought, this number is a Beverly Hills spoiled brat. Got everything she wanted but nothing she needed. I've met many others like you, girlfriend.

"Be cool," she wanted to tell Frances. *"You chose to get involved with this crackhead bad boy from the wrong side of Chicago. So get over yourself and let's talk about your future."*

Frances swallowed hard and reluctantly offered Fawn a handshake, disgusted that De Vito would want to do business with this behemoth.

Fawn shook her head and snatched the younger woman into a hug that seemed to go on forever.

"I don't think you two have been properly introduced," De Vito said, smirking. "Fawn Leibowitz, meet Frances Rofstein."

As they sat down to eat, Fawn said, "Men are just too full of shit. 'Want to give me a blow job? I promise not to come in your mouth.'"

Frances howled.

De Vito smirked. He knew that Fawn and Frances would get along just fine.

Back in Manhattan, Babs felt full of panic over what her son Chick had done. By now, everyone who cared knew about De Vito and Frances' illegal enterprise.

Chick had fled but Babs stayed put, believing that, sooner or later, De Vito would forgive her, mainly because it wasn't *her* fault.

"So it's a done deal," said Fawn as she gobbled up her dessert. "We all know what to do, right?"

Frances nodded, feeling much better now that they had professional help from someone who actually seemed to know what to do.

"Whatcha gonna wear to the funeral tomorrow?" Fawn asked.

Frances nodded. "All black. A skirt. Very little makeup. Just a cross for jewelry. Very dark sunglasses."

"Very nice. And you, De Vito?"

He sighed. "Simple black suit, be cool, keep my big mouth shut."

"Don't worry about Saul. With all the TV cameras around, he'll mind his manners. His public image means everything to him."

"After the service, do we go back to the house?" asked Frances.

"Maybe."

"Good enough for me," De Vito said.

"If possible," Fawn said, "keep the glass dick out of your mouth tomorrow. We don't want people to say, 'Look at the crackhead! What an asshole!'"

"Don't speak to me—"

"I'll speak to you any fucking way I like. After this is all done, you can go on as many binges as you want. But for the time being, you work for me."

De Vito sat back and pouted. Frances beamed.

Chapter 58
Hayley

Ricardo grabbed his junk on the way to the bedroom. He smiled. His package was nice and stiff, ready for some good lovin'. He'd show this white chick what fuckin' was all about.

As he entered the dark room he was nearly knocked over by a blast of frigid wind. Goddamn that cunt Lupe! She must've thrown open the window the whole way!

He felt his way to the bed and ran his hands over its surface. Son of a bitch! She'd *escaped*!

Lupe opened an eye and tried to figure out where she was. She tried to speak. All that came out was a gurgle.

A nurse hurried up and said, "Don't try to speak. I'll tell the nurse that you're awake." Half an hour later Dr. Byrne appeared.

"Where's my mama?" Lupe asked with a groan, abandoning her tough-chick persona.

Seeing that the patient was awake and at least partly mentally together, Dr. Byrne called the police and asked Detective Harrison to come over so he could take the victim's statement.

"Can't do it; I'm busy with another case. I'll send someone over to take her statement."

"Too bad."

"Maybe I will stop by tomorrow just for a moment. Will you be there?"

"I'll make a point of it."

The doctor went over to her patient's bedside and looked down at her.

"I wanna talk to my mama," said Lupe. "I want her to come here and take me home."

"So," Senator Greggins said on the telephone to Ricardo, "what's happening?"

"I'm concerned about Eduardo. I need to speak to you in person. Would you come to the community center tomorrow?"

"I'll be there."

Hayley ran and ran and ran, choking on the rain that pounded her head.

Chapter 59

Kayce

Nelson was there, and I wished he would fuck off, but he didn't. People didn't tell Nelson Skalbania to fuck off.

I wanted to say nasty things but that part of me that isn't into hurting people prevented me from doing so.

I felt angry at Nelson because he'd gotten a hummer from the world's biggest star, who then told the whole concert audience about it.

Of course, we'd had drinks together and we seemed really into each other, and I felt *so* honored that someone like him would be so attracted to me. But then I learned of his gobble job and that was a kind of kick in the balls to my considerable ego.

I sat back in my seat and tried to fall asleep. I wanted to be reasonably refreshed when we landed in D.C.

We touched down at Dulles just as the sun came up. I didn't care much about the time; I was just eager to hook up with Hayley's parents and see if I could be of service to them.

"It's too early," Nelson said. "Her parents will still be in bed."

I shook my head. "No chance. I mean, if you had

gone missing, would Lovey be asleep? No, she would be climbing the walls."

He nodded. "Yeah, she certainly would."

I didn't especially like him at that moment, but still had to admit he was the handsomest man around. *Nobody* had the right to be so rich and good-looking.

While we were twenty thousand feet over America, Nelson had made arrangements—something he was born to do. He called to have a limousine take us to the same hotel that the Colemans were staying in. Our suite would have two bedrooms and serve as an adequate base.

Just before we landed, Nelson, looking all hangdog, turned to me and said, "About what Ria said at the concert…She wants what she wants when she wants it, and at that particular time what she wanted was me."

"Poor baby."

"So I was in the shower, minding my own business—"

"None of my business, guy. Please don't say any more."

"I'm *making* it your business, and I need you to know that the time you and I have spent together has been *so* much fun. Ria and me? That's all very trivial. She means nothing to me."

"Apparently that blow job she gave you meant something to her."

"I have something in mind," he said.

"Do tell."

"Why don't we just start over? We can pretend that Ria doesn't exist." He smiled, and I thought once again that he was the sexiest thing on two legs.

I just sort of half-nodded, and he added, "Right

360

now we need to find Hayley. I have resources, and I'll do everything I can to help you in this matter. After we find Hayley, you and I can shake hands and start all over again. Sound like a plan?"

I smirked. "Sounds like."

Chapter 60
Hayley

After throwing a full-blown temper tantrum in the cold, darkened, empty bedroom, Ricardo fretted that the white woman had crawled out through the window and scampered off to the nearest police station so she could snitch him off.

How long had that cunt been gone? Couldn't have been that long. Had Lupe helped her? If so, God's mercy on her when he caught up with her.

Ricardo would *not* go back to prison. No fucking way. If the cops busted him, he would snitch like a motherfucker—he would tell them all he knew about Senator Strom Greggins and his knocked-up squeeze.

He grabbed his gun and hurried out to his pockmarked Geo Metro. Maybe he could catch up with her and return to the house with her. The only way that bitch was gonna leave was when he said so.

Hayley reached a major street but had no idea where in Washington she was. The only place clearly open was a bar, and she worried that bad guys, unseen by her, were checking her out and on their way to victimize her.

She walked as fast as she could to the bar, hoping

they had a pay phone she could use to call the police. The boys in blue would come and get her, maybe even drive her home.

Ricardo's Geo Metro crapped out on him and he nearly ripped the steering wheel in half. Piece of shit American car! Plus, the pouring rain didn't help his foul mood.

He knew that the only way to get his car moving would be to have it towed to a garage and have a mechanic fix it—for several hundred dollars. Well, the alternative was to borrow Lupe's mother's ancient Oldsmobile that mostly just sat in the driveway, unused. So he'd use it. If the old woman didn't like it, too fuckin' bad.

Swearing under his breath, he got out of his car and hustled the dozen blocks to where Lupe's mother lived.

Helping himself to her mama's car would be Lupe's punishment for fucking off and not telling her man where she'd gone. *Bitch!*

Hayley squinted as she looked up at the big, garish neon sign and pushed open the bar's heavy wooden door.

A tall, heavy-shouldered man wearing a black T-shirt hurried up to her. "No! Git out! I ain't havin' you bag ladies comin' in here an' hustlin' my customers for change!"

"You don't understand—"

"The hell I don't! Git! You need some help?" He grabbed her and flung her out into the street. She fell on her ass and wept as fat raindrops splashed down on her head. She had survived that kidnapping ordeal only to end up in the wrong part of D.C. and being thrown out of a bar by some bouncer who took her for riff raff. She realized then that she would have to loiter about the street till sunrise. She saw the recessed doorway of a pawnshop and limped over to it, grateful for the awning that kept away the wind and rain. She curled up and shivered in the unforgiving mean streets of her adopted town.

Chapter 61
Nelson

Nelson felt pleased with himself for having explained his sexual encounter with Ria to Kayce. Boys will be boys, he'd told her. She'd grinned, too. He thought she had such a lovely grin.

He had felt gratified to be able to offer her the use of his Learjet and have her accept his largesse. Although a zillionaire, he usually didn't live like one, mainly because his mother didn't want him to do so. But gassing up that aircraft and insisting that he and Kayce use it to zoom out to D.C. to take care of some of her personal business? Yeah, that was fun.

Nelson had also enjoyed saying to her, albeit not in so many words, 'I'm going with you; you're not going to be alone.' When his friends in Vegas discovered he had skedaddled, they would be most displeased...and when they figured out he had fucked off in his private plane, leaving them to find their own way back home, well, they would be that much more pissed.

Well, tough titties. He knew what he wanted and was going after it, regardless of the consequences. In that sense he was being his mother's son. Lovey

367

always believed that if you were smart enough to figure out what you wanted in life, you should go out and get it.

This was what Nelson knew for sure: Kayce was someone very special—better than, and different from, the other women he'd known. If Nelson had his way—and throughout his life he'd gotten what he wanted—some of her special-ness would rub off on him.

Nelson was determined to help Kayce find Hayley, and since Lovey knew everyone worth knowing, he'd called her on his iPhone and said, 'Help!'

After a few questions, Lovey, who always knew where to go and what to do, said she would make a few telephone calls and get back to him. She knew heavies in D.C. and, while her calls to heavies did not guarantee that the authorities would locate Hayley, they would certainly bust their balls on the case.

Nelson decided not to tell Kayce of his mother's intervention; the fewer who knew about it, the better.

Chapter 62
Kayce

I took a deep breath and knocked on the Colemans' hotel suite door. I had insisted to Nelson that I needed to do this alone; this crisis was not the time to introduce Nelson to the Colemans. Nelson was unhappy about being excluded from this meeting but agreed to stay in his suite while I went to see the Colenans.

Freddy Coleman answered the door and greeted me with a sad smile. He was tall and svelte, with a full head of salt-and-pepper hair; I hoped that Nelson would age so handsomely.

I wondered if he looked so distraught over his daughter's disappearance or Gina Roff's murder. I honestly didn't know which.

He put his arms around me and said, "Thank you so much for being here, Kayce. We've never been sure who our *real* friends are."

Just then his wife, Betty, came into view. A pretty, immaculately groomed woman, she was now disheveled and looked a hundred years old.

I told myself that her physical decline could not have happened within the past few days or weeks.

Something was seriously wrong with her, and her daughter's disappearance only added to her misery.

"Hey," I murmured, approaching her for a hug. She backed off like a timid three-year-old. "Where do *you* think she is?"

I had no idea, and didn't appreciate her sharp tone, as if she thought I should know, and if I did, why hadn't I said anything yet? And if I didn't know, why had I come here, anyway?

"But you two talked all the time. You were like sisters," she said, her face taut with anger.

I shrugged. "We stayed in touch. We were not 'like sisters.'" I swallowed hard at the sight of this angry, snarling woman who in no way resembled the charming lady who let Hayley and me monopolize the Colemans' TV set or who baked us cookies and drove us to the mall. Standing here before me now was one mean woman.

"So," I said to Freddy Coleman, "tell me what I need to know."

"He can tell you lots of things," said his wife with a sneer. "He can tell you all about his movie-star bimbo girlfriend who was murdered." She glowered at her husband, then burst into tears and fell onto the bed.

Freddy just shrugged at me with a fallen face.

"I'm very sorry," I said in a soft voice. "But right now we must think of Hayley first."

Freddy nodded. "I got a call from that detective. He wants us to come over as soon as we can. Maybe he's got something to tell us that we'll enjoy hearing."

Being asked to go to the police station didn't seem like such a good deal to me. Maybe she was dead and they had recovered her body.

Just then I started to understand what was happening. My longtime friend was missing and probably dead. Bummer!

Chapter 63
Monty Hendrix

Things were tough all over, especially for Monty Hendrix. As a young man, he had been told, "You're a handsome man. You should act in movies or on TV." He'd said, "Maybe I'll do that."

He did. Good-looking in a tough-guy way, he worked for years in minor parts, then became a stunt player. Throughout, he managed to eke out a livable wage until a stunt injury reduced him to subsisting on disability checks for a year. He'd done this and that for years afterwards, always getting bored and quitting or falling asleep and being fired.

On one recent day, his cellie from his three-month stay in jail offered him temporary employment as a house painter. His gig went well until he accepted a blow job from the wife of the customer. The man came home early and walked in to discover his wife deep-throating Monty.

Considering himself mostly unemployable, Monty accepted everything that came along.

His wife and two children disliked him and the bank wasn't apeshit about him, either. They were foreclosing on him.

Monty Hendrix didn't know where to go or what to do, when someone came along and made him an offer that changed his life.

But that was before his psychobitch of a wife tried to shoot him in the testes with his handgun. A neighbor overheard the commotion and called the cops, who arrived and quickly enough figured out that Monty's gun was stolen. They also discovered a pile of cocaine on his kitchen table. That was when they cuffed and stuffed him.

Hank didn't really give a shit until the cops told him that his stolen gun was the same weapon used to kill Gina Roff.

Hank had a problem, a *big* problem.

Chapter 64
Hayley

Ricardo ran as fast as he could through the heavy rain until he reached the dilapidated house where Lupe's mama lived.

He smiled at the sight of the pockmarked Oldsmobile that hadn't been used in the longest time. Its doors stayed unlocked so he didn't have to force his way in. The interior reeked of food and sweat and the upholstery was carved up.

Well, he didn't give a shit. A car was a car was a car. It would take him where he needed to go—to find Senator Horseface's knocked-up squeeze.

He hot-wired the vehicle, backed out of the driveway and zoomed off.

Feeling cold, hungry and terrified, Hayley pretended she was at home trying to decide which of the 700 satellite-TV channels she wanted to watch. She wished she could close her eyes and nod off for a few hours, but the street noise kept her awake. Cars honked and people screamed. About a block away some gangsters had decided to start a drag race. Their women cheered them on in shrill drunken voices.

Hayley wondered if any of them would help her.

No. To ask them for assistance would be suicidal. She knew the best thing was to stay put until the sun came up and the world woke up.

Still, she thought it would be nice to have a long nap.

Ricardo cursed himself for stealing the Oldsmobile, which, if anything, was an even bigger piece of shit than his own car.

He decided that Lupe was to blame for all of his current troubles. He'd been a fool to hook up with her. Teenage bitches didn't know anything about life and made all the wrong decisions.

He drove along slowly, looking this way and that. He felt sure that she was close by—she couldn't have gotten very far in such a short time. Also, he was feeling lucky, very lucky, and when that happened things just went his way.

Lupe's mother, Juana, got to the hospital very late, long after visiting hours. But when she arrived and explained to the night nurse about the trouble she'd had finding a sitter for Lupe's baby and, on top of everything else, some *maricon* had stolen her car. The nurse nodded and let her visit her daughter.

Lupe burst into tears at the sight of her mother. She cried over the many pieces of good maternal advice that she'd disregarded because she felt the daughter knew better than her mother.

Juana, a petite woman with a small strong body and leathery hands, hugged her daughter and muttered things in Spanish about Ricardo and how he must be the worst piece of filth that ever was.

Lupe lay there, too exhausted and full of pain to argue. Although much less bilingual than she should have been, she knew enough Spanish to understand most of what her mother said, and she nodded at the derisive things Juana said about Benito. The man was bad, even criminal, and seemed bent on dragging Lupe down with him. She knew the time had come to explain that Ricardo had made a deal with this Senator Strom Greggins to abduct this white woman and give her an abortion. She decided to tell her mama and, from there, to do whatever her mama felt should be done.

"Mama," she said in a breathless, tiny voice, "I have something I need to tell you…"

The more racket the gangsters made, the more they terrified Hayley. She huddled in her corner and shivered, wondering what those bad boys would do to her if they discovered her. She'd heard about how some homeless people were beaten senseless or even set on fire just because the punks knew they would get away with it. Plus, because she was quite obviously female—despite being fairly tall, she had quite noticeable breasts and long hair—they might rape and sodomize her as well.

At least when those Mexican people kidnapped her they gave her a bed to sleep in and even fed her once in a while. Now she didn't even have anywhere to sleep and no access to food.

What had she done to deserve this?

Answer: She had known Senator Greggins.

Intimately.

Ricardo drove as slowly as he could, looking every which way and cursing out the piece-of-shit car he was driving and the bitch who owned it. *Puta got to be aroun' here, she ain't been gone but an hour,* he kept saying to himself.

He shook his head and concluded that he should have handcuffed her to the bed, but Lupe kept saying they didn't need to do that. Well, what the fuck did Lupe know?

He drove some more and came upon some gangsters revving up their engines and laughing out loud. Ricardo then figured out that he had gone too far, literally, into a part of town ruled by the gangster whose dick Lupe had ridden and who had fathered her little bastard.

Ricardo had ventured out into their turf, and he needed to get back home, fast. If he had been in his own car, they would have spotted him already and begun the beat-down.

He needed to get the fuck out of there *now*, before they figured out who he was and that he was there, *alone*.

Hayley heard the squealing of tires. She smelled the wet pavement, and then she closed her eyes against the yelling and gunshots.

This had to be the worst experience of her entire life. She hugged herself and tried to sleep. Or die. It didn't matter which one at this point.

Chapter 65
Nelson

Nelson paced about his hotel suite, feeling a bit slighted. He was unused to being excluded from important things, but Kayce had said, 'Stay here. I'll go see the Colemans alone and handle this,' and he agreed. Still, he felt bummed out. Nelson Skalbania being told to stay out of the kitchen while something big was cooking? What a pisser!

He ordered coffee from room service and slurped it down as he watched the TV news. The lead story was about the arrest of someone in the Gina Roff murder case. They did not name that someone.

Did Kayce know about this arrest? He guessed not.

Nelson grinned. He figured she would want to know about it, since her boss was the lawyer representing the victim's widower.

He picked up the house telephone and asked for the number of the Colemans' room. Now that he had some important information, he had a good reason to invite himself to that important meeting.

Chapter 66
Kayce

When Dr. Coleman answered the door and saw Nelson standing there, I smiled in spite of myself as soon as I heard Nelson's deep, resonant voice. We were about to leave for the police station, and Nelson sort of invited himself along. I felt very glad to have him along, because while I'm normally supremely confident about my capacity to handle every situation I encounter—I wouldn't be much of a lawyer otherwise, would I?—by the time we left for the police station I had pretty much convinced myself that Hayley was already dead and done for, and that belief really freaked me out.

I'm about half an atheist, but I shot a glance upward, just in case He was indeed up there and I had His attention and He was of a mind to save Hayley's ass as a personal favor to me.

I knew that Hayley had the highest opinion of her boss, Senator Strom Greggins, and I wondered if he had something to do with her disappearance. Had those two been playing slap and tickle? Did she blow him? As a lawyer, I had learned never to say, "No way! That person would never do such a thing! That person would be above such behavior!" Frosty once said to me, "People are people, and sometimes they get weak and do stupid things. Those stupid things are sometimes felonies and those people end up in court, so they call you and me and say, 'Help! I'm in big trouble! Make it go away!'"

I wanted to know if the police had spoken to Strom Greggins. If not, they certainly should, although I wasn't sure how much information they would get. Guys like Greggins had gone far in life by dancing around questions they didn't want to answer.

So when Nelson knocked on the door and Freddy opened it, Nelson shook the man's hand and introduced himself. I wasn't sure if Freddy knew that Nelson was a member of the Skalbania family, but Nelson had news about the recent arrest of someone in connection with the Gina Roff murder, so he was a welcome addition to our little party. Nelson had sort of had that effect on people.

"I have a car downstairs," said Nelson. "We can all ride to the police station together."

So we did. I felt glad that his ride was a gray BMW instead of one of those ostentatious limousines he seemed so fond of.

I didn't know the identity of the person the cops had arrested, but my hunch was that the bad guy was the man who had been stalking Gina. Anyway, we were on East Coast time, so I couldn't call Frosty just yet and update him. But I sure felt eager as hell to find out as much as I could about the Gina Roff murder and the whereabouts of Hayley Coleman.

Chapter 67
Monty Hendrix

Monty Hendrix had been questioned many times by the cops over the years for a variety of reasons, but those two Beverly Hills scumbags? They were something else. They had dragged him into an interrogation room and kept him there all night, pelting him with questions as he begged them to let him nap for an hour or at least have a sandwich and a cup of coffee from the vending machine down the hall. He needed sleep and food, and he did not cope well when deprived of either one.

He decided his wife was to blame for this hassle. She, a teenaged stripper from Europe, had married him so she could stay in America; he had married her so he could spend every night fondling her beautiful blonde boobs. His two children were little assholes who refused to move out or pay for room and board.

After they were married, his old lady quit her gig at the strip joint and said, "You no more touch my titties. Understand?"

Shitfuck! Wasn't a husband allowed to feel up his wife? If not, what was the point of being married?

So he'd taken a job as a strong-arm man who collected money for wiseguys. Instead of turning in the loot like he was supposed to, he'd put it into his own safety deposit box.

Feeling good that he now had several thousand dollars stashed away, he invited his flat-chested, teenaged neighbor over for a drink. Then he screwed her, and just as he was about to shoot his load down her throat, his wife got home from her workday at Twin Peaks. She took out the gun, fired, missed his junk by inches and presently the cops arrived. They discovered the cocaine on the table and that his gun was the same weapon used to kill Gina Roff.

He was fucked up the ass in major ways...unless he could cut some sort of deal with the Man.

Chapter 68
Frances

Fawn Leibowitz said, "Frances, wear black to the funeral. Wear conservative makeup. You'll end up looking like your mother, and that's what we want."

She stared at herself in the mirror and sighed. Considered a breathtaking beauty, she wondered how many people knew about her fake nose and boob job. Then she decided she didn't give a crap who knew. Right now, half of her wanted to hurry back to Manhattan, lock herself inside her apartment and pretend that the rest of the world didn't exist. The other half of her wanted to go to her mother's funeral and let all the other mourners ogle her beauty and kiss her booty.

Frances often wished she could have some of De Vito's fuck-'em-all toughness.

She really didn't have the inner strength everyone seemed to think she possessed. The thought of seeing Saul "King Shit of Hollywood" Rofstein at that funeral made her want to vomit.

Saul, when angered, had always terrified his daughter. She remembered running and hiding in this nook or that cranny whenever the big man, face red and contorted, started screaming and flailing his limbs.

Frances decided she needed more than whatever

support De Vito or Fawn could give her. She needed Kayce, her bookish friend from high school who had grown into a big-hearted, caring person who would hurry to the side of a friend in need.

Kayce had promised to sit next to her at the funeral. But that was before the tabloid story and the ensuing scandal. Frances was unsure as to where Kayce's loyalty at that moment lay—after all, she worked for that guy Frosty, who represented Saul.

Frances decided to call Kayce and find out just exactly what that legal eagle could, and would, do for her.

De Vito had some serious *shit* going on. Doug Haslett was ultra-eager to have a business relationship with him. The two men wanted to start up a nightclub that was better than all the others. Nelson and Artie Jay, of course, were invited to get in on it if they wanted to do so. De Vito couldn't help looking at Nelson and Artie Jay and seeing two guys with unlimited capital to invest.

Fawn Leibowitz turned out to be just the person they needed. She knew everyone worth knowing, and in show business, personal contacts were paramount.

"I've got you all set up with a bunch of TV tabloid shows, and you're going to get your own reality show," she'd said. "De Vito, you'll be moving to L.A. permanently soon, so start figuring out what you'll want to do once you've gotten settled in."

De Vito couldn't stop smiling.

Fawn Leibowitz did not cry at funerals. In fact, they

were just too much fun. To her, funerals weren't places to mourn the dead, they were opportunities to be grateful she was still alive and to meet up with other folks who were still alive, too. She could smile and hug while whispering that she had a truly *tasty* project she should check out with the person she was hugging.

She felt most eager to arrive at the funeral and discover who was also there. Gina Roff, a celebrity, had an eclectic social circle and Fawn believed many of those people would be open to pursuing deals that Fawn could put together. She also knew that those at the event would take her seriously because she would arrive, and sit with, her two newest clients.

Hello, Mister Rofstein. I'm sorry for your loss if you are. Why, look at the little drama we have here!

Fawn got all dressed up in an enormous black dress and silver earrings. Before long she was ready to go.

As he got dressed for his wife's funeral, Saul Rofstein chose the clothes he would wear. He selected a simple black mourning suit.

Gina had been murdered. Now it was only *him*, and *he* would get all the attention. They would point at him and whisper things, and all because of his daughter, Frances Rofstein.

Frances. A restless child, a pain-in-the-ass teenager; as an adult, she had brought inexpressible ignominy to her family. Her father would never recover from the humiliation she had caused him.

At first, he'd let his impulses take over, so he flew out to Las Vegas to find his kid and tan her ass.

He'd also toyed with the idea of having some hit man kill her sleazy crackhead boyfriend. But upon his arrival in Sin City, he couldn't find her and assumed she had skedaddled back to New York. Then he cooled off and decided against having her boyfriend whacked.

Right now he wanted to disown her and give her inheritance to the Gates Foundation or something. Let her continue being a madam until she ended up in prison.

His housekeeper buzzed him. "Mister Frosty and Mister Bim are here to see you."

"O.K." He finished dressing and left the room.

Chapter 69
Hayley

Hayley pulled her hair out of her eyes and squinted up at the feeble sunlight, unable to believe she had actually *slept*, albeit not especially well. She hugged herself and shivered; her mouth was parched and she hurt everywhere. Yet she smiled after she yawned, because she had managed to survive the night and now could search for someone who would help her or at least could tell her where to find someone who could provide assistance.

With much care she straightened out and rose to her feet, unable to feel much below her knees. Although the rain had stopped, she still felt horribly cold.

Hayley had done a good job of curling up in the recessed entrance of the building. She felt pretty sure that the street urchins had remained ignorant of her presence. She wondered if she could now leave her hiding place.

She just stood there, unsure of where to go and what to do.

Senator Strom Greggins got up and took off early. He had spent the night tossing and turning about his meeting with Ricardo at the community center. "We got to meet. Got shit to talk about. Not safe over the phone," Ricardo had said. Strom drove out there expecting—what? Blackmail? If so, he would pay up. In his mind, he had pretty much run out of options.

He wondered about Hayley. Where was she? *How* was she? Had her abortion happened? He doubted it; Ricardo was just too big a fuckup.

Strom sighed. If Hayley was dead, could her death be pinned on him?

Shit, he said to himself. Just shit.

After Lupe told her mother all about the plot to abduct Hayley Coleman and give her an abortion, her mother told her to stay silent about the matter. Then the older woman knelt, prayed and crossed herself.

"You will never see that evil man again," the mother said. "I am sending you to stay with your cousin in Panama."

Lupe shook her head. "No. What about my *muchacho*?"

"I raised you. I will raise your *muchacho*. This thing you have done is terrible, but Jesus will forgive you. With Jesus, all things are possible."

Lupe nodded and smiled. Leave it to Mama to think things through and put things right.

Hayley looked this way and that, and as the sky lightened she could see more than she wanted to of the neighborhood that had been her home for the past several hours. Everywhere, she saw boarded-up businesses, vacant lots, half-finished buildings turning

390

to rust and the sounds of barking dogs.

Across the street she spotted the man who'd shaken his penis at her. She wanted to run over and ask him for help, but what could he do for her?

Well, now daylight had come and she was still alive. So was her baby. She started traipsing down the street, in search of a post office or police station where they were under some obligation to help her.

Never again would she ignore a homeless person she encountered on the street. If you didn't have the money to buy something to eat or make a telephone call, you were quite fucked.

Chapter 70
Kayce

We all piled into Nelson's car and headed to the police station. I chose to sit up front with the driver; Nelson sat in the back with the Colemans.

I checked my iPhone and saw that the time in D.C. was eight in the morning, which meant it was five back in Los Angeles. I certainly would not wake Frosty from his beauty sleep but was only to happy to call Chloe, my intern, and wake *her* up.

When she answered the phone, her voice sounded clear and giggly.

"You're up at five," I said. "I like that in a lawyer. You'll get a lot done."

"I've been up all night. I'm just getting in," she said, swallowing a laugh.

Up drinking and dancing, I thought. Bitch. "I need an update on the Roff case. Someone's been arrested. What's the person's name?"

"Huh?"

"Who got busted?"

"Not me."

"No, I mean, who got arrested for murder in the Roff case?"

"You tell me."

Blowing out an exasperated breath, I said, "I want

you to find out who was arrested for that murder, and then you need to call me back and tell me the name of that person."

"O.K."

I hung up and started asking myself questions about Hayley Coleman and what had happened to *her*.

Chapter 71
Nelson

Detective Harrison looked old, weathered, rangy and wise, a man who had seen way too much bad shit.

"Come in, Mr. and Mrs. Coleman," he said, gesturing to his office.

Nelson and Kayce thought they were invited, too.

"Who are you?" the cop asked.

"Friends of the family," said Kayce. "I'm a lawyer."

"Don't need a lawyer," said the cop.

"We're here as family friends," said Nelson.

Kayce tossed him a quick smile.

"Her name is Kayce White and I'm Nelson Skalbania."

The detective straightened up at the sound of Nelson's surname. *Everyone* had heard of the zillionaire Skalbanias. "Are you O.K. with having them here?" he asked Freddy Coleman.

Freddy nodded. "I'm glad they're here with us."

As soon as they had all crowded into the office, Freddy Coleman swallowed with some effort. "Is there anything you can tell us?"

Harrison nodded as he sat behind his desk and leaned forward. "We have made some progress."

"Tell us," said Mrs. Coleman, tugging at her hair.

"We haven't found her, but we've discovered that several calls have been made with her cell phone. We're sure she didn't make those calls, but it is an encouraging lead."

"Where were those calls coming from?" Freddy Coleman asked.

The cop shrugged. "One of the ghetto areas."

Mrs. Coleman groaned.

"Have you spoken to Senator Greggins and Hayley's colleagues?" Kayce asked, thinking that this deep-voiced old cop was a lazy bastard.

"Of course I have," Harrison replied, thinking that this tall blonde cutie who claimed to be a lawyer was sounding a bit bossier than he would like.

"How about her ex?"

He frowned. "Nobody said she had one."

"His name is Mark James. Look him up."

"Thank you, counsel." Harrison snarled a bit at her. "Don't know what I would do without you."

Nelson arched an eyebrow as he shot a glance at Kayce. He feared she would start yelling at the old cop. As a way of defusing the situation, he said, "Detective, where *specifically* did those cell calls come from?"

Harrison shook his head. "Can't tell you. It might compromise the integrity of our investigation."

"So the best thing for us is to go back to the hotel and wait for you to call with additional updates," said Nelson.

"Pretty much."

As soon as they left the station, Nelson called Lovey and asked her to call her own contacts and find out what was going on.

"Do it as soon as you can," he said.

"Mind your manners, Nelly."

The Colemans went back to their hotel room. Nelson suggested that he and Kayce have breakfast.

"I don't feel like eating," she said.

"Eat anyway."

"Why?"

"So you won't starve."

"Hope I won't have to identify her body."

"Next time you see her, you'll say 'Hi!' and she'll say 'Hi!' back. I guarantee it."

"You're such an optimist," she said.

He grinned. "Damn straight."

Chapter 72
Monty Hendrix

The public defender Monty got was named Finn Mulligan, a short, fat, bald man whose recent divorce had cost him his life's savings.

Finn had represented guilty clients for years, and most of the time he did the bare minimum for them. He wanted to rebuild his bank account and skedaddle off to Hawaii and spend the rest of his life sleeping late and screwing native girls.

He loved to sit back several times each day and fantasize about a life in Hawaii that had lots of fun and no worries. He had an easy time convincing himself that such a lifestyle awaited him in the Aloha State.

He hated Monty Hendrix right away. His new client was everything the attorney wasn't: Tall, muscular and handsome.

"Get me the best deal you can," Monty said, tugging at his hair.

Sure thing, pal. I'll get you a sweet deal that will put you in the slam for a decade, being boned by niggers and spicks who used to beat off to Gina Roff's movies.

"Write a confession," said Finn Mulligan. "Include as much detail as possible. That way, you'll get a lighter sentence."

Monty, hardly the sharpest tool in the shed, sat down and wrote that confession.

Chapter 73

Frances

The media love funerals full of good-looking, extraordinarily important people, and that's what they got at Gina Roff's funeral. The day started with a church service, followed by an outdoor burial service. Every famous high-tech CEO an entrepreneur had attended, along with every actor of significance. Plus the man on everyone's mind—Gina's handsome, omnipotent husband. Also there stood and sat Frances, the deceased's beautiful daughter, recently exposed as a Manhattan madam who wasn't entirely averse to gratifying a client or two when necessary.

The press lapped it up. All those stars and other rich folks! Saul was there! So was Frances! Just as promised! (By Fawn Leibowitz, of course.) The reporters, all dressed in black out of respect for the decedent. One of them, José Benitez, kept looking around for Kayce White. He had certainly disappointed her on their last date and felt eager to redeem himself with her.

Kayce might also have access to confidential information that she might tell him. As an entertainment reporter, he needed whatever he could get and as soon as he could get it.

José Benitez was a man who knew what he

wanted.

Fawn Leibowitz reached over and squeezed Frances' hand. "Stay strong, sweetie. This thing will be over soon enough."

Frances made a face; this was a funeral, not a dental appointment. She, Fawn and De Vito were sitting in a conservative black sedan as its driver took them to the cemetery.

Frances crossed and recrossed her legs. Meeting up with Saul again really freaked her out. As a child, she'd had nightmares about him and his big, menacing, handsome face.

Alas, Saul knew all about Frances and De Vito's prostitution business in Manhattan. How had she disgusted her father? Let him count the ways.

But Frances sat back and closed her eyes, reminding herself that Fawn had assured her Saul couldn't very well say or do anything to his daughter on this day and in this setting.

Fawn, sitting there in the black dress that, if anything, made her even more ungainly, reached into her handbag and took out the bottle of champagne she had brought. She handed it to De Vito. "Open it and pour us some," she said, holding up some plastic glasses. "We need this right now." To Frances she said, "You want some, girlfriend?"

Frances smiled and nodded. A few sips of bubbly were just what she needed. A nice buzz would be the best thing to help her get through this ordeal.

Saul Rofstein said to Bim, "Let's do it," and the two

men, along with Bryan "Frosty" Forst, headed out to the funeral. Saul had spent his entire life in show business, so there was little left in life that could scare him or freak him out.

Many people had speculated a great deal about Gina Roff's murder, but ever since the arrest, everyone had mostly shut up about the matter.

The police had said very little, but most people assumed that the stalker from out of state had been busted. Even Frosty didn't know for sure.

Saul remained taut-lipped with rage over the tabloid story concerning his daughter. Frances, always in Saul's estimation a dim girl, had burned with resentment over her parents' brains and charisma and their bond of love that left Frances feeling unwanted and alone.

Their relationship, as far as Saul was concerned, was over. He no longer had any use for his only child. He would leave his staggering fortune to a dozen charities and Frances would get nothing.

The funeral procession, especially for a public figure, was modest and somber. Gina Roff, an only child, had buried her parents years earlier. Saul had invited only a handful of their closest friends to be part of the line of black limousines following the hearse carrying Gina's body. Saul corrected himself—he *had* no friends; the people in the black cars were studio heads and other folks with whom Saul had had one professional association or another. Like Fawn, he found a career-enhancing opportunity even on the saddest of occasions.

Some helicopters chopped brutally at the

overhead sky, the men inside them taking pictures of the activity down below.

Even in death, Gina Roff could captivate the public.

Chapter 74
Monty Hendrix

So Monty Hendrix wrote a confession—a damned good one. His lawyer helped him with it, and he'd spent all day and half the night working on it. He included every detail he could, and he could remember plenty.

Nobody was going to throw his ass in prison for a murder he had been hired to commit. Fuck that nonsense!

You heard it: He was a hit man.

Someone had hired him to commit the murder, and he had no problem at all with naming names.

No problem whatsoever.

Chapter 75
Kayce

Ordinarily I would be falling desperately in love with Nelson. While I am nobody's idea of a romantic, I find him way too irresistible. I hate the fact that a handsome man appeals to me just because of the way he looks, but I do very often judge a book by its cover. Nelson was *GQ* material, yes, but he was also a *most* likable human being.

To paraphrase the consumer advocate David Horowitz, "If he seems too good to be true, he probably is." But then I remembered how he was taking a shower when Ria came in and gave him a hummer. He didn't shoo her away, which told me that he wasn't too good to be true; he was just a horny young man who got laid.

Anyway, I shouldn't be thinking of Nelson; all of my mental energies should go towards Hayley, who may already be dead, her body scored by local wildlife. All the while I'm falling in love with a man I will probably never see again after we part company.

He lives in Manhattan.

I'm in Los Angeles.

No chance for us.

Anyway, I'm sure he has myriad women offering themselves to him because for a dozen good reasons he is, as Robert Palmer sang, simply irresistible.

Not that I worship the almighty buck. I'm above that sort of behavior. It's what's *inside* the person that matters.

"Breakfast," Nelson said, ushering me into the hotel's dining room, "is the main meal of the day."

"Really, Mom?"

"I'll pretend I didn't hear that."

Our hostess led us to a booth. She licked her lips as she checked out Nelson.

Moments later, our waitress came by with menus. With much difficulty she pried her eyes from Nelson's smiling face.

That's how it would be if I was Nelson's woman—all the other chicks giving him the eye.

Why do I always choose the handsome men? Because they're handsome, and I have always had quite a weakness for such people. Life would be much easier without men, but not nearly as much fun.

"Want me to order for you?" Nelson was asking.

"What for?"

"Because you keep frowning at the menu."

"Having some trouble right now."

"Yeah. It's a trying time in your life."

"Hayley and I have been friends forever." I felt my voice grow husky. I swallowed, wishing very much not to cry. "She's always been sort of family to me."

"Then you should look forward to the fun times you two will have."

"Maybe she's already dead," I muttered.

"She's not. I promise you she's alive."

"How do you know?"

"Because I'm Nelson Skalbania."

408

I smiled in spite of myself. Then I checked my iPhone text messages. One was from Bryan Forst, clearly sent by his assistant because my boss wouldn't condescend to contact me by telephone. *You disappoint me, Kayce. Work must always come first.*

Eat my cunt, Frosty. Right now Hayley is way more important to me than you and your bullshit.

"Let's go, Kayce. I think I've got a way for us to find Hayley."

Chapter 76
Hayley

Hayley figured out soon enough that if you looked like a homeless person, people would get out of your way—even if you wanted them to walk up to you and say, "Hello, dear. May I help you?"

She thought of all those times when she, too, had made a point of avoiding slovenly, disheveled people she encountered on the street. Now that she very much resembled one of those down-and-outers, she despaired of getting anyone's assistance. With her filthy, matted hair, grimy clothes and missing shoe, could she really blame these people for scurrying past her?

A couple of drunks pointed at her and laughed. A handful of kids threw rocks at her and took off, giggling. Hayley ducked into another doorway and whimpered.

"Help me," she said as she choked back a sob.

"Good morning," said Senator Strom Greggins as he entered the community center. He lied; the morning was not good at all. He felt disgusted at being here and who he would have to speak to, even though he didn't altogether know what the other man wanted.

Eduardo sat waiting for him at a rickety wooden

table, scribbling something with the stub of a pencil into a discount-store notebook. He looked up and said, "You're a few minutes early."

Strom shrugged. "I have a hundred things to do today, so I thought I would get here early so we could do our business as soon as possible."

Eduardo nodded at a chair. "Have a seat. Make yourself comfortable. Our coffee machine is broken. Nothin' ever works aroun' here."

"I've already had coffee." Strom sat down. "So, what can I do for you?"

"It's my friend Ricardo." Eduardo put down his pencil. "I think he botched up the job. She's dead. You need to square our accounts because the job was done because you requested it." Eduardo's face darkened. "Ricardo is in big trouble."

"So…?"

"So I need you to offer him a job as a domestic helper or something."

"What good would that do?"

"It would give me some time to think things out," said Eduardo. "There's a notorious gangster in my neighborhood who wants to kill Ricardo, who needs a safe place to go while I figure out what to do about that gangster."

Strom frowned. If that gangster killed Ricardo, would that be such an awful thing? "Sorry, Eduardo, this is your problem, not mine."

Eduardo puckered his lips. "You refuse to help me, Senator? I'm not sure you have that option."

The two said nothing for a moment. Strom felt hostility in the air as powerful as an electrical current. He stood up, fighting the urge to run away from this awful man, this dreary community center and

412

forbidding neighborhood.

"Wish I could help, Eduardo, but there's nothing I can do for you."

Eduardo stood as well. "Too bad," he said. "But if *you* had a problem—say, your children were in danger—and you said, 'Eduardo, help me,' I would do all I could for you."

Strom nodded. Was Eduardo threatening to harm the senator's children?

The senator sighed. Why had Joni introduced him to these people and their awful place? Didn't she know how desperate and violent poor people could be?

By and by Hayley crept out of the doorway where she had huddled. People hurried past, on their way to work or whatever business they had, avoiding her as if she had leprosy.

She just needed to make a phone call. That was all she needed.

"Goodbye, Eduardo," Senator Strom Greggins said. "I can't do a damn thing for you."

He walked to the door, Eduardo right behind him.

"Too bad," Eduardo repeated. "I thought you were in the business of helping people to build better lives."

"If you don't like me, don't vote for me."

Strom opened the door and Eduardo peered outside.

"Raining again," said Eduardo. "You have no

umbrella. You go outside and the rain gonna ruin your beautiful gray suit."

Strom looked down at the lapels of his suit. Joni had bought it for him and he'd never especially liked it. If the rain ruined it, he would have an excuse for getting rid of it.

Just then an unmarked police cruiser pulled up and a tall, gray-haired detective emerged from the vehicle.

Strom scratched his cheek, thinking, *Oh, it's that asshole who was asking about Hayley. What does he want now?*

It was just one shitty day after another for Senator Strom Greggins.

Chapter 77
Kayce

I'm the bossiest bitch around, and Nelson was almost as bossy as I was, so that might have been a problem. But I felt sick with worry about Hayley, so whenever Nelson suggested that we follow a certain course of action, I said, "Yeah, O.K."

"I have information," he told me.

"What kind of information?"

"Quality information that her iPhone was last used in this part of town."

Ordinarily I would have bitched about driving through that creepy, seedy part of town, but I figured that driving around, looking for her, was better than sitting in that hotel room and waiting for news.

So we drove through the mean streets of D.C. in search of Hayley. D.C.'s ghetto looked like some YouTube videos I had seen of Detroit and Los Angeles.

"Shouldn't we get out of the car and look?" I asked.

Nelson burst out laughing. "Hell, no! What would *that* accomplish?"

"Well, what are we accomplishing right now? Just driving around, past one empty lot after another? We'll never find her this way."

"You sound really cranky. Want to go back to the hotel?"

I shook my head. "No, let's just keep looking."

Chapter 78
Frances

A number of people gave eulogies at Gina Roff's funeral, the last of whom was Saul Rofstein.

Saul cut quite a figure in his black suit, standing at the podium and pretending he wasn't mad at Frances for showing up with her crackhead boyfriend. The truth was, he couldn't believe that the two of them had the *chutzpah* to attend the Roff funeral.

He minded his manners because so many reporters were in attendance. At Bim's insistence he went over and gave Frances a Hollywood-style air kiss.

Saul spoke with deep eloquence about his late wife. As convincing a liar as any of the actors he'd hired over the years, he had many of the mourners wiping streams of tears from their faces.

But this was Hollywood, and everyone knew that Saul Rofstein would soon be keeping company with this or that young woman. People were already wondering: who would get first crack at him? In every possible way, Saul Rofstein was quite a catch.

Chapter 79
Nelson

"This must be the nastiest part of D.C.," said Nelson, shaking his head as he peered out the window. "Let's go back to the hotel."

"Let's try ten more minutes," said Kayce.

"We've been at it for an hour. Not sure another ten minutes will make much difference."

Kayce shrugged. "Maybe you're right."

"Hotel," said Nelson to their driver.

"Yessir."

Then Kayce shrieked. *"Stop! Stop!"*

"Why?" asked Nelson.

"It's her!"

"Who?"

"Hayley, for fuck's sake!" Kayce screamed, her face was contorted.

"Can't get out of this car in this neighborhood, you won't last two minutes," said the driver to Kayce's supple young blonde breasts.

"It was her, it was her," Kayce said, keeping her voice even despite speaking through clenched teeth. "I've known her all my life. She was back there a block or so away…"

Chapter 80
Hayley

"Why are you here, Senator?" asked Detective Harrison.

Strom ducked back into the entrance of the community center so as to get out of the rain.

I'm here to buy crack, Detective. Why else would I come out here?

"I am concerned about the well-being of our city's youth," Strom said. "Eduardo here fills me in on what's happening, and I do whatever I can to help."

Eduardo gave him the tiniest snarl.

The detective said, "Let's go inside. All three of us."

As the three men walked inside, the cop said, "Eduardo, I'm afraid I have some bad news about your brother…"

Hayley wished she could just lay down and die. Every street looked as desolate and forbidding as the others. Each person she passed made an ugly face and hurried past her.

She hugged herself and shivered. Every muscle ached. She supposed her unborn baby was already dead. Strom would be happy to learn that she, and their baby, were no longer his problem.

With a huge sigh she fell against a boarded-up storefront and closed her eyes. She would die soon, very soon. Surely it would be better than this.

She heard cars whizzing past.

"Hayley?"

A woman's voice called out to her. The voice of an angel, sent by God to collect her and take her home. Hayley was ready to go.

"Hayley! Hayley! It *is* you!"

Chapter 81
Uh-oh

In Hollywood, everything is unreal and surreal. Scandals happen often, and the entertainment-news media immediately try to sort it all out for public consumption.

There is always some kind of freaky shit going on and the showbiz community is seldom the least bit surprised.

But every once in a while something happens that freaks out even the coolest, hippest and most sophisticated people in the entertainment industry.

The Gina Roff funeral was one of those incidents.

Everything started off normally enough: the ride to the boneyard, the mostly sincere eulogies and lowering of the coffin.

Then came the *real* show, seen by all.

A half-dozen police cruisers. A bunch of cops. Two detectives who marched right up to Saul Rofstein.

Bim, Saul's flack, stepped in front of the detectives.

"Step aside," one of them said.

"Saul Rofstein," said the other one, "you are under arrest for your involvement in the arrest of Gina Roff. You have the right to remain silent; whatever you say will be used against you in a court of law——"

"What the hell?" yelled Frosty Forst.

Saul just stood there, saying nothing. As King Shit of Hollywood, he knew that these cops and the system they served could do nothing at all to him

Nothing at all.

Chapter 82
Kayce

Omigod! So much stuff has happened in such a short time that I feel *so* overwhelmed!

We found Hayley wandering the streets of D.C. and I almost didn't recognize her. But it's so wonderful to have her back!

I must thank Nelson for all he did. Must be nice, having a rich family that knows everyone worth knowing.

We went like hell to the emergency room. I held Hayley in my arms all the way there. Nelson got on his iPhone and called the Colemans and Detective Harrison.

A doctor named Byrne hurried up to us, snatched Hayley away and whisked her off to a treatment room. I sat with the Colemans in the waiting room.

Nelson sat right next to me. He answered the Colemans' many questions; he bought me coffee and candy bars. He took care of me very much the way the medical team was taking care of Hayley. That was weird for me, because I had always been so independent, never needing anybody's help in any way. But having Nelson there by my side was *so* comforting.

At some point they released Hayley to us. She

looked pretty zoned out on sedatives and Nelson carried her to his car.

Detective Harrison wanted to speak to her but Dr. Byrne said not yet. Harrison looked kind of pissed—he wasn't used to having people tell him he couldn't do something he wanted to do.

Dr. Byrne told us, "Hayley is suffering from dehydration, exhaustion and a bad cut for which we've given her a shot." Then she smiled and added, "But the really good news is that her baby is fine."

"What baby?" Detective Harrison asked, frowning.

"Yeah," I said. "Nobody told *me* about any baby."

"Well, now you know." Nelson squeezed my hand.

"She didn't mention that she was dating anyone," I muttered, thinking for a moment that she'd been riding her boss's dick, then hating myself for having such a thought. "Got to find out who the father is."

Nelson gave me a big smile.

Oh, my. Those perfect blond teeth. Those deep dimples. Those big, dark, smoldering eyes. Way, way too handsome.

Should I really be creaming in my panties at a time like this?

Probably not.

But I can't help it. But Hayley's safe now, so what's wrong with obsessing over Nelson now?

"I'm sure she would have told you when she felt it was your time to know," he said to me.

I suddenly felt completely exhausted. I just wanted to go back home, crawl into bed and cuddle Kurt Cobain for a while.

Nelson said, "I'm going to fly you home."

I replied, "But *I* live out west and *you're* up north."

"Let's go."

On the way to the airport, Nelson asked, "Where in L.A. do you live?"

"Why? You gonna have the plane land on my street?"

"Nope. Gonna open the door and throw you out when we reach your neighborhood."

We burst out laughing. As we reached the airport, his jet sat waiting. It seemed that whenever he snapped his fingers, he got whatever he wanted.

Nice work if you can get it, I thought with a grin.

I checked my iPhone. The local time was almost noon; three thousand miles away, in Los Angeles, they would be starting Gina Roff's funeral. They would have to do that thing without me.

Ain't that a shame?

No, not really.

The moment Nelson's Learjet took off, I conked out. I was just so damn tired. As I slept, someone, probably Nelson, put a blanket over me and a pillow behind my head.

I woke up a few hours later, and Nelson said, "I have news for you."

"Tell me."

"The cops busted Saul Rofsttein for the murder of Gina Roff."

"Couldn't happen to a nicer guy." I slept some more.

At LAX, Nelson had his car take us to my apartment. At my front door we discovered Richie, the wannabe screenwriter from Manhattan. At his feet sat his suitcase.

428

"My agent sold my screenplay, so here I am!" he called out.

I didn't recall ever giving him my address.

Richie beamed at me as if we were a couple. Nelson gave me an air kiss and skedaddled.

Later, Nelson, I said to myself.

I sighed, invited him in, cracked open a cold beer and handed it to him, congratulated him on his screenplay sale and reminded him that this was *my* home, not his.

He nodded that he understood. He was no dummy.

Over the next several days I learned many things. I found out that Saul Rofstein, in addition to being a zillionaire media mogul, was a man who knew people who did bad things. He also knew people who could help him when he got into trouble from consorting with the bad guys. So, despite being arrested for and charged with the murder of Gina Roff, he was released within hours because Bryan Forst posted a five-million-dollar bond. So Saul was back in his mansion, smiling and cocky. He felt sure that when his case actually went to trial—probably in four years—his jury would acquit him, for in Saul's mind he was an innocent man.

The beautiful and talented Gina Roff, Saul's missus, had ridden many men's dicks and sucked them off, and to Saul, every cheating wife deserved to die. He said to Frosty Forst and the investigating detectives that he had a couple of beers one day with an old friend, Monty Hendrix, that if he, Saul, knew of a hit man, he would pay the guy to cap Gina's ass.

"How could I have known that Monty, who needed money badly, would say, 'Show me the money and I'll do the job'?"

Frosty nodded that he understand. He was in the business of understanding things and people.

I looked at Saul and saw the meanest son of a bitch on two legs.

But Frosty, a legal eagle, knew he would have an easy time getting an acquittal for Saul, if it even came to trial.

Frosty was a badass lawyer.

And Saul *needed* a badass.

Soon thereafter, I quit Frosty's firm.

My dad said, "You should start prosecuting criminals instead of defending them. That way, you will have a much easier time sleeping at night."

Hayley had agreed to spend the Christmas holidays with me. I looked forward to getting all caught up with her and finding out the identity of her unborn baby's father.

Like everyone else, I had little idea of what the future held. But I promised myself that I would put my career first and stop letting handsome men do mind-fucks on me.

What about Nelson? Well, we had known each other practically all of our lives, and throughout most of it, he had been the handsome jock and I had been the brainy chick he had scarcely noticed. We were doomed as a couple; our essential differences won out.

Now I could get back to becoming the best damned lawyer in Los Angeles. I was free to be my own woman and do my own thing.

Epilogue

Frances was shocked but not surprised to learn that her father had killed her mother. She had a hunch about it all along.

Saul Rofstein and Gina Roff.

The perfect Hollywood couple.

Well, maybe not...

She felt convinced that Saul would be acquitted or not even be tried. He had the best criminal lawyer in town, that hotshot they called Frosty, who would file whichever motions he considered necessary to keep his client out of prison.

Frances stayed busy. Fawn said, "Let's exploit everything we can while we can," so they did just that.

The top TV talk shows booked her. Their hosts flirted with her, she flirted back and a star was born. Just as Fawn had predicted.

"You have to write a book about all this shit," Fawn said. "You have to say to the world, 'I am Frances Rofstein, daughter of Saul Rofstein and Gina Roff. I was their only child, and what a weird upbringing *I* had! Read all about it!' Your book will sell zillions!"

So Frances wrote her book in a number of days. Fawn found the right publisher and *A Hollywood*

Daughter's Story went straight to the bestseller lists. Presently Frances Rofstein became very famous, just like her folks.

De Vito shook his head and decided he'd had enough of being Mr. Frances Rofstein. That fat broad, Fawn Leibowitz, had fulfilled her promise to them and helped them exploit their tabloid scandal to the fullest. But now Frances was letting her fame go to her head and copping a shit attitude all the time. Mostly, though, the problem was that De Vito had been pushed into the background, and his ego definitely was not cut out for *that* bullshit.

Fawn was always like, "Frances, here's what I can do for you," and De Vito was like, "Hey, *I'm* here, too." So Fawn said, "Maybe I can line up a reality show for the two of you—how you're getting along after all you've been through." Alas, that show failed to materialize, which surprised De Vito not at all. Hollywood was all about thinking up shows and pitching ideas and most of the time none of that shit ever went anywhere. But that fuckin' Frances got an offer for her own show just because of her retarded book.

So De Vito said, "Fuck this shit!" He didn't give a good goddamn about Frances or the life they'd had. He had a dozen ideas for potentially lucrative things he needed to develop. Anyway, he and Frances had pretty much called it quits without saying as much. He wasn't going to worry about her; she could find herself a new man in fifteen minutes.

Both of them had settled in Los Angeles and the lifestyle agreed with De Vito. He had started hanging out with Doug Haslett. Doug, a guy who was down for whatever paid well, had started up a business with De Vito that Silvera knew very, very well: Turning out struggling actresses who were desperate enough to go out on dates with ugly guys who had big money. De Vito had said to himself, 'My pimping gig worked out great in Manhattan, so why shouldn't work out here in California?' Amazingly, his logic worked out just fine.

Hayley recovered very fast. Determined to put her ordeal behind her and get on with her life, she decided to move back to Los Angeles with her parents.

Strom and Joni Greggins visited her in the hospital. Hayley, too much a lady to tell them to piss off, shook her head in disbelief. Strom brought his wife! God, did that guy ever have a pair on him!

"Hayley, we think it was just *awful* that you went through this," said Joni, putting a box of designer chocolates on Hayley's bedside table. "Strom was just *sick* with worry."

Oh I'm sure, Hayley thought.

She could not have said with absolute certainty that Strom had something to do with her ordeal, but the guy was sure having trouble looking in in her direction.

Hayley tried to remember why she had once loved him. She could not, so she decided to forget about him and start life anew.

"Have the police solved the case yet?" Joni asked.

Hayley shrugged. "Nobody's told me anything."

A day or so later the doctor signed her discharge order and she left town with Strom's baby growing inside her. She would have his child but never permit him to see their offspring. That would be his punishment.

Ria continued to dominate the music charts and do sold-out concert tours. She also made love to myriad young men and women. She decided that sex with four partners was more fun than one on one.

Sometimes, while sucking this one's cock or eating that one's pussy, she thought of Nelson Skalbania and what might have been. She convinced herself that one day they would meet up again and go down on each other. Maybe she would even tell him about her romp with his father.

Or maybe not.

After all, it was none of Nelson's business.

Dr. Byrne and Detective Harrison began dating each other. Both of them were busy, cynical people who believed that romance was for young folks, so when they began having evenings of dinner and dancing, neither could quite believe that such a fun thing was happening to them.

José Benitez received a promotion to weekend TV talk-show host. His job was to review each week's showbiz news and what it all meant. Viewers loved his smartass manner and Latin good looks and José loved being in the studio and not having to go out into the field and try to interview people who might actually be rude to him.

One person who didn't love him was Kayce White. She refused to reply to his texts and didn't even call to thank him for the flowers he had sent her.

Tough titties for Miz White, he thought.

Lupe returned from Central America with a new attitude. After spending some time with her indigent relatives, she decided to take life more seriously and to value what little she had.

She resolved to become a better mother. She had missed her baby and mama; she would start minding her matters and stop cutting class.

After the Epilogue
Kayce

A few hours after my phone call to Nelson, he and I got it on. How was he? Better than I could have imagined or expected.

We did it again and again, and each time it was better than the last one.

What will become of us?

I have no idea. He lives I Manhattan and I'm located in Los Angeles. He won't move to my city and I won't move to his.

But one thing I know is this: some things are meant to be, and that includes us. We'll *make* it work out.

www.ingramcontent.com/pod-product-compliance
Lightning Source LLC
Chambersburg PA
CBHW051512250626
47156CB00001B/61